Honest And For True

Honest And For True

by

Jane Lebak

Philangelus Press
Boston, MA

Also by Jane Lebak:
The Wrong Enemy
Seven Archangels: An Arrow In Flight
Seven Archangels: Sacred Cups
Seven Archangels: Annihilation
The Boys Upstairs

 Coming Soon:
Forever And For Keeps

ISBN: 978-1-942133-10-0
Library of Congress Control Number: 2015939604
Kindle ASIN: B00W47ZGUG

Cover: C.K. Volnek

Dedication

I talk out my plots to myself, and sometimes I rope in the closest person. I was hashing through the germ of this story one night while making dinner, and as I started forming up a rough outline of Bucky, my Patient Husband said, "And he has a strange fascination for the Rumours album."

That was the moment the whole story gelled. My husband knows just how to cut through a lot of the writer-fog that would otherwise keep me living in my own head all the time. So for the laughs, for the patience, for the insight and for the decades of marriage, I dedicate this story to my husband, James Lebak.

Chapter One:

A strange fascination for the Rumours album

If the customer was any more in my face, I'd be tasting her mouthwash. "You were supposed to give me an estimate!"

We don't have bullet-proof glass at the garage, so I raise both hands. "But we didn't—"

"I was waiting right here for the car." The woman's angular cheeks go purple, and she's got a white-knuckled grip on her purse. "If you think I'm paying for that, you can forget it."

I thrust her the keys and the paperwork. "You don't have to. You're free to go."

For a moment she huffs in the otherwise-still waiting room. Passing cars hum outside the windows, and a whiff of exhaust hangs in the air. Finally she says, "What?"

Poised to dart back from the counter, I circle the total on the invoice. $0.00. "The car is fixed. You're all set. Have a nice day."

Two regular customers are pretending not to watch. I'd like to think both men would save me if she attacked, but this is Brooklyn—they'd have bolted outside before their abandoned *Daily News* pages finished fluttering to the floor.

The keys crunch together as the woman slips them into her coat pocket. "It's fixed?"

Breathe, Lee, breathe. Crisis averted.

This late in the day, the vinyl floor bears a salt and dirty-snow grime, and I'm as tired as last month's Christmas decorations. My last cup of coffee happened four hours ago. At least, I assume that was coffee. I found it in the coffee pot, so that should count for something.

I grin at the customer. "Our test drive confirmed the gasoline odor in the car, but that wasn't the smell of a bad fuel pump. Your gas cap had a cracked gasket which was letting fumes get sucked back through the trunk whenever you accelerated." I slip onto the stool beside the computer, bringing myself up to eye-level with the woman. "Since a locking gas cap isn't standard on the Taurus, we popped the trunk and found the original cap rolling around the spare tire bed. New test drive, no odor, no charge." Leaning forward, I rest my elbows on the counter. "If you aren't satisfied, we'll provide a full refund."

Silence for five seconds.

She bites her lip. "The first mechanic swore it was the fuel pump."

"And agreed to change it for $300," I venture, "while throwing in a new gas cap for free?"

She bursts out laughing. That's less than a week's rent, but hey, money's money. "Tell the mechanic I want to marry him."

I make my eyes big. "That would be me." When she steps backward, I add, "But I'm happily single, so I'll decline your proposal."

Now I've shocked her twice. "But you're a girl."

I stare down at myself. Yep, still the same me: grease-stained pants, work boots, and a denim shirt with our logo.

Although they pretend not to be watching, the other customers snicker.

The woman shifts her weight. "I ought to pay something."

I shake my head. "At some point you'll need to get your car fixed for real, and you'll come to the honest mechanic. Here, tell your friends, too." I hand her five business cards that proclaim *Mack's Auto: We Repair Anything!*

The woman takes the cards. "Thanks. Lee, huh?" She prints my name on the reverse of one. "You're right—I'll be back."

No kidding. She's got a 2006 Ford Taurus. Of course she'll be back.

Five minutes later, I'm on the next repair. Ladies and gentlemen, in the center ring—I mean, repair bay: a hundred-ten pound mechanic versus a factory-driven nut rusted in place since the second Bush administration. Who will prevail?

"Hey, Bucky," I whisper. "You there?"

No response.

"Bucky, you'd have stepped in if she attacked me, right?"

Again, silence. I wonder what's going on.

I'm going to be a bad girl. On the metal shelf behind me, I keep a twenty-year-old boom-box that has only ever played one tape, and now I turn it on.

The other three mechanics look up. Carlos says, "*Rumours* again?"

"It's the only thing everyone agrees on," is all I ever say. You'd better believe I won't ever tell them the real reason.

"Secondhand News" starts up, and I enjoy the echo of my voice against the undercarriage. It's a good thing I work in a garage: when it comes to singing, I'm a great mechanic.

By the time the second baum-baums have started, I can see Bucky, leaning against the lift riser.

It's convenient to have a guardian angel with a strange fascination for the *Rumours* album.

He's awesome. I've been able to see him since forever, and sometimes it still knocks the breath out of me. He's got a squarish face with short brown hair that curls at the edges like an afterthought, and his smiles carve a dimple on his right cheek. There's no dimple now; no smile either.

"Why are you so scarce today?" Teeth clenched, I have another go at the bolt. The other mechanics won't hear me over the music as they work on their own assignments. If they do, well, all of us talk to the cars we're fixing. They won't care that I'm apparently holding a conversation with mine.

He still doesn't answer.

"Wasn't that the neatest thing about the gas cap? I just knew that woman was being fleeced by another mechanic. She was so cagey describing the problem." I touch the air where his arm appears, but my fingers pass through. Today he's wearing blue jeans and a sweatshirt that says HEAVEN. "Where were you before?"

He shifts away from me so his wings flare, showing his brown feathers with white speckles, even the yellow bars across the shorter ones. "I'm not all that happy with you right now."

I look away from the engine to meet his brown eyes.

His mouth tightens. "Would you care to guess why?"

I'm in for it. But you can always delay the inevitable: I drown the bolt in WD-40 and slip some PVC piping over the edge of my wrench to make a longer tool for more torque. As I get it ready, I venture, "Does it have to do with last night's date?"

Bucky has the most arresting eyes I've ever seen, but at times it's hard to appreciate how they shine. Like now, when he's staring into me as if someone has shouted "Fire!" while I'm holding a wadded-up newspaper, a gas can, and a flame thrower.

"I couldn't help it." He's still glaring: he must think I could have. "It was great until he wanted to know what I do for a living, and he wouldn't let me joke it off." I glance sideways. "Why didn't you distract him?"

"You can't distract me," he says, "and I'm asking why you did what you did."

I should know by now. "What's the big deal? So I told him I'm a secretary for a political action committee."

"The big deal is that you aren't a secretary for a political action committee." Bucky's wings close as he leans back on the riser. "There's nothing wrong with fixing cars."

The song has changed to "Dreams" as I finally get the bolt to loosen. "I know that."

"Then why lie about a job you love?" Bucky's still got a tightness around his mouth, and one hand clenches. Uh-oh. "It's not like the man was pining for a delicate flower. You met him at a bowling alley, for Pete's sake. You can't even claim he thought you were just watching the other mechanics because he saw you paying for your games, which were pretty good by the way."

"Thanks!"

"And...?"

I let off a long sigh, then set about removing the heat shield. Something's still blocking it.

"The guy didn't ask you to teach him needlepoint. You two talked hockey while feeding quarters to a game of Duck Hunt." Bucky makes that *figure it out* circular motion with one hand. "Where in all that did you get the idea he'd climb out the men's room window if you told him you inflate radial tires rather than collate radical flyers?"

"I didn't want to ruin the fun." I sigh. "I'm never going to see him again, so why does it matter?"

Bucky says, "Why care what he thinks if you're not going to see him again?"

"We have this discussion every time," I say, and Bucky shoots back with, "Then maybe you need to listen to what I'm saying every time. What kind of person would roll his eyes at the mere mention of your job?"

I lower my wrench and regard him patiently.

He flinches. "Well, other than her."

We're silent for a moment. Bucky says, "You might want to remove that heat shield if you don't intend to become a secretary."

"You're done lambasting me?"

"I can see I've had a great effect on you." He looks up into the engine as if he can see a salt-encrusted flange preventing the heat shield from sliding loose. "Maybe I should start scanning the *Heavenly Times* classifieds. Or place one. *Wanted: Guardian who stands a chance of turning someone into an honest woman.*"

"No fair! I don't want a different guardian!" I try again to slide the shield loose. "I'm up-front about everything else." I pause. "Is there a *Heavenly Times*?"

Bucky opens his hands to create filmy image of a broadsheet that does indeed say *Heavenly Times*, with a banner headline about the music of the spheres being in concert.

Bucky's dimple tells me he's fighting a laugh.

I say, "Honest and for true?" Then we both crack up, and the image disperses.

"You're the best guardian." I throw my weight against the metal, and it slides only a bit before it catches again. "I may have a teensie problem with the truth, but I'm not totally dishonest. Have I ever ripped off anyone here? You know how easy that would be. 'Yeah, your thermostat needed a new torque sensor, and then I laced up your CV boots.'"

When he concedes the point, I add, "It's not as if I'd lie to you."

"Do that and you won't see me again."

I pivot toward him. "You wouldn't leave!"

"I want you to quit lying." He draws up to his full height, staring into the heart of me. "You've got me at the end of my rope."

I turn my back so he can't see the tears in my eyes or the way I'm biting my lip. Ironically, it's by turning the wrong way that I finally slide the heat shield free. I set it on the ground and pick up my wrench to start dismantling the exhaust system.

When I think my voice will be steady, I chirp in a kid-voice, "I love you, Bucky!"

He says into the air, "Here's a note to all guardians everywhere on Earth: It may be cute when they give you a nickname at age three, but consider whether it will sound cute when they're fifty-six."

"I'm not even thirty." I glare at him. "Unless you're implying it feels like you've been stuck with me fifty-six years."

Bucky sheds sparkles at me like the crackling of a fire.

I smirk. "Hey, shine a little this way so I can see the exhaust system better, will you?"

"Oh, is my new name Maglight?"

I'm about to retort that there are worse names when my boss shouts so loud I drop my wrench. "Lee! Get in here!"

Well, *that* doesn't sound good, does it now?

The other mechanics smirk as I head for the narrow office behind the waiting room to talk to Max, the non-eponymous owner of this garage ever since he realized that "Max's" would immediately make people think "he maxes out your credit card."

Over sixty, graying but with a full head of hair, Max is visible from the chest up behind the towers of paper walling his desk. "Listen, I know I don't pay you near enough, but I can't accept your resignation."

I roll my eyes.

He snaps a paper with a thick shortened finger, the victim of a distracted moment under an engine twenty years ago. "And you ought to learn to spell my name."

I choke down a laugh.

In addition to the tightest fists on earth, he also has the most concrete deadpan. "You're in the shop today. Why'd you waste a stamp mailing it?"

I run a hand through my hair. "Are you also mad at me for not signing in my own handwriting?"

He studies it. "You're right. This isn't even close."

I need the laugh. "If I may ask, where did I say I was going to work instead?"

He crumples the letter. "The Post Office."

My eyes widen. "My mother's getting desperate."

Max lays it up into the trash can. Two points. "At least this time you're not quitting to work in the back room at Target." He swivels toward his computer, dislodging a stack of junk mail with the chair's arm. "Give your mother a free oil change and get her off my back, will you? Maybe change her wiper blades too. Oh, and nice catch with the gas cap, but you should have charged her for labor."

Yeah, that wrist motion of turning the gas cap? Nearly did me in.

Max adds, "Take the rest of the day off, on me."

I glance at the clock. Fifteen minutes early. Impressive. "Thanks."

Max tells Ari to finish my repair, and I'm free.

In the four-by-four bathroom, I stand practically on top of the toilet to replace my work gear with jeans and a fresh flannel shirt. My hands turn pink from scrubbing, but eventually they're clean.

This is the life. I can't imagine going back to being a legal secretary or schlepping on the subway every day.

As I leave through a parking lot surrounded by a razor-wired chain link fence, I pause: where is my bike? Oh, great—am I about to make another friend on the NYPD?

Then I remember, I drove to work today because it's my niece's birthday. In less than an hour I have to enter Battlefield Mom.

Chapter Two:

Points In Heaven

I will now describe my mother in one sentence: after nine years and three boys, she was pregnant with me, due February 1st, but managed to go two weeks overdue so I would be born on Valentine's Day.

Then she named me Juliet.

There are no pictures of me before the age of fifteen wearing anything but pink.

Lacy pink.

Gossamer pink.

Pepto-Bismol pink.

What changed when I was fifteen? I started buying my own clothes. And I discovered how to put dye in the washing machine. I accidentally ended up Goth before Goth was even a style. How was I supposed to know you don't need quite that much dye for one load of pink clothes? Or that the next few loads of clothing would also turn black? Or how much it costs to call in a washing machine repair man? Bucky laughed until he saw the trouble I got in.

I should add that she hates "Lee." When customers got squicked by the idea of "Juliet" working on their cars, Max printed a new name-tag, and I loved the nickname.

When I arrive halfway across Brooklyn at her apartment, Mom buzzes me in, and by the time I've lugged my niece's gift up two flights of stairs, she's finished unlocking most of her apartment door. The last thing to clank is the Master Lock deadbolt. In her heart of hearts, she longs for a portcullis.

I'm greeted by a double-take. "What on earth did you bring Avery?"

"Hello to you too, Mom." I maneuver the box enough to kiss her on the cheek, then shuffle inside.

I wasn't the only victim of The Pink: my mother also dresses herself in pink. Plus cream, yellow, lavender, ice green, pastels I haven't got a name for. The air around her carries a sweetness as she moves, and at sixty-five, she remains unwrinkled without the interference of plastic surgery. Time hasn't touched her for two decades—I'm of the opinion it's afraid to.

She sizes me up, nose wrinkled. "Randy's going to be ten minutes late. Traffic on the Belt."

In other words, just enough time for my mother to re-lock her entire door.

I leave my jacket on the couch, then hide Avery's gift in my mother's bedroom. As I'm heading back to the kitchen, Mom intercepts me. She pushes me into the bathroom, thrusting a faded Mickey Mouse towel into my arms. "You smell like an oil change. Shower. Now."

Next thing, the door slams with the finality of a judge's gavel.

"Five visits running." Bucky settles on the edge of the sink. "We have a trend."

Based on past experience, the best course of action is surrender. I drape the thirty-year-old towel on the rack beside my mother's satin-trimmed deep-pile towels that weigh five pounds apiece. Is it my imagination, or did they scoot away from it?

Bucky doesn't disappear when I turn on the shower.

"Do you mind?"

He shrugs. "No."

I fling my socks through him, and he laughs, so I splash water in his general direction, getting drops all over a mirror that doesn't reflect him, and then I rat-tail him with the ancient towel. It cracks in the air like

Indiana Jones' whip. He casts up his hands before vanishing.

Bucky hated it when I hit puberty. I gave serious thought to showering in my bathrobe, no matter how much he assured me that he had no interest in that kind of thing. "Think about it: I behold the mysteries of the cosmos. Human romance has no appeal. It would be like offering you a candle-lit evening at a five-star restaurant featuring a seven-course meal, finished off with cheesecake so dense it has its own gravity field, all served up while you listen to the Moonlight Sonata and enjoy a sunset over the Grand Canyon, and instead you say, 'Thanks, but I'd rather sit in the freezing rain and eat mud.'"

Bucky offered to appear as a female to placate me, but in the end we worked out that he could do whatever he wanted, just as long as I couldn't see him doing it. He still hassles me, though.

With my hair shampooed and rinsed, I hunt in futility for a bar of soap.

Mom's shower stymies me. She has four types of shampoos, two kinds of conditioner (one for everyday, one to strip your hair, or maybe prevent stripping) and five different scents of body-wash. Me, I get my shampoo at the dollar store. I wash my body with Dial. Cheap. Comes in *two* colors. Claims it kills bacteria. What more could I want?

In the next moment, I shriek because what I should have wanted was for the Thrilling Fifty-Degree Hot-To-Cold Alternating Shower to remain above body temperature. Instead icicles hang from the soap dish, and I'm jammed in the corner while my toes freeze to the ceramic.

I rinse with inhuman quickness and flee to the embrace of the threadbare towel.

When my teeth stop chattering, I realize I'm staring at a silky blouse in pale purple and a knit skirt. Like Bucky said, we have a trend: she did this last time too.

When you work in a garage, flannel shirts and jeans cover your wardrobe needs. One glance tells any normal person I don't do silk and lace. I'm short. I work out four times a week. My nose is too "cute" and my eyes too big. Put me in silk and I get handed the kids' menu at Denny's—although I like it when they give me the crayons too. I'd save a bundle riding the bus for half-price. But no, not worth it.

Finally, not to put too fine a point on things, I don't have the body to wear this stuff. It's not just my job that's boyish.

Oh, and good grief—sitting on the counter is a name-brand bag with shiny underthingies nestled in crinkly pink paper. These might decrease my coefficient of friction just enough that I'll lie on a gurney to push beneath a car and go shooting from my jeans and out the other side of the vehicle.

"Mom," I call, "give me my clothes."

"Just wear that. You'll look so pretty."

For Pete's sake. "Theft is illegal."

"I didn't steal anything. I threw it in the wash."

Stealing the hot water from my shower, too. Should I just give in?

Oh, wait. The one thing my mother forgot was shoes. Just imagine her face when I clump out in a skirt, nylons, and work boots.

No, really not worth it.

Bucky is my intelligence officer. As if I'm a soldier behind enemy lines, I say, "Is Randy here yet?"

Bucky inserts into my thoughts an all's-clear.

"Then I'll need you to help cover my nakedness, or something else Biblical."

Bucky laughs.

Wearing the towel, I follow his directions to the bundle of clothes my mom stole from me during the last visit, at the bottom of her closet tied in a plastic bag like a dead animal. I drop the substitute outfit on her bed and leave the towel in her empty laundry basket. Ladies and Gentlemen: my mother at the top of her game.

It takes two minutes to transform from sky-clad to company-worthy: pants, shirt, five yanks with a comb through my black hair (short, part-free) and I'm set. When I'm not at work I wear silver studs so I don't have naked ears, but jewelry's a safety hazard working with engines. My first day on the job, Max's wife Allison told me about a guy who wore his wedding ring at work. One electrical shock later and the guy was forever known as "Frodo."

In the kitchen I find my mom frosting Avery's cake, and I smell lasagna. There's crusty Italian bread on the counter, but when I reach to break off the end, my mother raps my hand with the flat of the spreader. Bucky snickers.

She gives my clothes a disgusted look, but she all she says is, "Are you doing anything Friday?"

I shrug.

"Good, because you're going on a date with a doctor I met at Manorside."

I said she was in top form, didn't I?

My mother describes one Paul Warner, a surgeon who visited a patient at the nursing home where she is an administrator.

Ah, but this time I have a weapon. "You told me never to marry a doctor."

She puzzles. "I did?"

"You said he'd never be home."

"But don't you see that's perfect for you?" She beams. "He won't be underfoot when you want to do your things."

"I have another way of keeping him from being underfoot." Surely she can't argue with this. "He can date someone else."

She huffs a "pshaw!" while giving a wave of her hand. "He's earning decent money, he's good-looking, and he's interested in you."

This ought to be amusing. "Why? What did you tell him?"

"That you're a private duty nurse, that you're almost thirty and never married, and that you've got an interest in the theater."

How my mother manufactures this stuff is beyond me, but at least Bucky can attribute my lying to good breeding. "Didn't you tell him I pilot the space shuttle?"

"Don't be ridiculous." My mother sprinkles silver dots over the cake, the kind that guarantee a root canal if you bite the wrong way. "Honey, it's your thirtieth birthday in only a few weeks. If you haven't met the guy of your dreams by thirty, you'll never get married."

Have I heard this before? Yep. Before my twenty-fifth birthday to be specific. I'll no doubt hear the same before my thirty-fifth, fortieth, fiftieth, sixtieth, and seventy-fifth birthdays. Maybe at seventy-five I'll concede, but that's okay. Seventy-five is a bit old for skydiving anyhow.

I snitch a bit of frosting off the cake plate. "I don't care if I never get married."

My mother sighs. "Sometimes I wish you were the daughter I never had."

Even as my ears get hot, Bucky squeezes my shoulders. *Points in Heaven.*

There isn't an angel standing around with a chalkboard making tally marks every time you bite your tongue. But damn it, there should be. *Five points to the gal in blue jeans who isn't screaming.*

I'll award you ten, Bucky replies. *Seven more seconds and you're off the hook.*

I count them. Seven more seconds and the doorbell rings. I buzz in my brother and his family, then proceed to unlock the knob lock, two dead-bolts, a chain, and the sliding bar.

"Don't forget to look through the peephole!" my mother yells.

I look through the peephole. Surprise—it's still my brother.

My brother and his wife troop in with their children: birthday girl Avery who turns fourteen tomorrow, nine-year-old Brennan, and seven-year-old Susanne. The three of them share my brother's round face and his propensity to squint while smiling, their mother's straight brown hair, and child-pitch voices that hurt my ears whenever they shriek with laughter.

Randy rubs tired eyes as he gathers coats from three kids, then hangs up his own and Corinne's. Finally he lifts mine from the couch. "Hey, Grease-Monkey, have you ever heard of the 'coat hanger'?"

I peer at him, baffled. "Heard of *what*?"

"I thought so." He looks over my head and whispers to someone he can't see, "Hi, Bucky."

Unheard, Bucky returns the greeting.

I hug Randy, then follow the kids into the living room where Susanne has already dumped a bag of My Pretty Ponies. Brennan has a hand-held video game in front of his face. Avery has eyes downcast, but when I ask what's going on, she glares at the wall.

Randy guides me by the sleeve into my mother's bedroom. Corinne sits on the bed beside the discarded girly outfit, and she hasn't bothered turning on the lamp.

"Whoa," I whisper as Randy shuts the door. "Don't tell me you're expecting again!"

Corinne says in a low voice, "Avery is in serious hot water, but we don't want to tell Mom."

Randy steps close so that even if all three kids press against the door, they won't hear. "After volleyball practice, a bunch of them went to one girl's house where they raided the parents' medicine cabinet and took random pills, 'just to see what would happen.'"

My eyes widen. "Did any of them get hurt?"

"One was throwing up all night, which is how we found out. Mostly they took things like expired antibiotics, but there were painkillers too." Randy folds his arms. "We punished Avery for not telling us, but she didn't take anything."

I frown. "They're only thirteen! That's crazy-young to be experimenting with drugs."

"No kidding," Corinne mutters. "Imagine if there was heart medication? One of them could have had a heart attack!"

Randy says, "She's having a rough time of it. The other volleyball players are mad, so she's getting bullied for having stayed out of it, and some of them are vicious."

He doesn't have to tell me.

Corinne has steel in her eyes. "I'm livid. I can barely look at her. She knows better than to go along with other girls who are doing that."

I say, "Volleyball is through the school, right?"

Corinne says, "And I spoke to the principal about it, you'd better believe. She didn't want to admit this could happen, but I'm beginning to think the private schools only give them access to more expensive drugs."

Randy says, "We don't know for sure the girls are doing street drugs."

Corinne snaps, "I never grabbed a handful of my grandmother's medication just to see what would happen!"

"Back up a bit." I hate it when Randy and Corinne fight, especially when they're on the same side. "Will you pull her from the team?"

Randy looks unhappy. "They're supervised during practice. It's afterward."

"I'll pick her up." I nod when they both look at me. "I could shift my hours to be free Wednesday afternoons."

Randy's brow furrows. "And then?"

"We live in New York City—there's got to be something we could do." Then I grin. "Never underestimate the power of a Cool Aunt. Especially a Cool Aunt with a restored 1965 Mustang."

Corinne bites her lip. "Oh, that makes sense. Play games with drugs and get afternoons with your aunt."

I glance at the crumpled lavender blouse still with the tags. "Look, Mom's always on my case because I don't have a *family*." Randy hugs me across my shoulders. "I don't have to shuttle my own kids anywhere, and I don't have a husband who requires a hot meal on the table at six. Let me take her out. We can have dinner. I'll help with her homework, and I'll drop her off at your place around eight."

"I like it." Then Randy smirks. "Only not the homework. I remember your grades."

I blow him a raspberry.

Corinne rubs her temples. "I still don't know."

Randy puts his hand on her arm. "We don't need to decide tonight."

We head out of Mom's room to find Brennan engrossed in his game while Suzanne arranges her ponies in families and Avery braids their ridiculously long manes in dozens of cornrows.

When Avery sneaks a guilty look at me, I keep my face impassive.

Nah-uh, Bucky sends, along with the impulse that she knows we were talking about her, and like any level-headed teen, she knows I'm going to hate her forever.

Weird that she cares. I'm just her crazy aunt.

I wrack my empty head for wise, witty and wonderful thoughts that will enlighten her world.

Unfortunately, I'm hardly the Dalai Lama, so I drop to the floor at her side. "How do you do that? Those braids are tight."

"Practice." She's flushed.

I say, "Can you show me?"

Before she can reply, Mom calls us for dinner, and everyone crowds into the dining area. She serves the lasagna, and I finally get my crusty Italian bread. Randy and Corinne have assured the kids could dine with royalty if necessary, so dinner isn't a pitched battle over using silverware or not talking with one's mouth full, but there's chatter verging on mayhem, and it's entirely too much fun at the table.

After dinner comes the cake, and after cake comes the gift-giving. My mother produces a pile of tiny packages for Avery: jewelry, a light sweater from the Gap and a gift card for Aeropostale, plus hair gadgetry in a velvet bag. Avery is thrilled.

Then I haul out my box, as big as her kid sister, and Corinne groans while the younger two cheer. "Aunt Lee always buys cool gifts!"

I can't help but grin as Avery opens it. "Awesome! I love the *Titanic*!"

"You're assembling that model with her," Randy murmurs just loud enough for me to hear.

Avery heaves over the box to look at the pictures of the model when it's assembled. "It's got to be like three feet long!"

Corinne says to me, "You're also installing a shelf for it."

I kneel on the floor beside Avery to show her the intricate parts of the model: the lifeboats come out; the decks raise to reveal the lower levels; there's thread for rigging. I bring out the paints, plus a set of brushes so small you can paint a 1:400 doorknob, plus tools the folks at the hobby shop said you'd need to do this right. It's got to be a great gift if it requires specialized tools.

Corinne interrupts to say, "Avery, maybe you and Aunt Lee can put that together this Wednesday. She's going to pick you up from volleyball."

Well then. Corinne's got a fast turnaround time.

Avery looks from her mom to me and back again. "But—"

I interrupt before she tips off my mother. "I'll pick you up in the Mustang."

She's staring. "You will?"

"We don't have to do the model, though." I shrug. "We can go someplace. Maybe spend your gift card. Have dinner."

Delighted, she strangles me in a hug and, I roll with it so she's inadvertently tackled me. My mother yells at Avery to be careful, and Randy pulls her off.

Yeah, every kid should have a cool aunt, and every aunt should have a niece who knows it.

Driving from East Flatbush back to Park Slope, I think about Avery and prescription drugs and Corinne battling tears. I think about my mother and points in Heaven. I think about four weeks before I turn thirty to find a guy I'd want to marry. I think about the popular girls united against my niece.

"Bucky?" I can't see him, but he prickles the edge of my senses. "What happens when someone makes one really stupid decision?"

His voice blends into the hum of the engine. "Bad results."

"A bad choice now would ripple out to touch everything." As I cruise up the ramp exiting the Prospect Expressway, I bite my lip. "She's just so young."

Unspoken agreement.

"Damn." I brake at a red light before the turn onto Seventh Avenue. "She needs someone to help her."

Bucky agrees, but I get the sense he considers it already done.

Chapter Three:

It's short for Hallelujah

My roommate has made our apartment smell delicious.

"We need to eat eighteen eggs by Thursday." Beth doesn't look up from the paper in her fingers. "There's quiche in the fridge."

I drop my jacket on the pantry knob. "Eighteen eggs? Can we do that?"

"We got nine wishbones last fall, didn't we?" She's still staring at her work. "Blow them out of their shells. I'll make brownies for the church coffee hour, which leaves nine if you have two at breakfast."

Scattered around Beth on the dining room table are the half-formed origami carcasses of a creature I can't identify. That in and of itself is not unusual: too may times I can't even identify the finished product. But the sheer number of botched attempts points to a ridiculously difficult creature, like a centipede that actually has a hundred legs.

Like most brownstone apartments, ours is arranged like railroad cars. The hallway entrance opens straight into the dining area (with kitchen, pantry closet and bathroom offshoots) and to your right is a small pass-through room: Beth's bedroom, because the realtor swore on his mother's grave that it was absolutely, undoubtedly, amazingly legal to have a bedroom serving as the only access to half the apartment.*

Following that is a common area for our TV, computer, couches, etc. Its eight-foot French windows stream with afternoon sunlight. We call it France because it also has French doors that divide it from the middle room.

Off that room to the right is the real bedroom with a door and the only closet. The dresser drawers bang into the twin-size bed when you open them, but you can fit a desk. Beth needs more space, so I get the privacy.

This brownstone was built in 1904, and I feel bad that I missed its centennial birthday, like someone should have given it a cake. The stairs are thick wood, and every other step emits a groan no matter how lightly you walk, alternating with a creak. The wallpaper has an ivory and olive paisley pattern, only it's faded a bit since World War II. Because the tenants don't live in the hallway, our landlady Mrs. Goretti sees no need to illuminate it with more than a fifteen watt bulb.†

At the table, Beth continues creasing pieces of paper to within an inch of their lives, assuming papers live. I gesture toward the pile. "What are you making? Something for the preschool?"

"It's a woman symbol," Beth says. "March is Women's History Month."

Of course. I wonder why that didn't occur to me? Perhaps because it's insane.

Beth and I are the same age and the same build, although she's got unassuming brown eyes and wears her hair in a chin-length bob parted on the side. We tell everyone we're sisters because we like the resulting look on their faces: she's Filipino and I'm Caucasian.

---

* *And then took a call from his mother.*
† *For the record, I have no idea where Mrs. Goretti finds fifteen watt bulbs. They don't sell them at Key Food.*

It's even funnier if you know her personality. Beth can find a rag in a garbage bin and casually toss it over her shoulders so you'd swear it was a hundred-dollar scarf from Lord and Taylor. With an ineffable sense of how things go together, she decorated our apartment. It's all secondhand stuff, but if we washed the dishes, *House Beautiful* could come tomorrow for a photo shoot.

I shove my hands into my jean pockets only to hit the receipt I tucked in there when I bought lunch. I toss it into the trash, drawing a squeal from Beth. I snatch the thing from the can and she plucks it from my hands. This she carefully straightens, then lays on a stack of paper by the doorway.

The way Bucky thinks it's a crime to lie, Beth thinks it's a crime to throw away paper. Paper can be turned into origami.

I apologize, Beth forgives me, and we're all back on solid ground.

In the kitchen, I open a can of soda and lean against the entrance. "Do you have any idea what I can do with my niece? I'm supposed to take her somewhere this week."

Beth shrugs. "She's a bit older than the crowd I teach. You're baby sitting?"

I stand taller. "Avery got into some trouble at school, so they want her to have a stable adult influence."

Three minutes later, with Beth still laughing so hard she can't sit up, I fold my arms and stare at the floor. "I really don't think that's warranted."

"They wanted a stable adult, and they picked you?" She didn't need to lean into the *you* as hard as she did. "No wonder the kid's in trouble!"

With a sigh, I return to the kitchen to open a bag of chips. "I'm not that bad."

"Lee, you're my best friend and you're an awesome roommate, but when I have a kid who needs career counseling, I'm not sending her to you."

I return to the dining room. "This, coming from someone who spends three hours a day folding paper puppies."

"Then you need to trust me that I know *immature* when I live with it." She squeegees the tears from her cheek, then looks at me and surrenders again to the laughter. "Call them back. Tell them in retrospect, you'd rather they sent out for pizza, and when the delivery guy arrives, size him up to see whether he's a stable adult."

I stalk back to my room, thinking how unfair Beth's being. For one thing, I did deliver pizza once for six months.

She has a point. Just a tiny, tiny bit of a point. But wouldn't Randy and Corinne have noticed if it was the bad plan Beth says it is?

Two rooms away, Beth is still giggling. Well, we've got her verdict.

I pick up the phone, and shortly Randy's on the line. I blurt out, "Is this really a good idea?"

"I wouldn't be trusting you with my daughter if I didn't think it was." Randy chuckles. "Here, I'll give you Avery."

"Aunt Lee!" Avery chirps into the phone so loud I nearly drop it. "I was thinking about all the stuff we could do!"

The objections melt out of my head like a multi-layer braze around a hot spark plug. The kid trusts me. Her father trusts me. Heck, even the pizza delivery guy would trust me if I tipped him enough. We'll make it work.

It's seven o'clock when Bucky tells me I need to get out of bed.

No, I don't.
Yes, you do.
No, I don't.
Yes, you do.

I'm not getting out of bed.

Yes, you are. Beth needed to bring those brownies to the coffee hour, but she overslept.

"Go wake up Beth," I mutter.

Get up.

You can't win an argument with an angel. Technically speaking, he's a saint, and therefore he has the patience of one. If I repeat a thousand times that I'm not getting out of bed, he'll tell me a thousand and one times that surprisingly, I am. I'd have to keep it up until it was too late to bring brownies anywhere, but by that point I'd be awake anyhow.

I could tell him to go away. But what if he did?

Two minutes later, I've put myself in the shower, hunting for the perfect balance of hot and cold water that doesn't leave me shivering but doesn't make the pipes sing.

You know those flow-restricting shower heads that leave you never feeling quite rinsed off? No, the people who built this house didn't know about them either. Water erupts like a blast from Old Faithful, an experience I call "instant wakefulness" and more effective than a cup of coffee on mornings when I could never surmount the coffee bootstrap problem. Bucky didn't hassle me about disappearing this morning. He knows my limits.

As I awaken, I have a thought. *Just why is waking up a different human being beyond your mysterious angel-powers?*

Quit your whining and bring the brownies.

The Coffee Bootstrap Problem, documented by one Kimberlee Chestnut Chang, is the difficulty one has making coffee before one has consumed her first cup of coffee.

For today's entertainment, let's look at Exhibit A: a coffee maker that seems to be brewing and yet wheezes dryly like an exasperated old woman, dripping no coffee into the carafe. It figures. Jesus started the Apocalypse by rapturing my Folgers.

I pull out the carafe and see it has no lid, and without a lid it doesn't trip the "pause and serve" lever, and without tripping the "pause and serve lever" it leaves the coffee nowhere to go. This breed of trouble-shooting, ladies and gentlemen, is what you seek in an auto mechanic.

I lift the top and find what I expected. "Hey, look, Bucky! It's a cone of coffee!"

Quite a thrill. Get a move on.

With a sigh I shove the now-lidded carafe back onto the heater plate, and liquid awareness cascades into the pot with a sound more joyous than the seventh trumpet.

By 7:45 I'm heading out the door, jacket on and keys in hand, when Bucky says, "And the brownies are where?"

I return to the fridge. Beth has arranged them on a paper plate. At last, my pizza-delivery prowess will come in handy as I transport brownies to the church.

Since I can see Bucky, I know there's a whole spiritual realm out there, but Bucky refuses to tell me exactly what. I know he would love me to attend some kind of religious observation all the time, but right now he's got to settle for me going when I feel like it. This may be his attempt at getting my butt on a bench.

You have to believe me when I say every religion is represented in New York City. I had a few criteria when I screened them (the religion had to have angels or the equivalent, for obvious reasons; since Bucky talked about God, it had to have a God) but within that range, I've checked out everything: centuries-old buildings with grand statues and an organ larger than the one at Shea Stadium; medium-sized buildings with the latest in cold-war shoebox architecture; congregations you have to pay to be a member of; services conducted entirely in languages I'd never even heard (but Bucky understood); and store-front churches with signs like "Franco's Iglesia y Bagel Shop: If You Have The Keys To The Kingdom, We've Got The Lox."

Nowadays I go with Beth, and here's why: Beth's church is across the street.

In the vestibule, I check the bulletin board for Max's flyer and business cards: one fewer than last week. Call it job security. In the church hall, a couple are setting up a vat of coffee and laying out concoctions involving bleached flour and cane sugar, plus one fruit tray that looks so lonely I feel sorry for it, like a bespectacled librarian at a night club.

I ask the woman setting up the coffee where to put Beth's brownies, and she calls "Hal?"

He turns.

I blink at him. Hello! *Hal* has got to be short for *Hallelujah.*

It's not that he's gorgeous, because he isn't. It's his eyes and the way he carries himself. His nose is a little too big, his chin a little too small, but his clothes are neat, a shirt with a button-down collar visible beneath his forest green sweater. He cocks his head as he smiles. I look away before I stare.

"You can put them over here." He comes closer as I set the brownies on the table beside some cookies. "You made these from scratch?"

I find myself ensnared again in his eyes. "My roommate did." My brain is a cyclone, factoids whipped around with no regard for coherency. Those eyes are a luminous blue against his jet black hair. I think they call it "black Irish." I don't care what they call it. "We, um— We need to use eighteen eggs by Thursday."

He chuckles. "You could make quiche."

"Already done." Hal, huh? I push my hands into my jacket pockets. "We need to find homes for nine more."

"Omelets." Hal rubs his chin. "Have omelets for dinner."

I shrug. "Like I have any clue how to make an omelet."

"It's disgustingly easy." He moves to another part of the table to position napkins and coffee fixings. "Get a cookbook. You'll figure it out."

I follow Hal, setting out plastic spoons and fake sugars in both pink and blue, plus the real thing in white. (He adjusts them after I'm done.) There's fake milk with designer flavors in a plastic jar beside pitchers for real milk. Hal sorts tea bags while I put out hot chocolate packets.

Okay, that woman, is she his girlfriend? No, she's got a ring. His wife? Because if he's married, I'm going to get as far away as possible in the next thirty seconds. "I usually hit the ten o'clock, so I haven't seen you two around. I'm Lee."

"I'm Hal," says Hal, who then looks at the woman and says, "and you're—" He snaps his fingers a couple of times as if trying to jog his own memory, and my heart sinks because the only time you'd do that is if you have a longstanding relationship.

She throws a sugar packet at his head.

"Oh, right," he says, snatching it from the air. "You're my sister, Alicia."

Sister?

I win. I completely win.

Alicia wrinkles her nose. "Usually my husband helps set things up, but Andrew got sick, so I tapped this joker."

Hal asks, "Are you sticking around?"

I'm not proud. Yes, I will find it in my heart to sit through church this morning.

I help Hal drag folding chairs to the rows of tables. Alicia finds a brown basket in the kitchen for donations. I put paper-lace thingies on the tables to make them look nice, and then Hal repositions them so they look nicer. When it's time to head upstairs, I sit with Hal and his sister, and shortly their friends stop by, asking her how Andrew is doing and not asking Hal about anyone in particular.

This is good. This is very good. So far this morning I have delivered brownies, made my guardian angel happy, and enjoyed the presence of a guy who makes my pulse do the fandango.

Hal turns toward me after the Mass ends, again I'm transfixed by that gaze. When he says, "You want to stay for coffee?" I follow him downstairs.

After we drop our coats at a table and get on line, Bucky says to me, *You're going to ask him out, right?*

What are you, in high school?

Very funny. Are you going to ask him out?

I narrow my eyes. *Did you wake me up early just so I could meet him?*

I received orders to make sure you brought the brownies. They didn't say why.

We get our coffee and a bunch of little snacks (including Beth's brownies) and sit at a table with Hal's sister and some of their friends. It turns out they've been attending this church for years, but we've never met: eight versus ten, the Great Divide.

One of the friends asks me what I "do," and Bucky prickles at my conscience, so I say "I breathe, I sleep, and not much else," then turn the conversation toward hobbies.

When there's a lull in the conversation, Hal says he's getting more coffee, and I too discover my cup needs a refill.

Would you please make sure Beth is awake? I ask Bucky.

Would you please ask him out already?

Bucky has always been straightforward, but he doesn't get that you can't walk up to someone and say, "You have incredible eyes. Can I look at them over dinner?" Actually, maybe some people can. I can't. Right now I'm so nervous I can't make the coffee spigot work.

Hal asks if I need help, and yes, I do, but I tell him no, and then I get the coffee out of the vat and into the cup, and the next insurmountable task is how to get the sugar out of the packet.

I try to sound casual. "How do you make an omelet?"

He ticks off ingredients while I stir the sugar. "Three eggs, lots of butter, whatever you want inside. A frying pan, a spatula, and about five minutes."

Oh, I get it. "Kind of like scrambled eggs."

"Nothing whatsoever like scrambled eggs." Hal arches his brows. "Haven't you even watched them made at a breakfast bar?"

I shake my head.

"You can Google it."

As we head back to the table, I say, "You could show me."

He turns to me with a curious expression. "You have three eggs and a frying pan on you?"

I nod. "Sure. I carry them everywhere."

"I left mine at home." Hal smiles, and that's the first time he's ever smiled at something I said. "Really, it's easy. I'm surprised your mom or dad never taught you."

My mom did. That is, she tried teaching me to cook, but I never made sense of her instructions, and I was always doing something wrong. I learned more from Beth and frightened exclamations from Bucky (*"Lee! Don't eat that!"*).

Hal says, "If you're serious, I can stop by later and show you how to do it."

Be still my heart: that worked. "I'm very serious. I wasn't looking forward to more quiche." I should follow up with something, though. "And then I'll owe you dinner." Dating tip: finagle two for the price of one when you can.

As Hal takes a seat, he says, "Why do you need to finish nine eggs by Thursday?"

"Preschool project."

He nods. "Gotcha. Say no more."

Good, because right now, I know no more. I assume the kids are coloring them, but as fast as they grow up nowadays, they may be pasting in microchips to make tot-sized cell phones.

In high school, I never could have managed the previous exchange. I'd have fretted for weeks, asking my friends to ask his friends what his interests were and feigned excitement for them. Then after an impromptu trip to throw out my trash that just happened to coincide with him being there too, I might have asked about going somewhere romantic, like walking to the Principal's office to pick up a permission slip, and then run back to my friends to squeal.

It's easier now. Who has that kind of time? But still, it's pretty neat thinking we went for coffee refills as two single people, and we're back at this table with something like a date.

Chapter Four:

Please tell me you don't cook with a hammer.

I pass Beth on the way home and tell her we're featuring a guest chef for dinner, and I'll be sand-blasting the apartment if she needs anything. She begs that our maestro use many, many eggs.

Upstairs, I swing a security-camera eye around the apartment. I see twenty-seven days worth of dishes in the sink. Those need to go first. I'll scour the bathroom, herd origami women chimeras off the table, stack paper in all the corners, and mop the hardwood floor. I'll corral Beth's pre-tested preschool projects into one place, although technically they are in "one place" because "the entire apartment" counts as one place. I turn on *Rumours* and get to work.

Halfway through my self-imposed to-do list, I remark at Bucky that it'd be nice if he could magic away the dirt, but he doesn't respond. I look up to make another smart remark—and then stop.

Bucky sits at the table, his eyes fixed on Something, his lips half-parted in a smile as if he's been taken by surprise. There's a relaxation to the way he holds his wings, but his hands are clenched as if disbelieving.

For a moment, I can't speak.

Sometimes I forget what it means to be an angel, that this friend I pelt snowballs at can look right into the heart of the universe and comprehend it all, all the little ways creation interlocks like a big machine and all our separate realities mesh like gears, one of us turning the next turning the next. I bet right now he's looking down the corridors of time and marveling at how all these things you never thought would go together are somehow coming together like they never should have been apart.

I turn back to drying dishes, leaving Bucky to his moment.

Beth and I spend the half hour before Hal will arrive blowing eggs out of their shells, on the grounds that the process looks dorky.

Lightheaded from blowing, I settle myself on the linoleum floor. "Why are we doing this?"

"I'm going to fill the shells with Jell-O." Beth pokes holes in opposite ends of yet another egg, then whips up the yolk with a poultry pin. "You block the bottom hole and fill it, then chill it until the Jell-O hardens. The kids can peel the egg shell off and have a Jell-O egg."

I gasp. "If I score a nineteenth egg, will you make me one too?"

Beth says, "Get me a twentieth and I'll make one for that role-model-deprived niece you're supposed to be helping."

I blow her a raspberry.

With five minutes until the appointed hour, I take myself to the bench in the second floor foyer. Mounted to the wall is a mirror bigger than a queen sized bed, and I get my daily "thrill of risking death" by sitting beneath it.

The tenants all use this entrance, the grand entrance, the one you need to climb a flight of stone steps outside the house in order to reach. When you think of Brooklyn brownstones, those are the stones you're thinking about, and they're pretty impressive. A servants' entrance is tucked under the steps downstairs, but in one of those strange ironies only our landlady Mrs. Goretti uses it

Biting my lip, I reach with my heart for Bucky.

"Why are you worried?" His touch tingles against my scalp. "It's just eggs."

"I know." There's no reason Hal should give me butterflies. "Any idea where he is?"

Bucky turns his head. "Yes, in fact." And the doorbell rings.

"You could have warned me," I mutter.

There are two sets of doors. The outer entrance and the inner entrance both have glass panels, and each weighs enough that I wish we had a winch.

Hal takes in the fifteen-foot ceilings. "Nice place."

Nice eyes. I can't stop my compulsive grin. Hal is bundled into a blue Land's End jacket, a tan scarf peeking out from the collar. The duffle bag in his gloved hands strains the straps.

"We're not done climbing yet." I lead him upstairs while the steps serenade our passage.

At the top floor, I let him inside the apartment and introduce Beth. She studies him. "I've met you. I can't remember where."

Hal returns the look. "You're dating Stuart, right? He's in my book club." With a clang, he hefts his bag onto the table. "I hope you don't mind, but I brought my own equipment."

Ah, is that what he has? Up until that moment, it hadn't occurred to me he might be packing heat, planning to kill us and pillage our apartment. ("Officer, stop him! He stole five hundred origami animals! Wait, what am I saying? Officer, please, don't stop him!")

I take Hal's coat, and some quick thinking tells me the polite thing is to hang it up, so I carry it to my bedroom to hang in the only closet. Hal's still wearing the sweater and button-down shirt from church, still the docker shoes and the khakis.

When I'm back in the kitchen, he's still unloading the duffle bag, which arguably holds more than Mary Poppins' carpet bag. He's removed four lunch bags, the paper folded neatly, and a loaf of Italian bread. He removes another package in brown paper that's long and wrapped flat, and then something bound like a mummy in a plastic bag. This he opens without laying it on the table first: a cast-iron skillet with low sides.

Now that's one prepared guy. "We're going to have world-class omelets, aren't we?"

"Absolutely." I might as well have said *You breathe oxygen, don't you?* "Assuming the eggs are fresh."

"I got them Saturday afternoon," Beth says.

Hal surveys our kitchen, me at his back. He's got the faintest whiff of Old Spice, and his hair fluffs at the edges as if from a recent hair cut. When my nephew's hair is like that, I can't resist running my hands over it; in Hal's case, I resist.

I notice his expression. "The landlady doesn't do renovations often," I say, "but these appliances are the best the Vietnam era had to offer." I put a hopeful note into my voice. "And avocado green goes with everything."

He turns, worried. "Do you have a man who delivers blocks of ice every morning?"

I try to look earnest. "If this horrifies you, don't venture into the bathroom. The tub has feet."

He ventures, "Does the toilet work on a pull-chain?"

When I say, "What toilet?" that finally coaxes a smile from him.

"I guess I can work in here." He sounds uncertain. "Oh, and you might want to move your egg shells so we have some room." A pause. "So you teach preschool?"

I lift the boxes and say, "Yeah."

Bucky yells "Lee!" so loud I jump.

Hal pivots. I'm shaking. "I'm sorry—I thought I heard something."

In the dining area, I try to get myself together. *I'm sorry, Bucky.*

When are you going to stop being sorry and shape up? He's pushing at my heart. *Tell him now—tell him you have no idea why you said that! Tell him what you really do!*

Back in the kitchen I find Hal wiping down the countertops we just cleaned. "Uh, actually, I misspoke." I swallow. "Beth is the preschool teacher."

"Oh?" He chuckles. "What do you do?"

Heart pounding, I whisper, "Would you believe I'm a top-secret spy who works for the NSA?"

I'm reasonably certain the Virgin Mary never did anything that made the Archangel Gabriel smack himself on the forehead.

Hal laughs. "You'd tell me, but you'd have to kill me?"

At least one of us is laughing. Bucky certainly isn't. But hey, at least this time I didn't lie.

Before I have to answer the real question, Hal has reverted to that worried look. "Um— You keep a hammer with your spatulas and ladles?"

I nod. I mean, it's right there in the drawer.

"Please tell me you don't cook with a hammer."

Is this a trick question? "Not that often."

"You'd better not tell me more about that." Hal holds our chef's knife to the light. "Have you got a sharpener?"

Back on solid footing. By the time I locate one, he's removed a cutting board from his bag of tricks, and then he starts opening paper bags.

Fresh parsley. Portabella mushroom caps. Cubed white meat chicken. A block of cheese. Canadian bacon.

Hal works with full attention on the food, and for a moment our kitchen seems a sacred space. He decides that even sharpened, our knife is too blunt; from a brown paper wrapper he draws his own chef's knife. This atom-splitting blade flashes over the food and leaves behind slices a hundred times smoother than a ball-bearing. He has a smaller pan to fry the portabellas; he even brought his own butter. He shows off a special long-bladed omelet spatula.

I had no idea you needed so many tools to cook! For my birthday I should ask my mom for a gift certificate to Kitchen Universe. She'd break open her pink piggy bank.

For half an hour, Hal dominates our kitchen. He prepares garlic bread with real garlic and butter. He asks me to brew some coffee.

"Are you watching?" When I assure him I am, he grins. It's a confident, showy smile. "Good, because ostensibly I'm here to teach you."

His hands are so quick. He adds a tablespoon of water to a bowl with three eggs in it and whips it with a tiny whisk (did he bring his entire kitchen?) while melting a chunk of butter. With the layer of butter sizzling, he dumps in the egg. After the bottom sets over the heat, he lifts the edges with the omelet spatula, tilting the pan to spread the liquid parts under the bit that's already set.

Periodically he gives the pan a shake. He says it's to keep the egg from sticking, but after the amount of butter he used, he could be making an omelet from three tubes of superglue and a cup of Quickcrete and it wouldn't stick. This thing is going to take three months off my life. I'm going to enjoy every bite.

He looks at me. "Do you think you could do this?"

I'd rather watch him. "You're making it seem easier than it is."

"You want all the liquid to get under the solid parts. Then when it's cooked nearly all the way through, like now, you put in the fillings." He sprinkles chunks of chicken over half the omelet, then portabella pieces. The kitchen smells like Heaven, assuming they cook in Heaven. With a flick of the wrist, he folds the omelet along its diameter.

That's when he flashes me a smile.

"I'm in awe." About more than one thing.

He stands taller.

A minute later, he slides the omelet off the pan and brings it to the table. Beth divides it in thirds, we all have coffee, and there's garlic bread. I'm floating, like being dizzy except not as distressing.

Time for the second attempt. He has me do the water and the whisk, and he tells me to put more butter in the pan (yikes—it's already a frightful amount) but he takes over when it's time to make the egg run under itself. The kitchen is warm. He's right beside me.

Omelet #2 has chicken and cheddar and parsley. Then he tells me I'm flying solo.

Again we butter the pan (is it considered homicide to use an entire stick of butter for three people's meals?) and I whip up the eggs. I pour them into the pan, and then I freeze.

"Let the bottom firm up." He's close enough to breathe against my neck. "Okay, now."

I pry the edge up, but the egg won't run. He reminds me to tilt the pan, only it's still not working. He reaches around my waist, putting his hand over mine on the handle, and demonstrates how to swivel the pan.

"Use the spatula," he prompts, because for a moment I've forgotten we're cooking eggs.

Dear God: Thank you for not having me take Home Ec in junior high so that Hal could teach me today to make an omelet.

He lets go. I'm tempted to botch it again—like when I told blue-eyed and funny Patrick MacElroy I couldn't do algebra—but instead I do it the right way, and the egg starts turning into an omelet. Then, at the end, I put in Canadian bacon and portabellas, which land in clumps. When I fold the omelet, it looks crooked and amateurish. Hal tells me his first was worse.

"Because you didn't have you to help." I crinkle my eyes at him. "You're a terrific teacher."

"You're the first to think that." He flushes. "Everyone says I'm too nit-picky."

Afterward we linger at the table. Beth offers to clean Hal's paraphernalia, and while she's in the kitchen, I coax Hal to talk about himself. It turns out he cooks as a hobby, taking classes at a culinary institute in Manhattan and then experimenting with dinner parties (people still have dinner parties? I guess so). "Desserts are the most fun, and I bring them to the book club all the time, but I've brought more than a few entrée experiments to functions at the church."

"And nobody ever died," I offer.

He snickers. "No one they can trace back to me." Then he looks around. "Are you infested with paper parasites?"

I chuckle. "The origami? It's Beth's."

He nods. "And which of you is the reason you're overrun with angels?"

Looking around, I realize just how many I've accumulated. I've put angel sun-catchers on the windows, angel statues on the shelves, angel prints on the walls. Every so often I'll start an angel-hunt through gift stores and craft fairs until I find one I've never seen before.

Hal tells me he never thought about angels that much, something I've heard a lot. I tell him I could talk for hours, but I'll spare him this time.

We repack his paraphernalia, him taking special care wrapping that chef's knife. The bag is lighter than before because of all the food we consumed, and also because I "forgot" his whisk. It gives me an excuse to call him later. Yes, it's an underhanded trick. Yes, it works fantastically.

I walk him downstairs. "I owe you dinner for teaching me. When do you want to collect?"

He studies me for a moment. "To tell you the truth, I'd much prefer someone to cook for. Maybe you could drop by sometime next weekend? Saturday night?"

I may have the whole day free, but always say you're more busy. "I could be there by five."

He smiles—and that's the first moment I think he's interested in spending time with me rather than just cooking. "Five o'clock on Saturday, then. You could bring Beth. See if Stuart will come too. It's better to cook for more people." Hal pulls out a business card and writes his address on the back along with his email address and phone number. "Let me know by Thursday." He looks up. "You can tell me all the things about angels you didn't have time for today."

I can't help but smile. "It's a deal."

He looks uncertain for a moment, as if he's not sure whether he should shake my hand or bow or make some other gesture to formally end the evening. I solve his problem with a hug. "Thanks for the omelets. I had a great time."

Then he's out the doors and I'm alone in the 15 watt brilliance of the hallway but glowing inside. Please join me for a moment in thanking God for interesting men, without whom I would spend all my time surfing the net and eating Hamburger Helper.

Chapter Five:

Now everybody is happy

Back upstairs, Beth and I do nothing but stare at one another for half a minute. Then she breathes, "He's a catch."

I nod, mute.

She retrieves a box of origami paper off the sideboard. "I remember him now. Stuart mentioned six months ago that he roped a guy into the book group because he'd just broken up with his fiancée. The guy brought snacks for everyone, and at first Stuart thought he was trying to bribe them." She chuckles. "I bet it's him."

"Six months, huh?" That's long enough that he won't be a rebounder. I count it a service to all the women of New York when I date a man on the rebound, figuring I'm enough fun for the guy to get his confidence back and that when he's ready to dump me for an actual relationship, I'll be just about bored with him. If it's been six months since Hal was dumped—or dumped his girlfriend—he might be ready for the real deal. That's bad.

Maybe I should call this off. "Any idea why they split?"

"Cheating?" Beth frowns. "Stuart said the guy—we don't know for sure it's Hal—was devastated, and it had

Stuart really shook up. He made me promise that if I ever felt like cheating, I'd have the decency to dump him."

That's really the way to go. Whenever I juggle guys, they always know about each other. But if you're exclusive, you really owe it to the guy to break up with him before you date someone else.

I finger my hair. "Nothing else?"

"I'd warn you if he kept suggesting books about necrophilia." Beth sorts paper squares on the table. "If it's the guy I'm thinking of, the worst that could happen is you'll get fat from the yummy desserts."

"Bring 'em on!" I lean my elbows on a chair back. "That reminds me. He wants you to come for dinner with me on Saturday. I said you would."

Beth recoils. "Like hell I'm going to dinner with you two!"

"You and Stuart."

She frowns. "How about we have him cook for all four of us, and then Stuart and I cancel at the last second and you two can snuggle on the couch wondering where we are?"

"I've got a better idea. How about you come for dinner?" I head into the kitchen to grab a Coke only to quail at the sight of Mount Dishmore. "Did he just use every plate in the house?"

That's what I hate about visitors. You clean up for them, and when they leave you have to clean again.

Beth and I look at one another with a tacit understanding. She goes back to folding her origami, and I grab my bag to head for the gym. But first I check on our landlady.

Mrs. Goretti doesn't answer right away, so I call through the door. "I'm going out. Do you need anything?"

She opens up. "Would it be any trouble?"

Mrs. Goretti believes in never shopping on Sunday, and as a result, she's gotten caught with no milk for her coffee some Monday mornings. The gym is on Fourth Avenue; Key Food is on Seventh, so it's not on my way home, but she's an old woman. I'll run a little less on the treadmill.

She asks me to pick up milk and grated cheese ("Lucadell," she reminds me twice. It's always "Lucadell." Imagine my surprise after six months to learn it's actually *Locatelli*.) She gives me two dollars and tells me to be careful.

Mrs. Goretti is seventy-five and takes no guff from anyone. She rents us the apartment for less than a fortune because Beth and I sweep the steps in the fall and shovel them in the winter; we drag the trash cans to the curb and back again. I climb ladders to change her fifteen-watters (while she hovers beneath urging, "Careful! You'll fall!") She also has me climb ladders to wave flaming newspapers beneath her smoke detectors once a month (while Bucky hovers beneath urging, "Careful! You'll set yourself on fire!")

Mrs. Goretti knows the value of a dollar. She asks me to buy ten cans of tomato sauce, then gives me five dollars and a dollar-off coupon good only at Pathmark. I pick them up at Key Food for five dollars and throw away the coupon because it's not worth the hassle. I give her the tomato sauce cans and one dollar "change," which she tells me to keep. Now everybody is happy:

- Pathmark is happy because they didn't sell ten cans at a loss.
- Key Food is happy because they ripped me off for a buck.
- I'm happy because I didn't drive to Pathmark.
- Mrs. Goretti is happy because she thinks she saved money, and because she thinks she gave me a dollar.

It doesn't get any better than that.

Mrs. Goretti's two dollars and I head to the gym. It's a store-front with panes of glass so passers-by can recoil in horror. I drop my stuff in the locker room, change, and head to the publicly displayed torture chamber.

Before I get to the Iron Maiden—or is it a stair master?—there's a friendly voice. "Hey, Lee!"

I turn. "Bill!" Chocolate eyes, dark skin, square jaw: it's the physical trainer who refers to me as his dial-tone girl, there when you feel like picking up the phone, not there when you don't. No expectations, no frills, no strings. I've known Bill since...well, since I got my membership. He made a point of copying my phone number off the contract. I liked his style.

Since I've only got a few weeks before Mom decides I'm forever unmarriageable, I give him that half-squint-plus-head-tilt that makes guys grin. "I thought you left the country to avoid me."

"I'm back." He gives me a chuck on the shoulder. "How are things going in the political world?"

Due to a verbal mishap, I kind of told Bill I work for a political action committee. We'd gone to a bar near the gym, and when I mentioned something about the shop, Bill gaped as if I said I vivisected kittens. "What do you mean?"

I don't know—I'd thought maybe guys might find car-fixing to be cool. So instead I blurted out some job I saw on a discarded newspaper further down the bar.

That was the first time I ever used that particular dodge, and it keeps being my career because no one knows what political action committees do. Even better, no one cares. It's like saying *Insert instant change of subject matter.*

Bill leans against the counter. "Want to do something on Saturday?"

"The evening's taken. A master chef is throwing a dinner party in my honor." I squint while thinking. "And I'm working in the morning. Friday night is free." I'll be seeing Hal the next day, but it's not as if Hal owns me. "What did you have in mind?"

"Anything." That's what I like about Bill: you can't call him driven. "Movie? I've been thinking about *Thrillseeker II*."

My nose wrinkles. "You can't think of anything more exciting than a movie?"

Bill laughs. "Indoor glow-in-the-dark paintball? They opened a place on Third Avenue in one of those old warehouses," and I catch myself just before I squeal. Paintball? That's so cool!

That's what I'm talking about. I could take or leave the guys, but man, I love New York.

At the garage ten-thirty Wednesday morning, we get a walk-in, a short woman with a five-year-old boy bundled into a lime-green parka. She needs a tire patched; it's in the trunk. She hands over the keys, and I head to her Honda Accord to fetch it.

I open the trunk, and the next instant there's a shove against my chest as the lid slams down like a guillotine.

Bucky's between me and the car, eyes ablaze.

I stammer, "What the hell?"

He's flushed. "You're welcome."

"Yeah, thank you. Sorry." Keeping clear, I lift the lid again, and once more it drops. A third time, but now I don't let go while I make my expert diagnosis. I return to the waiting area.

"Mrs. Zhou," I say, "your car tried to kill me."

She looks puzzled. Then, "Oh, you have to prop the trunk with a broom handle."

"Ordinarily there's a piston that keeps it aloft." I open our parts catalog to get a quick quote. "We could replace it if you'd rather use your trunk without risking amputation."

The woman looks blank.

I wait her out, then give up. "Would you like the trunk lid to stay up without a broom handle?"

It turns out she would. When trunk pistons don't appear in the table of contents, I set Max on the trail of the correct part, and then, with the help of the broom handle, I retrieve a tire flatter than my mother's soufflés.

Eventually I find a puncture so tiny it shouldn't have deflated anything. I circle it with a grease pencil, patch it, refill it, and balance it. I roll it back into the waiting area, charge fifteen bucks like a good little mechanic, and then roll the tire back to the car for our customer, who holds the trunk lid aloft like the Statue of Liberty.

"I'll track down that piston and give you an estimate," I say.

Mrs. Zhou shrugs. "I've kind of gotten used to it."

Inside, I take the next ticket to find a hand-printed list of requests taped to the form. Oil change, tire rotation, radiator service, check all the belts. Nothing's wrong with the car, at least not that the owner knows. Sounds good.

I glance at the owner: he's the five-foot-five white-haired gentleman sitting with his cane between his knees, cursing at the sports section of the *New York Post*.

He catches my glance. "Overpaid bunch of morons. Have you ever seen such inept playing in your life?"

Uncertain which overpaid bunch of morons he's talking about, I say, "Mason's not too bad."

"Not basketball!" He huffs. "Hockey! Hockey used to be for real men, but now they're all a group of crybabies. You ever see blood bouncing on the ice?"

With Bucky pale at my back, I confess to having missed such a spectacle.

"I'm not surprised," he mutters. "Back in the day, you weren't a real player until you lost four teeth."

Ah, yes. I flee to the company of his car.

There's no mistaking exactly which one it is: the 1987 Cadillac. It's the kind of car where you say, "Hey! Caddy!" followed by, "Oh, good grief, 1987." The book value must be the same as the price of the oil it leaks when you trawl around the block hunting for a space big enough to wedge the thing.

I get inside the car to pop the hood, and—wow. If "cigar smoke" is a type of aromatherapy, then I'm all therapied up for the next five years. I also detect Eau Du Dog, that special scent where you turn on the heat, and suddenly it's as if that dog you owned during the Clinton administration is right back with you in the car.

In my head I hear Bucky: *It's not that bad.*

I let off a long sigh.

Bucky adds, *Well, no, I don't have a sense of smell.*

I spend the next half hour working on a car from the Good Old Days when ten miles per gallon was fit for kings, and because the owner is so nice,* I clean out the interior, vacuum the salt from the rugs, and wipe down the dashboard with a rag that, to be honest, may not have been washed since the car was assembled.

Mack's Auto has three other mechanics and Max. I got my job two years ago when I was knee-deep in restoring the Mustang. One morning, tired of waiting for one of the mechanics to get around to doing whatever it was I didn't have the right tool for, I told Max I was going to take his unused bay and pay him for his time. He was fine with that for the same reason you'd be fine with finding a twenty dollar bill in your loaf of Wonder bread.

When I pulled out, another customer demanded that I couldn't "go on break" without changing his oil. Much to Max's amusement, I did it. Max gave me three more oil changes and a tire rotation, and when his wife stopped by, he laughed it up with her.

They ogled my Mustang. We talked cars, and they found out how much I hated my job as a legal secretary. *"Egomaniac and Stuckup, Esquires. This call is being billed at $92 an hour. How may we pervert the justice system this morning?"* Two weeks later I started my new

---

* *By which I mean, "Because I'm delaying out of a desire not to discuss bodily fluids some more."*

job at Mack's, doing the boring maintenance in the mornings, then venturing into the cooler, more difficult stuff under Max's supervision. I took classes at night to get certified.

I knew my mom would blow a gasket. That's why I didn't tell her for two months, until she called me at work and found out the hard way. Hard for me, that is. I held the phone two feet from my ear while the entire waiting room got treated to my mother's opinion.

The money's good. To be honest, though, I'd have done it just for the tools. Every morning when I walk into the garage, I open the storage closet with the same feeling as in 1994 when I took the subway to Wall Street to watch the ticker-tape parade celebrating the Rangers winning the Stanley Cup, paper streaming from the office windows and everyone hollering as they pushed to glimpse, just once, New York City's heroes.

Also, I love the guys here. Max and his wife Allison are like a cool aunt and uncle. The other mechanics are Carlos, who works both for us and part-time at a track to support his wife and kids; Ari, who worked for two years to bring his bride over from Pakistan while completing college at night; and Tim, as old as Max and as verbose as Calvin Coolidge.

And I love the cars. Even—yes, even—this 1987 Cadillac.

I'm recording the mileage for the oil change sticker when my phone rings. Caller ID says it's Avery. "Hey, girl."

"Aunt Lee?" she says. "I hate everyone."

Noting the film of cigar smoke lining the windshield, I'm tempted to agree. Instead I put some hurt into my voice. "Me too?"

Instead of absolving me, she says, "Shelly is an idiot. She keeps staring at me and then I can hear them whispering, and no one will do anything about it."

"Take a deep breath." I wipe the windshield but it looks like a job for Mr. Windex instead of Mr. Rag. Or maybe Mr. Sand Blaster. "I'm going to be there at four. That's five hours. You can deal with anything for five hours, right?"

She's quiet. Then, "I guess."

"Hold your head up. Look them in the eye. You've got nothing to be ashamed of. Okay?"

My phone beeps, but I don't want to grab call waiting.

"I hate this," she whines. "They were supposed to be my friends." Then, "Gotta run. Bye." And she hangs up.

Well, I guess I can pick up call waiting after all. Before I do, I think, *Bucky? Can you check on her?*

A quick assent. I think toward his departing self, *And maybe break those girls' pencil points while you're at it.*

I pick up the call waiting. "Hello?"

"Hi, Lee? It's Hal Baxter, from last Sunday." My goodness, does the master chef accountant sound nervous? Nervous of me? "Are you okay to take calls at work?"

I chuckle. "I answered, didn't I?"

"I guess." Yeah, definitely jittery, but he plunges ahead. "It occurred to me that I don't know if you have any food allergies or aversions."

I scrub in vain at cigar residue that may be as old as the car. "I eat everything."

"Everything?"

"Well, everything except American cheese."

He gives a sniff. "American cheese is not food."

"In that case, yes, I've eaten everything I've been served in my life so far."

A pause. "Sea cucumber?"

Oh, toughie. "It comes wrapped in foil, right? Pickled, served at room temperature? A bit salty and gelatinous, but not bad."

"You're braver than I am." That's raw admiration in his voice.* "I wasn't thinking of anything quite that

---

* *Or maybe pickled admiration.*

adventuresome. Stuart's tastes run more toward well-done hamburgers."

I've eaten with Beth and Stuart. Beth would eat live spiders if she had to. For Stuart? Hold the ketchup.

I'm about to say this when I see Ari lift the pneumatic impact wrench. Before I can mute the phone, the whine shrieks through the garage.

"Whoa," Hal says. "You okay? Aren't you at work?"

"Uh—" I don't try to speak until Ari does the rest of the lug nuts. As he slides the wheel from the axle, I say, "You still there?"

Hal says, "What was that?"

"I'm—" My heart pounds. Bucky isn't around to give me that glare. "It's— It's just some machinery."

Shock in his voice: "Where are you? What do you *do*?"

Where else do they have machinery? "At the gym?" Swallowing, I choke out, "I'm a personal trainer."

"Remind me never to enroll there. Doesn't it affect your enrollment if they die before they renew?"

"Yeah. Um—" Bucky's going to kill me. Angel or not, he's going to slay me where I stand. "About the menu, don't cramp your style on my account." I finally see light through the yellow film coating the windshield, but that only highlights the parts that haven't yet succumbed. Right now the interior smells more of ammonia than dog, which I would have thought impossible. "Cook until your heart's content."

"Thanks," he says. "I think I will. See you on Saturday."

"See you."

I step out of the vehicle to find Mr. Hockey leaning on his cane, watching. "Sir," I say, trying to avoid a lecture about being on my cell phone, "you shouldn't be in here."

He murmurs, "I was just admiring the sexiest thing in the shop."

What the hell?

Then I realize he's not looking at me but behind me. Neither is he looking at Ari, who appears ready to run. He's got his eye on my Mustang.

Max allows me to bring the Mustang on slow days, and when there's no one around, sometimes I'll knock any one of six dozen items off my perpetual to-do list.

Mr. Hockey runs smooth fingertips over my car's rear quarter panels, then peers inside. He pops open the door and has a long gaze.

Moving toward him, I say, "It's a beauty, isn't it?"

My Mustang is blue, a metallic navy hardtop coup with a 170-cubic-inch, six-cylinder engine and a three-speed manual transmission. Snicker if you like, but it's the "secretary" model. It has 101 horsepower, which is laughable by today's standards when a Nissan Maxima or even a Honda minivan packs 240, and given that the car is heavier than the Nissan Tin Can, it's not an overpowered monster.

But boy, does it look like it could be. The lines on my baby make pedestrians' eyeballs bulge. I've spent enough hours on the engine that it purrs and growls like a kitten. When I'm driving, it's a homeostasis: I know when a belt is slipping or the brakes are thirsty just by the car's sound or the smell. I have rewired everything in the dashboard, replaced everything in the car except the car itself. Many women my age carry a diaper bag; I carry half a disassembled engine in my trunk. I've restored the leather seats so they're supple as a baby's cheeks, and I redid the paint job so it sparkles in the winter sunlight.

Mr. Hockey says, "Can I sit in it?"

I assent, hoping the leather interior won't pick up residual dog smell. The man slips into the passenger side. I lean in through the driver's side window.

"Definitely a beauty." The wrinkles around his eyes relax. "It reminds me of my brother's first car."

Before I can ask if the Cadillac was his first car, I stop myself. I also stop myself before I ask if he has a thing for old cars. In fact, I can't think of anything polite to say at all due to an overdose of sarcasm.

Finally I say, "You can enjoy it for a little longer. I'll be done with your car in five minutes."

While I'm scrubbing the remainder of the windshield, I feel Bucky return, and a moment later he says, "This is an unusual way to bench press."

"I'm sorry," I whisper. "Hal heard the air wrench, and I panicked."

Bucky sighs, but there's no lecture and no bloodshed. I guess because it's hard to clean blood out of a leather interior.

I vacuum out the car. At least, I do until the shop vac chokes, followed by the whine of a blocked hose. Pulling the nozzle from beneath the seat, I find a Christmas card sucked firmly across its face. A moment later, I'm looking at a picture of the New York Rangers.

I shouldn't, but I open the card to discover the signatures of the entire team.

My hands are shaking. I stand away from the car. "Mr. Rossman? This Christmas card...is yours?"

Unimpressed, he waves a hand. "My grandson sent it to me. Thinks he's doing me a favor. I forgot to throw it out."

I'm numb. "Your grandson?"

His grandson is, he tells me, Paul Rossman, goalie for the New York Rangers. He tells me to get rid of the stupid thing.

He might as well have said, "Those gold doubloons? Toss them in the trash!"

I muster, "Can I keep it?"

He laughs. "You like that bunch of pansies?" He whips out his wallet and pulls out two tickets. My heart pounds in my ears until I'm not sure how I'm standing upright, and he extends his hand. "Take them. My grandson keeps giving me this garbage. Such wimps."

Chapter Six:

A good old-fashioned New York assessment of my character

I don't take out the Mustang often, especially during the wintertime when I can hear the salt in the undercarriage singing "Mmm, mmm good!" But today I de-mothballed the car for Avery.

While waiting, I run my hands along the dashboard, feeling the power in its firmness. I trace my fingertips along the stick shift knob, snuggle lower in the seat and let the car engulf me. The tan and chrome dashboard, sparse compared to today's overcrowded panels, impresses me with its chiseled lines. The car surrounds me and fills me with its potential.

My Acura is my everyday car, which I can park on the street. That's a 2009, but it's only got thirty thousand miles. No joke—a little old lady who only drove it to church asked us to do an inspection before she sold it. The car was a peach. When she said the nice ~~thief~~ young man at the desk had offered her five thousand bucks, I pulled out the blue book, showed her where Ted had "misread" the column, and I offered her ten grand on the spot. She actually drove me to the bank.

Ted, by the way, didn't only have a problem misreading the blue book. I've never seen Max as mad as the day Ted got canned. Some people you just hand a credit card and fraud happens. At least the police were laughing when they cuffed him.

My Acura and I: we're okay. But the Mustang and I are a team. We can hit the road for anywhere, and because this is an engine from before the days when computers ran everything, there's nothing to come between us. I can diagnose and repair anything that could go wrong. Just me and an engine and a little cab to keep us together.

Oh, here we are, girls exiting the school, so I exit the car. They've got that *look,* the one that leaves me tense inside. How they toss their heads, the way they walk just a little too close and put their hands on one another's arms. They keep their jackets open to the chill: you can't be cool if you're warm.

Leaning against the side of the Mustang, I let my breath curl into frost. More girls emerge, Avery walking hunched among them. She doesn't wave when she sees me, but where the walkway splits off at the sidewalk, she veers in my direction.

Some of the girls call, only Avery lengthens her stride. Two of them follow.

I fold my arms. They catch up to Avery as she reaches me.

One of the girls smirks. "Nice wheels."

"Thanks." I grab Avery's backpack. "You ready to go?"

Another girl gasps. "You're here for her?"

I nod. "Girls' night out."

The first girl flags over the others at the walkway. The second says, "This is your Mustang? Is it an antique?"

I say, "I rebuilt it myself."

The other girl says, "You went in the engine and fixed things?"

"Fixed things, replaced things, repainted things." I look at Avery, who has a grin ghosting her lips. "It was a blast."

By now half a volleyball team surrounds me, and they all have questions: does it have a radio? No power windows? How fast does it go? Do you race it? Why does it have three pedals?

After the girls' interest wanes, I open the door like a chauffeur. As she's getting inside but before the girls turn away, Avery says, "Aunt Lee is teaching me to drive."

A collective gasp. Then they look at me.

Like fun I was going to teach her to drive—and on this car?

But they're looking, so I say, "As long as she can get the brake and the clutch to the floor, why not?" I slam Avery's door, then walk around the front. "Nice meeting you!"

I keep smiling as I start the engine, but she won't mistake my flat tone for approval. "I'm teaching a fourteen-year-old to drive?"

"I'm sorry, Aunt Lee." She hunches up again. "It's just—"

"They're that bad to you." I rev the engine, then launch onto the road with a force that jerks Avery into her seat. Goodbye, volleyball team! I now know again how it feels when someone talks about you behind your back.

I'd planned on the mall or the library or just hanging out at a coffee shop. Corinne had assured me it didn't matter where we went, as long as we went together, so I drive to the mall. The cars are all snuggled up by the entrance with none in the overflow lots, so to the overflow lot I go.

I set the car in neutral. "Get out."

Avery looks confused. "Isn't this far? Aren't you coming in?"

"Come around to my side." I slide the seat all the way forward and get into the passenger seat, then make Avery buckle herself into the driver's side. She's short: the steering wheel is in her lap. "The pedal on the far left is the clutch. Hold it down with your left foot until I say to stop."

Avery depresses the clutch. The engine seems alive under her hands, banging the wheel even though the car is still.

"Push the brake with your right foot. Can you get it down all the way?" She can. "Now turn the wheel." I show her where to place her hands, and she experiments with just how far it turns in either direction.

"Take the stickshift." Making sure she keeps the clutch depressed, with my hand on hers over the knob, I slide the car into reverse, into first, into second, and into third. (Only a three speed manual transmission for me. Bucky says I can't be trusted with five.) I slide it back into neutral.

She looks confused. "I don't get it."

I chuckle. "I'm teaching you to drive, silly."

Avery grips the wheel tighter. "Really? You're not mad?"

"Keep your foot on the clutch." I sigh. "I don't want to make things worse for you."

Head down, Avery gives a shy smile. "I didn't mean to make you. It kind of popped out." She bites her lip. "I just wanted... I just thought if maybe I did something cool—"

"They'll find a reason to hate you if they're looking for one." I let out a long breath. "Either you're too good or you're too bad, or you're too ugly or you're too beautiful. People are too demanding to destroy yourself for their approval." I gesture to the dashboard. "Next you're going to put it into gear. But first, there's two ways to make a car go forward and two ways to make it stop."

I give her the same lecture Uncle Mickey gave me when he first taught me to drive, along with tips Randy had shared with me.

Then the tough part: teaching her to shift.

Ten minutes later, Avery sits, red-faced, tears in her eyes. "I'll never get this! How do people learn to drive?"

Great way for me to build up her confidence, huh?

"You're not as bad as I was when I started." I make sure she's got the clutch depressed and take it out of gear.

"How'd you end up with a car this old, anyhow?"

"This used to be Uncle Mickey's. He wanted to get rid of it. I thought it was cool, so I bought it. And then he offered to teach me how to fix it." I smirk. "Aunt Mary said it was too much trouble to do it himself, but not too much trouble to spend five times the hours showing me how."

Avery grins. "That must have been fun, though. Uncle Mickey's a riot."

"Well, I got tools and I picked up the know-how, but I had no clue how to drive it." I laughed. "Back in those days, I had to use the *phone book*. I called someone and got two driving lessons for manual transmission cars."

She nods. "And—?"

"One day I went out to his place, and without telling him, I took it out on the street. Within four blocks I'd stalled fifteen times. That's when the guy behind me laid on the horn and treated me to a good old-fashioned New York assessment of my character, my heritage, my morals, my intelligence, and my right to own a vehicle more complicated than a tricycle."

Hint: it was not complimentary.

Avery clenches her fists on the wheel. "What did you do?"

"I panicked?" I laugh. "I fought it into gear one last time so I could buck to the side of the road, and there it died while I just broke down and cried."

Her eyes are as wide as golf balls. "And?"

"A stranger older than Uncle Mickey knocked on my window, and against all common sense I opened it. He said, *First time driving a standard?,* and he didn't sound like he thought I was the daughter of unwed dogs. He said, *Mustangs shift really hard. Eventually you're going to have huge muscles on your right arm.*"

I rub my upper arm. "He was right, too. I asked him to drive me home, and then he wouldn't take any money and he wouldn't even give me his name so I could send a gift."

Avery says, "Lucky you that he came along."

I squeeze her arm. "Don't feel bad when you stall. Once upon a time, I was the worst driver in the city of New York. You'll catch on."

Avery and I appear to have beaten Randy home. With that instinctive teenage sense of what she should not tell her mother, Avery yells, "Thank you for taking me to the mall, Aunt Lee!" and dashes into the bedroom she shares with Susanne.

I join Corinne in the kitchen, which smells like spaghetti sauce. It takes one look to realize she's holding herself together by a thread.

Oh, great. Either Randy's dead or he's leaving her.

I glance at the stove to make sure nothing is going to boil over, then take a seat catty-corner to her.

She says in a low voice, "I talked to the school again about how the girls have been harassing Avery. And—" She plucks a tissue from the box before her. "It's my fault. They're all saying that Avery made them do it."

My eyes are huge. "Would you care to run that by me again?"

In a dangerously low tone, she continues, "Because I take antidepressants, you see. Obviously I've taught Avery that pills make you happy."

Now I want to kill. "Is this a witch hunt?"

"I got it from the school secretary, and then from the principal." Corinne wads the tissue and presses it into her eyes. "The coach threatened that if I didn't stop raising trouble, she'd boot Avery off the team."

My heart hammers. "Are you going to pull the kids from the school?"

"I'd like to." Her voice cracks. "If this is going to happen, why not just send them to public school where at least I won't pay for folks to put the knife in my back?"

I scoot my chair closer so I can hug her.

She tenses under my arm. "My kids would be better off with no mother at all."

"Don't say that!" I grab her tighter. "How are antidepressants any different than taking insulin or antibiotics?"

She sounds flat. "Good mothers don't get depressed."

My brain is whirling—I'm not a mom, but that can't be true. "How can they think that?"

The water for the spaghetti boils over. I dart to the stove before she's even out of her chair, and the burner snaps off with a click. "When will Randy be back?"

"Soon." She looks deflated. "I would have fed the kids earlier, but I couldn't think."

"No problem." I test the spaghetti. The table isn't ready, so I put on four place settings. *Bucky, could I ask you to go afflict someone with boils like those Biblical angels?*

You could try. He sounds unamused.

How about you just remove the fruit from their fruit-on-the-bottom yogurt?

No response. I get the pitcher of water and a gallon of milk from the fridge, then look for parmesan cheese. Corinne still isn't moving.

This isn't fair. These parents hurt her because they don't feel like thinking their own kids made a mistake. Corinne was an easier target, and she took it through the heart.

Before I say something I'll regret—although maybe Corinne needs someone to get good and angry on her behalf—I go into the living room to tell Brennan and Susanne to get ready for dinner.

They're playing with a plastic Noah's Ark. Brennan rams it into a throw pillow, crashing it over on its side.

Waving a tiger, Susanne squeaks, "Aaah! The Ark hit an iceberg! Everyone into the lifeboats!"

Brennan falsettos, "There aren't enough!"

"Noah has to go down with the ship," calls Susanne.

Brennan continues in a high-pitched voice, "You can't come onto the lifeboat, Tiger! You're a sinner!"

"Uh, kids?" I'm not sure whether to guffaw or scream. "You'd better get your hands washed for dinner."

As soon as they're arguing about who uses the bathroom sink first, I return to the kitchen.

Corinne rubs her temples. "Were they still playing with the Ark?"

I swallow. "I'm really sorry about that."

"Avery keeps talking about the *Titanic* as if it's romantic to suddenly drown." She sighs. "Brennan and Susanne tossed that into their Cuisinart brains, and you heard the result." She pauses. "Did the big fish come yet to eat Noah?" When I shake my head, she says, "After three days, it spits him out, and then the dove flies to the lifeboat with some of Noah's hair in its beak."

I can't tell if Bucky just flinched or smothered a laugh.

Randy saves my bacon by coming home just then. Corinne hugs him before he's even put down his bag.

He gets a slightly longer version of the story than I did, complete with names (*I hope you're taking notes, Bucky, for afflicting these people with boils*).

His response: "How did they find out you're taking antidepressants?"

She gasps.

"You specifically didn't tell people at the church or the school, not after you heard them gossiping about Sylvia's problems."

"The only one who knows is—"

Corinne goes white.

Randy throws his coat into the closet and slams the door. "Terrific. We've not only got drug-experimenting volleyball players and parents who don't feel like parenting. You've also had a confidence betrayed by the pastor's wife."

Chapter Seven:

I officially can no longer win this one

Friday morning: I look up to find Mrs. Zhou, she of the guillotine trunk lid, with her five-year-old a pace behind.

"Good morning!" I wave to the boy, who smiles as if I were Mr. Goodwrench herself. "I was going to call when we found a trunk piston."

She looks puzzled, then says, "No, I was wondering about the tire you patched. Should it have air inside it?"

Now that's a loaded question. "It should."

We return to her vehicle where she props up the trunk so I can verify that no, there is no air inside the tire. I remove the tire, she lets the trunk slam, and I roll it into the garage.

The patch held. What's the deal?

Max examines the whole tire with me and finds bad news: a crack in the sidewall, the kind you can't patch. I return to our customer while Max fetches a replacement.

She's remarkably good-tempered about having made a second trip, and when I price the replacement, I deduct fifteen bucks for the unsuccessful patch.

When he comes from the back, Max encourages her to buy a pair of tires instead of just one; she declines as the opposite tire is itself new. Max asks to look at it, which I know will result in the tire being badly in need of replacement. Maybe she suspects it too, because she says it's on the other car, three miles away. Breaking into the conversation before Max offers to drive there, I offer to just attach the new tire to the old rim and fill it with the kind of air that stays put.

The job takes twenty minutes. I roll the tire to the trunk, heave it in while she holds the lid, and then remind her that I'm still searching for a trunk piston.

"No rush," she tells me.

I return to find Max glowering at the computer. "You undercharged."

"I refunded the tire patch."

He shakes his three-quarter finger in my face. "Did she ask for a refund? She did not."

Well—yeah. "Good customer service?"

He scowls. "It's not good customer service if she didn't ask for it."

I open my wallet and hand him a twenty. He bats it away. "Don't do that again. I don't mind you missing the crack on the sidewall. If it brings her back a thousand times, I don't care. But don't be giving away my money."

You know what? I disagree with our octogenarian patron who thinks the Rangers are a bunch of wimps. I'm enjoying the hell out of this game.

Our friend with a little too much bloodlust has gifted us third-row seats. This close, we feel the chill of the ice. If someone were to bleed, we would in fact see the blood freeze.

The second "garbage" ticket found a home in Bill. Why? Because when I told him I couldn't justify playing paintball for twenty bucks when I could watch the Rangers get pummeled for free, he offered me a kidney for the other ticket.

Of course I said that wasn't necessary: I would never take Bill's kidney. Bucky says none of my internal organs require replacement yet.

Oh, and Bucky's here too because Bucky doesn't require a ticket. But now you're wondering, how does Bucky like hockey?

He's standing on the back of my seat, shouting, "You're missing a great game, Ref!"

No one is sitting. Well, maybe the forward's 98-year-old great-grandmother. Everyone is screaming. It's a blast.

Bucky cheers at an interception. There's an obvious foul, but no call, and he shouts, "Hey, Ref, are you totally blind, or just legally blind?"

Thank you, Mr. Hockey. You rock.

Bucky's wings flare. "Hey, Goalie! Your mom's on the phone! She says you're a loser!"

"Bucky!" I exclaim. "That's just mean."

He bounces on his toes. "Don't play hockey if you can't stand a little critique."

Oh dear. Although to be honest, the things the rest of the crowd is screaming make Bucky sound complimentary.

At the end of the game, Bill and I take the subway back to Park Slope. Once there, on the grounds that it's way too early to call it a night (only eleven) I suggest we hang out. Bill suggests his apartment, and I suggest pizza. We walk a couple of blocks to Pino's Pizzeria.

While waiting at the counter, a glance shows Bucky back to his normal self.

Do they have sports in Heaven?

He shrugs. *We have games, but no organized teams. Certainly not leagues.*

I imagine several thousand of Bucky suggesting an angelic referee get a pair of glasses, and it's not pretty. *Who referees?*

We don't argue with God. A pause. *Well, not most of the time.*

Oh, terrific. Now I'm trying not to imagine the Archangel Michael yelling at God, "It stayed fair! I saw it!"

Angels don't foul each other, Bucky said. *That wouldn't be sportsmanlike.*

Glad to hear it. The pizza arrives. We eat while I trade opinions with Bill about whether the Islanders did the stupidest thing in their entire history (which would have to be pretty stupid) when they fired their coach in the middle of the season. We're on opposite sides; he thinks it was dumber to hire the guy in the first place.

Bill says, "So what have you been up to?"

I shrug. "My niece got in trouble with some girl-bullies at the high school. So I'm going to mentor her."

Bill laughs so loud that a guy behind the counter drops his pizza pan.

"Very funny," I mutter.

"You?" he says. "You're mentoring some kid?"

Jaw clenched, I pay very close attention to sprinkling parmesan cheese on my pizza.

"Babe, don't get mad. It's not that I don't think you'd do a good job—"

I wait him out, an excellent technique for verifying that someone has no idea how to get out of the hole he's dug himself.

When the silence has lasted longer than some insects' life spans, I put a chill into my voice. "Do you have any better ideas?"

One of Bill's hallmarks is his skill at extracting himself from certain death. "You should take her to a women's self-defense course."

That might be fun. "But I don't want her to get expelled for fighting. Girls don't bully that way."

"The point isn't to beat them up." He pours more Coke from the pitcher. "The point is to carry yourself with confidence because you know you *could* beat them up."

I sigh. "They made her a social pariah."

Bill says, "Knowing she can walk away will make her more attractive to everyone. They'll know she doesn't need them."

Is that true? Maybe that's why I'm never short of a date.

After midnight I don't feel guilty about wasting an evening, so I suggest heading home. Bill wants to come with me. There's some good-natured tussling, resulting in playful kisses and him trying to get his arms around me. I sidle free and say, "No."

Bill's a good sport. He drives me the three blocks home, and I kiss him goodnight before heading inside. Yes, I have to remind him, yes I'm sure he's not coming inside. Thank you for coming to the game, etc. He's gone, and I'm back upstairs alone.

Eighteen years ago, I begged Bucky to be my first kiss.

It's not what you think. After my mother gave me The Talk, rather than ask her questions, I asked Bucky. It's a truism that kids ask their friends, and since Bucky actually knew what he was talking about, he and I had endless discussions about the fascinating changes awaiting me in the next years.

That is to say, it couldn't have been fascinating to him. Regardless, for a couple of weeks, all our talks were about intercourse, puberty, secondary sex characteristics, tampons, and biological processes. The only question he couldn't answer was what sex felt like because he had no personal experience.

By the time I was twelve, Bucky had covered STDs, unwanted pregnancies, and emotional complications. In his angelic opinion, I needed to do something radical, something only six thousand years of human history could have devised: married monogamy. I needed to pick one forever-guy before having sex.

I'd heard the radio often enough to know two things. First, true love fails all the time. And secondly, if you didn't have sex, you'd die. He assured me the Angel of

Death would not actually be reading magazines on my couch.

Eventually I agreed on the following grounds: in the current culture, virginity is the ultimate non-conformity. *Nothing* would shock my mother more.

Plus, if I ever decided virginity wasn't working for me, that could be remedied. But pregnancy, AIDS, herpes, and the emotional issues attached to multiple bed-partners weren't so easily reversible. He made sense then, and it keeps making sense: since the purpose of sex is babies and emotional bonding, if I don't want a baby and I don't want an emotional bond, I need other entertainment.

Yes, sometimes it's difficult. Yes, I've been dumped because of this. And you know what? I don't care. Eventually it dawned on me that sex in a relationship is like fifth gear in a car: sure, it'll be fun, but it'll be harder to corner, and I don't know if the relationship is rated for that kind of performance. Plus, think of how hard it would be to cool things off with Bill if he thought of me as an easy booty call.

During one of those conversations, I asked if Bucky would be my first kiss. He wanted nothing to do with it. I told him it should be someone special, and he said he was sure it would be.

I pressed on. My oldest brothers had already moved out. My dad had died. My grandfather was in the final stages of lung cancer. My best friend had just broken up with the hottest guy in the school. The message was clear. By contrast, Bucky had stuck with me for over a decade already, so this was a relationship with longevity.

"Please?" I perched on the edge of my bed, clutching a stuffed panda in a death-grip. I had cranked the *Rumours* album so my mom or brother wouldn't hear my voice.

Bucky sat amidst the clutter on my desk, looking about sixteen years old. "You make a great case. No."

A pain stabbed my heart. "What if no one ever kisses me and I have to become a nun?"

Bucky tucked up his knees and wove his fingers around one another. "Consecrating your life to God shouldn't be a last resort, for one thing, and for another thing," he said, talking louder over my protest, "no matter what your life evolves into, whether you're married or single, I will provide whatever support you require."

I sat forward. "But— But I'd miss out—"

Even as he raised his wings, Bucky's eyes went steely. "I am not your boyfriend. If you can't get that through your head, I'll appear to you as an eighty-year-old woman."

I was a philosophical preteen. "Eew!"

He tilted up his chin. "I would walk through fire for you. I will dedicate the next century of my existence to you. If I were able to die, I would die to save you. But I'm not going to kiss you."

I trembled, and then inadvertently I drew the ultimate blackmail. "You think I'm ugly!"

Bucky stared in horror as my tears overflowed. "I can officially no longer win this one." And he vanished.

When new guardians get assigned, their friends ought abduct the newbie to a quiet restaurant, and there they could have an assignment shower. On the gift registry: a two-by-four with a handle (aka a "clue-by-four,") a highlighted copy of *The Beginners Guide To Guarding A Soul* (fifth edition, expanded), ear-plugs for when the child starts any instrument more complicated than the kazoo, a flashing LED sign for the very obvious realities that the human will miss, and one other very important thing: the *In Event Of Teenage Hormonal Meltdown* emergency case. Within is a sense of humor (naturally in the shape of a rubber chicken.)

I can picture it now. Behind the newbie guardian lies a jumble of wrapping paper. As he holds up the sense of humor, his best friends mutters, "You're gonna need that."

The upshot was, within three days I got my first period, I moved on to collecting pictures of Hootie And The Blowfish, and as you've seen, I haven't had a problem finding someone to kiss every now and again.

At home, I find a note taped to the outer door. *"Leigh."*

Hal. If I've got nothing else to do, he suggests, since I was so interested in learning about omelets, I can come early tomorrow and he'll demonstrate some other techniques.

He's sweet. He really is.

At the table, Beth uses clear nail polish to shellac paper frogs, some no bigger than her thumbnail. "How was it?"

"Awesome. We went for the fights, but a hockey game broke out." I hold up the note. "Hal says if I come early he'll teach me more about cooking."

I'm about to drop it into the trash when Beth fixes on me a look that would curdle milk. Chastened, I hand over the note, which she unfolds, flattens, and then lays atop the stack of paper on the sideboard.

I wonder at what point we passed 'fire hazard' and moved into "Mrs. O'Leary's Bovine Delight"?

"You've got him snared." Beth paints polish on a pink frog, then gets a sly expression. "Although I have to tell you, Stuart laughed out loud when I told him."

I stiffen. "Why?"

"Apparently Hal 'likes his women to look like women.' That last girlfriend was a graphic designer, played the flute, and even got Hal to take ballroom dancing."

"Oh, God!" My eyes widen. "I can't compete with that!"

Beth laughs out loud, and a moment later I'm in stitches. "Clearly he's done with girly-girls," Beth says, even as I exclaim, "How evil was she if he's resorting to *me*!" and then Beth adds, "If it doesn't work out with you, maybe next he'll go for Stuart."

By this time, I'm gasping. I drop into a chair, surrounded by frogs and the reek of nail polish. "He's cleansing his palate."

"Whoa, watch it with that culinary vocabulary." Smiling wickedly, Beth turns back to her plague of frogs. "I'll see if I can't make Stuart late, so you have some time to *learn to cook*."

I roll my eyes, but hey, I'm not going to stop her. Tomorrow I'm going to find out how a chef heats things up.

Chapter Eight:

A special measuring cup

Hal meets me at the elevator on the fourth floor of the Ansonia Clockworks, a converted clock-making factory between Seventh and Eighth Avenues. Again I'm overtaken by that smile. He's wearing khakis and a polo shirt, and his shoes are Dockers. Does he even own jeans? Again I'm transfixed by his eyes. He doesn't object.

"I'm glad you could come early." He shifts his weight, as if unsure how to greet me. Maybe in Victorian England they had rituals for this kind of thing, like kissing your hand. We're Americans, so we have to wing it.

As we walk to his apartment, I say, "About your note—it's Lee like the jeans. My real name is Juliet."

He tilts his head. "You have brothers named Romeo and Othello?"

"Hamlet, too." I sound serious. "Either that or a delusional mother."

As he lets me inside, he says, "Sorry about the archaic means of communication. I'd have invited you in person, but you weren't there."

Plus, we haven't advanced to the point of exchanging email addresses, although he could have phoned. You know what that means? He wanted to see me.

"I scored free tickets to a hockey game, and— Oh wow, nice place."

Hal's door opens right into a living room. It would only just fit our dining room table, but the way he has it set up I can't imagine it larger. A tan loveseat fills one wall, its breadbox-thick cushions poised to engulf you the instant you sit too far back. No decorative pillows, only a fleece throw blanket, cream, draped over the back.

With no windows, Hal's made do with a painting in the center of each wall. Over the couch, a landscape by Albert Bierstadt looks upward into the Rocky Mountains. There's an impressionist vase of barely-opened tulips over the far wall, and over the television a seascape, sunrise twinkling across waves that, rather than incoming, seem to be undertowing back toward the ocean.

While he takes my jacket, I register that the apartment smells delicious, although at first I can't identify all the scents. Garlic and onions, as well as olfactory evidence that someone baked something. ("I've got the solution! It was Hal in the kitchen with the cake pans!") He hangs the jacket in the world's narrowest closet (no joke, the door is twelve inches) and then shifts his weight. "So, you, uh, wanted to learn a bit more?"

He leads me into the kitchen. I halt, open-mouthed.

All the square footage for his unit has converged here, with more counter-space than a McDonalds and half of that serving as storage space for gadgetry. I hear violins, but I'm relatively sure that's a symphony courtesy of the CD player, not angels rejoicing.

I cross the white-tiled floor to the center of the kitchen to stare at all the tools. He's mounted racks to the wall, loaded with spatulas and several mutations of spoons (with slots, with holes, in twisted contours.) Over the island, clear except for a cheese tray, a hanging rack dangles spotless pots and pans.

Pulse racing, I head for the counter bearing the most gadgetry: a coffee maker with more buttons than the Acura's dashboard; a coffee grinder and, heaven help me, a coffee roaster; a bread machine and an instant marinator and a Kitchen Aid mixer with a dozen attachments.

I spin toward him. "This is incredible! It's the Holy of Holies of food!"

Chuckling, he comes alongside me. "I did my best."

"You have to show me all these things!"

Hal begins a running tour. Let's meet our cast of characters, shall we? We have:

- A microplaner with teeth sharp enough to strip the shell off a nut
- A mandolin you push through vegetables or potatoes to make matchstick-sized pieces or waffle-cut fries
- A two-level wire whisk.
- A food processor which slices, dices, et cetera.
- Silicone spatulas, which he says he could no longer live without.
- A magic corkscrew, which can remove the cork from a wine bottle without any danger of pushing the cork into the wine.

His newest acquisition: a mortar and pestle to crush the herbs he grows and dries by the window. The ceramic makes a gratey sound as I play with it.

A magician's bedroom might resemble this, every drawer erupting with wonders. If I owned this kitchen, who knows? —I might even cook something.

"That's a cute one." I point to the smallest frying pan I've ever seen. "What's that for?"

He hesitates, then says, "It's the perfect size to fry one egg. It was a gift to myself about six months ago."

Oops—that's unsafe territory. I recognize a break-up gift when I see one.

Hal changes the subject by displaying what he's making for dinner, and I render the appropriate oohs and ahs. He's made roast beef with a béarnaise sauce and scalloped potatoes. He's roasting asparagus. He's prepared a tray of neat appetizers for a visit in the oven, and in the fridge awaits a tomato-basil salad with mozzarella balls, home-grown basil leaves and quartered plum tomatoes. The aroma—I want to keep inhaling forever.

Hal pulls a book off a wall-mounted rack. While he rifles through, I glance at the other titles: *Gastronomique, The New Professional Chef, A Clove of Garlic, Smoke and Spice, I'm Just Here For The Food, Professional Cooking, The Silver Palate Cookbook.*

"Here." He swivels it around for me. "Instructions on how to attach a hair dryer to a gas grill to turn it into a blast furnace."

I gasp. "Today?"

He shakes his head. "Sometime this summer, though."

Holy cow! Mrs. Goretti would never let me into her back yard again. Nor renew my lease. Nor let me back into the building to get my things. I wonder if Randy...?

Bucky, sitting on the counter, says, "No."

I frown. *You said you couldn't read my thoughts.*

"I don't have to." He folds his arms. "No."

Try and stop me.

A wicked grin flashes across his mouth. "Is that a dare? Let's see how well it works when the power goes out, the doorbell rings, the grill won't light—"

I shoot him a nasty look. *I won't burn down all of Brooklyn.*

"No," Bucky says. "You won't."

Sighing, I watch Hal replace the book.

Hal chuckles. "When I do it, I'll be sure to invite you." Then he shows me a shoebox-sized hibachi that on occasion he has clamped outside his window sill on a metal tray. (I'm aghast—why didn't I think of that?) "Later, the super told me about some weird complaints he'd gotten. Luckily he never asked if it was true."

I wonder where I can get a couple of clamps—

"No," says Bucky.

Again I sigh.

Hal brings me to the final quadrant of the kitchen to reveal a rotisserie oven and a pizza stone and a rice cooker and a garlic press. And then, with the gravity of Thomas Jefferson handing over the final draft of the Declaration of Independence, he opens a drawer to present me a dry-measure cup. A *special* measuring cup: it measures two cups. He had to look for over a year, but now when he makes cakes, he can do the two-cup measure and not the one-cup measure multiple times. I'm not sure anything will top that.

It gets quieter. Hal presses a button on the under-the-counter mounted CD player, and classical music returns. He asks if Beethoven is fine, and I say it is. I recognize this piece from Loony Toons.

Now, the culinary tour concluded, Hal uneasily tells me he has to make the soup. If I was uncertain before about his motive, I've got it nailed now. Although ostensibly I'm here to learn, he doesn't have me do anything. On a stool from the island I chat with him while he washes mushrooms, fries mushroom stems and onions, and slices mushroom caps.

(Again with the butter. If I ever need to drive away Hal, I'll open a tub of margarine. Like sunlight to a troll.)

Hal clears his throat. "Before I get to know you any better, I need to ask something."

A chill settles over me.

"Why did you have a hammer in with your kitchen supplies?"

Oh, nothing bad. "For when you need one."

"That wasn't a meat tenderizer."

I laugh. "We don't use it on meat."

He shivers. "You're implying you use it on something."

The conversation pauses while he whirls fried mushrooms in the food processor.

While he's scraping pulverized mushrooms and onion into the pot, I say, "The brown sugar gets hard."

He shrugs. "You can keep that from happening."

"But bullion cubes come square, and sometimes it says a teaspoon of bullion."

Hal's head jerks up. "You break it apart?"

"I'm not in your class." I look at my lap. "I'm not worthy to wash your two-cup measure."

He steps so close I could wrap my arms around him. "The next time you need bullion, I'll show you a better way."

"You do that," I murmur.

For a moment we're in one another's orbit. I've got goosebumps.

He reluctantly draws away to stir the soup. "How'd you manage to get free Rangers tickets?"

"Oh, some guy at work didn't want them."

Hal looks up. "Does one of the Rangers work out at the gym?"

I feel Bucky blaze up inside me. I drawl, "...not exactly..."

He says, "So tell me about your job."

If you were to compare the hot seat I'm on with the hot burner those mushrooms are on, I'm not sure which would win. "It's not that interesting. Tell me about yours."

He says, "You've carried a burning ember in your heart for years that could only be quenched by hearing about the life of an accountant?"

I lower my eyes and do something guaranteed to distract. "Is that why I'm warm when I'm with you?"

Silence. I look up to find Hal either thrilled or terrified. Finally I take pity on him. "Accounting is interesting. I'm math-challenged."

He's still off-balance. "I'm fitness challenged," he says, a blatant lie. "I've been talking the whole time. It's your turn."

And so I give up.

I tell him about the gym patron who used the leg machine on her arms and insisted she was supposed to lie flat on this tiny bench, and the guy who shot himself over the top of the Stairmaster. They're Bill's stories. Well, not now they aren't. Now they're mine.

I can't see Bucky, but boy, can I feel him.

I describe for Hal the mythical "weight-lifter face," whereby perfectly normal men who can lift a quarter ton with ease suddenly develop a strained rictus before a mirror. Hal laughs out loud. "The mirror increases the weights."

Then I say to Hal, "My favorite, though, are the ones who drive two blocks so they can run for thirty minutes on the treadmill."

Hal said, "I always wondered why there's a handicapped space in front of most gyms."

"Several disabled gym members work out for therapeutic reasons." I shrug. "But no, the seventeen-year-old guy in the black Land Rover isn't in denial when he fails to hang a handicapped placard. He's just a jerk."

Hal chokes on a laugh.

I smile wickedly. "I used to carry computer-printed signs in my gym bag, for placement on said vehicle. They read, in 96-point font, *The cops are too chicken to tow this car!*"

Hal gasps, "You didn't!"

"I placed five before he stopped parking there."

He tries so hard not to laugh, then gives in. "My goodness—you're insane."

I wink at him.

As Hal replaces all the whirled-up soup back in the pot to keep warm, the intercom buzzes, and I leave to let in Beth and Stuart.

Out at the elevator, Beth and I whisper for a moment while Stuart rolls his eyes, and only then do I realize how long the hallway is and how identical the doors. Luckily Hal emerges from one of them, and then we're all inside.

This dinner will inspire me for months. There's the music. There's the cheese and crackers I already mentioned (although you'd be nuts to fill up on that.) We begin the meal-proper with stuffed mushrooms and a spinach and artichoke hors d'ouvre on round slices of bread, which he broiled for just a moment to make it delightful.

After that first course which could have served as its own meal, out comes the cream of mushroom soup, and then the roast beef. (Broiled asparagus is nothing like the limp boiled stalks my mom used to serve. It's wilted, but the flavor is nutty.) He's too fit to eat this way at every meal, but goodness—how can he resist?

Is it my imagination, or does Hal get physically taller when we praise the food? I don't think it is. In fact, I think he's glowing.

Given the size of the dinner, we vote to delay dessert.

I'm always up for a new board game because Bucky likes them, so I ask if Hal has any. It turns out he does. Stuart, Beth and I wait while he finds them in his bedroom.

Beth and Stuart sit on the couch, which faces an eleven-inch television/DVD combo declaring SONY across the bottom. Hal keeps the remote on a gleaming end table tucked into the corner, and on that, a small rack of CDs. Curious, I clack through them. Not an ABBA album in sight. Instead, culture. Taste. Manhattan Transfer. Mozart's Divertimentos. Claude Bolling's *Suite For Flute And Jazz Piano*. Vivaldi's *Four Seasons.*

Hal returns with four games, some I've seen before. There's Monopoly, Carcassonne (a perennial favorite of mine,) Scrabble, and a game called Queries.

Stuart says Hal bought Queries as an ice-breaker for the book club. While it has a board, movements are determined by points the other players award based on how well they think you answered personal questions. Since the only ones in the group who don't know each other well are Hal and myself, I request Queries.

While Hal sets up the board, he says to Stuart, "You must be jealous as hell about the Ranger tickets."

Stuart says, "Which tickets?"

Hal says to me, "Oh, I'd assumed Beth went with you."

I shrug "I went with a guy I know from the gym."

Hal tenses. Beth says, "It's just Bill. He's been hanging around for years."

"Oh." Hal's voice is a little lower as he sets the game out on the coffee table.

We'd better let that blow over as fast as possible. Beth and I mock-fight about which one of us gets to be red. "Red always wins!" Beth declares, and I shoot back, "That's why I wanna be red!"

The questions begin simply: what is your favorite color? (Red, because red always wins.) What is your favorite pastime? If you could meet anyone from history, who would it be?

I take the top card. "Who is your role model?"

Hal says, "My father."

I lean toward him. "Aww, that's so sweet."

He recoils. "You don't look up to your father?"

I shrug. "My dad died when I was five."

He flinches. "I'm sorry."

"Don't be." I trace a small circle on the table-top. "It's just something that happened."

Leaning against Stuart's shoulder, Beth says, "He was a firefighter."

I nod. "He saved two children from a burning house. He knew the place was coming down, but the kids were trapped in their bedroom on the third floor. The stairway collapsed, but he got them out."

Hal swallows. "That's brave. Your father was someone's hero."

I let out a long breath. "Yeah. But my role model would be Teddy Roosevelt. Speak softly and carry a big stick."

Hal gives me five points. Maybe he feels sorry.

Stuart's card says, "Do you judge people based on their cars?"

Beth, Stuart and Hal all stare when I snort. "Absolutely I do."

Beth says, "That is so not right."

"To a point it is." They're all still aghast. "Okay, if a person buys used, he's limited. But if he buys new, he's telling you a lot about himself. There are umpty-skillion cars, option packages, and colors. Why would the manufacturers do that if people weren't making choices based on who they are? And if someone's buying a Hummer, he'd better be getting shot at."

Hal laughs. "But other than that—"

"If you see someone driving a brand new Lexus," I say, "then you know he either has money or else doesn't mind a lot of debt, and he values performance but doesn't put a premium on it. If that same person plunked down that same money on a high-end Volvo, you'd know he wanted performance and safety. If he owned a BMW, you'd know he liked a fun drive and wanted attention. And if that rich guy bought a Hyundai Elantra, you'd know he thought of a car merely as transportation."

Hal cocks his head. "How do you know all this?"

My heat stills. I can't very well tell him I see hundreds of car owners every month, can I, now?

But I can bluff. "It's obvious."

Stuart laughs. "Not to everyone else."

Stuart doesn't know I'm a mechanic. I mean, he did know for three minutes, during which time he laughed so hard I thought he'd burst his appendix. When he kept going on and on about it, I thought Beth was going to unleash a plague of origami locusts on him, so I spared us the whole booking-for-murder hassle by claiming I worked with Beth. This seemed so much more sane that he patted my hand and said, "Good one."

Hal perks up. He might as well have a light-bulb illuminated over his head. "If that's true, that the car makes the man, then reverse it. Tell me what kind of car I drive."

Stuart says, "Yeah! Do it!"

Beth laughs. "You're in for it now."

Bucky?

I've had a brilliant idea: tell him you're an auto mechanic. That will neatly resolve this whole problem.

Not in front of Stuart I'm not going to. For one thing, after a meal of that density, he'd rupture his spleen if he laughed as hard as before.

I could flee down the hall, but then I'd miss dessert. Instead I study Hal. "For starters, you only reluctantly bought a car in the first place. You weren't dreaming of one from the day you turned sixteen."

"Accurate." He's still relaxed. "But I do own a car, so what is it?"

I squint as if reading tea leaves. "You're a sedan guy. You bought it new, but it's more than a few years old, paid off. You wouldn't lease a car."

Hal says, "Because I'm smart."

"Many smart people lease cars. You had better reasons not to." I rub my chin. "Based on your personality, I'd guess either an older Volvo or a five-year-old Camry XLE or the same age Accord EX."

Stuart laughs out loud, and Hal looks rattled. Then he forces a grin. "What color?"

Stuart and Beth both cry foul.

I shake my head. "Not unless you tell me the model."

He refuses.

"Fine, be a pain. Maroon Volvo, silver Accord, or dark green Camry."

Hal whistles. "Okay, I give up. What does it mean if I own a green Camry?"

I lean close to whisper, "That you're easily impressed?" I wink. "Or maybe that I'm going to get five points for this question?"

Laughing, Stuart awards ten.

Hal looks pouty, but it only makes him cuter. "What car do you have?"

"Acura." I shrug. "I'm really, really lucky to have found the right car at the right time."

I probably won't date Hal long enough to show him my real car. Of all the guys I've ever gone out with, only three ever saw the Mustang. Another thing I could save for marriage. Picture the scene: after the reception I could have the limo drop us off at the garage I rent on President Street. My husband raises the garage door and then carries me through. Once inside, I lead him by the hands toward my tarp-covered vehicle, first lifting the vinyl cover a fraction so he can get the briefest hint of the experience to come, letting him run his hands over the quarter panels beneath the protective sheet, and then when he's crazed with anticipation, with a flourish I whip off the tarps from my Mustang, and my new husband gasps with ecstasy.

Still sullen, Hal pulls the next card. "What was your earliest memory?"

Oh, God, these questions got hard-hitting all of a sudden.

Beth laughs. "Walking the dog with my grandfather."

Stuart says, "Eating M&Ms. Just me at the table, sorting M&Ms by color, saving the greens for last."

Hal turns to me.

I drop my gaze. "I'm not sure."

Of course I could answer. In my earliest memory, I'm being held, tiny in the arms of someone so strong, and I know from the way I'm held and the way we move that we're dancing. It's a snapshot in my head, a single grainy moment as someone sways me to sleep against his chest. Broad shoulders, a comfortable place to rest my head. It's either my Dad or Bucky.

I won't ask. I keep the memory ambiguous, sometimes holding it close when I long for my Dad, sometimes knowing with all my heart it must be Bucky instead. Finding out for sure would keep my dancer from being simultaneously both.

I do remember back when I was three, quite clearly, asking for Bucky's name. He refused. He told me to give him a nickname instead, and I picked one. Again, I don't remember why. Maybe because my brothers watched Battlestar Galactica and I liked Starbuck. Maybe because of Buck Rogers. Or maybe Bucky Dent. I'm sure it's only coincidence about Lindsey Buckingham.

He's got to be following the lead of the Biblical angels that always reply with "Why do you ask my name?" but I just want something to call him that doesn't make him flinch. I'm sure he wasn't "Hey, you!" for six thousand years until I happened along. But again, that's not something I'm about to share with this crowd.

So I say, "Yeah, really, nothing."

Hal sounds incredulous. "You must remember *something*."

"I'm a total amnesiac." I grin. "Who are you again?"

Laughter all around. Hal says, "My first memory is being lost in a department store. I was three."

Beth pulls the next card. "What's the most embarrassing thing you've ever done?"

A frisson of relief shoots through me, and I say, "That's easy!"

After the game, Hal roasts some decaf coffee beans. I'm not kidding: he opens a bag of greenish-brownish beans and measures them into a tube that resembles an upright hair dryer. (I've got hair dryers on the brain now. I've got to make Bucky relent.) The beans whip around the tube in steam-generated gyrations while the smell of roasting coffee infuses the kitchen with airborne happiness. After three minutes, the browned beans snap as their shells burst.

I shift onto my knees, my eyes level to the counter.

Hal puts a hand on my shoulder. "It's okay to drink it, but don't worship it."

I stick out my tongue. He laughs.

The roasted beans go into the coffee machine (which grinds by itself) and shortly afterward, coffee exists. We enjoy individual fruit tartlets covered in whipped cream.

After that, unfortunately, it's time to head home.

Hal hands me my jacket. "You didn't tell me about angels."

"Maybe next time." I pull his whisk out of the pocket. "I forgot this last time."

Eyes sparkling, he slips it back into my pocket. "Too bad you forgot to give it to me this time, too."

His hand brushes mine, and I'm dazzled.

At the last second, he grabs his jacket and accompanies us downstairs. On Seventh Avenue, I turn to say goodbye, but he says he'll walk me and Beth back to our door, even though Stuart is here. Hal and I drop a few paces behind.

"That Ranger game," Hal says in a way that makes my heart sink. "Was that a date?"

I make a noncommittal noise. "I've known Bill for years, and sometimes we go out. When the free tickets came my way, I called him."

Hal looks down. I assure him, "The food was lousy."

He frowns. "I'd have gone with you."

I recoil. "Did you think omelet lessons meant we were exclusively dating each other?"

"Well—no." He sounds tense. "But I didn't think you were fitting me into a roster of men either."

"It's one guy, one night, and a lot of fun. That's the point of going out, isn't it?" I shrug. "I'm not pining away for my one-and-only."

Hal says, "If the right guy did show up, would you be open to him?"

"I hope so. I'd at least consider it." I run a hand through my hair. "You don't need Mr. Right if Right Now is enough."

"Doesn't having the wrong thing just make you hungrier?" Hal's trying to sound sensible, but his voice carries a higher pitch than usual. "If you want a fruit but you have a sandwich instead, you'll still be craving fruit no matter how many sandwiches you have."

"Then I'll know when I stop being hungry, won't I?" I rest my hand on his arm. "If I found the right guy, yes, I would stop running around. There are two million ways to have fun in New York. Why not see hockey games and go roller-blading and walk on the beach at Gateway National Park? If I hadn't met you, I wouldn't know how to cook an omelet or that you could broil asparagus. Or that blast furnace gas grill trick."

About to reply, Hal falls quiet.

No, I can't have him pouting. "With all that available, why not play? Being married is a lot of work."

He mutters, "How would you know?"

"My brother and his wife are the perfect couple, but they laid a lot of groundwork." I swallow. "They have absolute trust in one another, but they still struggle with the waves. And it's the big waves that drown you," I add. "No one needs help getting through the good times, but during the bad times, it's hard to stay afloat together when you're both swamped."

Hal says, "Then they're in it together. The continuity is their lifeboat."

"It's not a fairy tale." I pull him closer. "Being married isn't three hundred sixty-five days a year of dinner parties. Being married is about doing laundry, scheduling an oil change, and running the rent downstairs to the landlady."

"Stability isn't overrated." Hal shrugs. "Sometimes it's nice to be predictable."

"And when I feel like that," I say, "I decide no, I'm not playing paintball this week. This week I'm watching TV every night."

When we get to the brownstone, I hop onto the lowest step and turn back to rest my forearms on his shoulders.

He fixes me with those stunning eyes. "Is your life exciting enough right now?"

I feign a sad sigh. "I'm afraid it isn't."

That's when he kisses me for the first time, almost just a brush-by, and before he pulls away I bend my forehead closer and press it against his.

"I want to see you again."

He says, "You have to. You have my whisk."

I release him and he takes a step backward. "Good night," he calls up the steps to Stuart and Beth at the door. He looks back at me and says, "Sweet dreams."

I find myself delving into those incrediblue eyes again. "See you tomorrow," I say, only I wish he didn't have to go home.

Chapter Nine:

Yes, Ma'am, right turn on green is permitted

This week, Avery's volleyball got moved to Tuesday to accommodate a game on Wednesday. I pick up my niece in the Acura rather than the Mustang because I'd rather lose her some social capital than lose my Mustang's clutch.

Again the volleyball players leave in groups. Again Avery walks hunched. Again it's cold both in the weather and in their hearts, and inside me it's cold because I remember being part of the first group and not the second.

"How much damage did I do?" I whisper.

We never know how much damage we did.

"You never damaged anyone." I offer a smile even though I can't see him; he'll feel it. "You're the angel, remember?"

Thanks—I'd forgotten.

I chuckle.

Avery joins me. The girls ask where's the Mustang, and I say this will be an easier car to learn on. Gasps all around: Avery *really* had a driving lesson? Avery looks miserable, so I say we need to be leaving. Randy already warned me the girls had escalated.

"They're so friendly in front of me," I say as we pull away. "You'd almost never guess they hate you."

She grimaces.

"Why are you still playing with them?" I glance at her sidelong. "Don't you get tired of looking for the knife in your back? Join glee club or something." Glee club might be cliquish too, but it always sounded thrilling, a club full of glee.

When she doesn't answer, I sigh. "How do you feel about ice skating?"

Avery perks up. "That would be great!" She hesitates. "Can you skate? Because I'm not very good."

I snort. "Didn't I ever show you my Olympic medal? No?" I smirk at her. "I keep from falling over. And I go forward. Sometimes."

Prospect Park has Wolman Rink, home to amateur hockey leagues for women (no, don't even ask—imagine Bucky if I were actually in the game) but open skating at other times. Avery and I will glide in circles on rented skates (or fall on our behinds) for an hour. Then I can take her to the library at Grand Army Plaza to do homework. We'll grab fast food for dinner. Maybe we'll have time to sneak in some driving.

As we head to the park, I ask Avery, "What really happened? Back when all the girls got in trouble."

She hesitates. Then, "Jan was talking about some stuff she did at her cousin's. Felicia said Jan would never do that. So she pulled out all this stuff from the medicine cabinet and showed it around. And then Felicia dared her to take something." She twists the strap of her backpack. "Lisa dared me to take some pills. She said she'd tie me down and make me. Then Ashley said about how she steals her brother's cigarettes, so Jan got her mom's and smoked one on the balcony."

"Just cigarettes?"

"Marlboros. Nothing terrible."

Avery mustn't know what they put in cigarettes.

"And when she came back in, everyone was like *Ooh,* and Felicia is such a showoff, she couldn't stand that Jan had everyone's attention, so she opened one of the bottles and took what was in it. There were like five pills."

There's a red light staring me in the face, and it's a good thing because my hands have begun to shake. "She didn't check what it was?"

"I couldn't pronounce half the stuff. They're all these long words. Pseudo-whatever, something-cillin. I kept backing off. And they said I was a coward." Avery bites at her fingernail. "Jan got nervous then because her parents were coming home, so she hid the containers at the bottom of the trash."

We lurch forward with the traffic. Back when I was younger I did some monumentally stupid things, but they were normal kid antics. I have no idea what to say. I shouldn't have asked.

But I did ask. "Which one got sick?"

"Felicia. She couldn't stop throwing up, but I guess all she took was a ton of antibiotics."

"That can burn out your stomach lining, especially if you haven't eaten."

"She tried not to tell the doctors, but eventually she did, and the doctors told her parents, and her parents told everyone."

"And everyone said you instigated it even though you hadn't taken anything."

Looking miserable, she bites her lip. "And now they're telling me Mom's a mental case. I wish they'd all die and not get up in the morning."

"Hey—"

"I walk into school and it's like barbed wire in my stomach whenever I see any one of them. I get there first and then one by one they show up and I just know nothing's going to go right. Sometimes one of them stays home, and I imagine all day she's dead, or she got arrested for being a jerk." She shakes her head. "I hate them. I hate all of them."

A noble-minded person would say something like we have to get in touch with the human side of our enemies, or that bullies only lash out because they're lonely. I must suck because I can't. She's hurting so much.

The angst of high school entangled me too, when the drama was everything because we had no other experience. Everything was *big*. You'd die if you didn't pass that calculus test. You'd have to leave town if your best friend told anyone that secret. Six years later you can't remember whether you passed the test, and you mention the contents of that dreaded secret during a game of Queries.

But there's no way to tell her that now, not when she's neck-deep in a drama that could have taken the life of one of her friends, or her own life, and that will definitely cast her into the wilderness to find a new social circle, maybe even a new school.

So all I say is, "I don't blame you." I can't take away the pain, but at least I have her back.

When I drop off Avery at eight o'clock, I find my mother at Randy's, papers spread around the kitchen table. Her information for income tax?

"Your jeans are filthy," she says. "You smell like antifreeze."

I kiss her cheek. "I love you too, Mom. We went skating."

"Aunt Lee's really good. She only fell about five times." Avery kisses my mother too, then heads toward her room.

Randy's filling out a form, and as Avery passes, he says, "Did you do your homework?"

"All done!"

"We grabbed dinner after skating, and she did it there." I pull up a chair. "Avery's a natural skater. Soon she was teaching me tricks."

"It's so dangerous," my mother says. "Must you corrupt her too?"

"I'm glad she's getting physical exercise," Randy says, "and it's not what they're doing as much as being together."

"Take her to a museum." My mother stares me down, tight lines around her eyes. "If it doesn't matter where you go, why turn her into a little hooligan?"

Corinne says, "Last week they went to the mall."

"And probably played that dancing game at the arcade." My mother folds her arms. "Did *you* actually go shopping?"

"We didn't buy anything." There, that's not a lie. "She's having fun."

"But she needs someone..." and my mother stops.

"Someone respectable and married whose paycheck doesn't involve grease?" I lean back in my chair. "You're doing income tax before March?"

"Here." My mother hands me a sheet of paper.

"She's registering with a firefighters' widows' group," Randy says. "They'll put Dad's name on an online memorial, and Mom can counsel families that have lost a member on the job."

I look at the paper in my hands, expecting to find a brochure. No, it's a letter from a travel agency. "What is this?"

"You're hired!" My mother beams. "I filled out a job application for you, and you start on Monday."

I crumple the paper and turn my gaze to Randy, who's staring openly at my mother. I say, "You want me to write something?" as I toss the paper over my shoulder in the direction of the trash can, hoping Bucky thinks fast enough to swoosh it.

"Uh, no, I'll write it up. Nice throw."

Thanks, Bucky.

No problem.

My mother sighs. "I wish you'd reconsider."

I don't take my eyes from Randy's. "What can they use?"

I'm worthless for stitching memorial quilts, but if they need someone to drive a widow for groceries—oh, or someone to fix an aging minivan!—I'm in.

Randy chews on the pen cap. "I'm not sure. They're just starting up."

I smile wickedly. "Maybe Max could donate a decrepit station wagon."

Randy laughs out loud. Right after Dad died, someone "donated" us a decade-old vehicle with no seat belts that smelled of vinyl and gasoline and always made our brother Kerry vomit.

Brennan wanders into the kitchen while Randy and I insult the old station wagon, which my mother ran into the ground due to not having money for a replacement.

Brennan pours himself some milk. "How come there aren't station wagons anymore?"

"Because they saw ours and swore death was superior." Randy turns to me. "Hey, Gear-Head, did you reach for the wrenches because of all those times Mom had to call AAA?"

I laugh out loud even as Mom gasps, "Absolutely not!"

I arch my eyebrows. "Hey, some of those AAA guys were cute, especially the ones who would tell Mom she just didn't know how to start the car, then repeat everything she'd done and discover hey, they couldn't start it either."

Brennan says, "Does anyone still make station wagons?"

"Subaru makes one. Ford had a Taurus wagon." I shrug. "But none of the high-end manufacturers."

In between gulps of milk, Brennan says, "You mean Cadillac doesn't make a station wagon?"

I wink. "It's called a hearse."

Brennan spits milk all over himself even as Randy applauds.

My mother rolls her eyes. "My daughter is polite and refined. But somebody stole her and replaced her with you."

I'm a mile from home, exiting the Prospect Expressway. Styx "The Grand Illusion" plays loud enough to buzz the plastic on the dashboard.

The light turns green. The woman in front of me doesn't move. I snarl, "Yes, Ma'am, right turn on green is permitted in Brooklyn."

She idles through the intersection and trudges up Seventh Avenue.

I'm right on her bumper. "The one on the right! Push it and the car goes forward!"

I feel Bucky trying to calm me, but I don't care. It's not like he'll take the wheel: he won't drive because he doesn't have a license. Maybe that's why I need a husband—to collect the keys when I'm ready to floor the accelerator and wipe out a corner bodega.

Ten minutes later, I've passed every stupid driver in the city of New York, wedged my car into a great tightness (I wish parking were an Olympic sport—I'd get a gold) and stomped up two flights of groaning steps I wish would shut up.

Beth isn't here. Good.

In my room, I pull off one sneaker and hurl it at the foot of the bed, then again with the other because it makes a loud crack.

Bucky's voice: "Let me guess. Your Mom?"

I hope Mastering The Obvious is an Olympic Sport too, just so Bucky can show off his own gold medal.

I throw my belt-pack at the bed. "Someday she's going to kvetch one time too many, and I'm going to detonate all over her."

Bucky appears on my dresser—safely clear of my target practice. "You handled it well."

Next the jacket. It doesn't make a thump. "I damage my soul every time she starts in on me."

"You did fine." Bucky half-closes his eyes, and the room fills with the scent of tea leaves. "You need to get your mind off her."

I'm out of things to throw.

Bucky's hair has hazel sparkles. "Let's play Carcassonne."

"I want to play Carcassonne the same way I want to get married."

"I didn't ask what you wanted to do." Bucky places his hands flat on the desk and sits up straighter, then tilts his head. He probably suspects how adorable he looks that way, only it runs a serious risk of backfire right now. "I checked on Beth and we have time to play a whole game. Please?"

You don't want an angel pestering you.* "Fine. But you always win."

I fetch Carcassonne's square green box off the game shelf in France. A glance down the length of the apartment reveals Beth's forest of origami trees has marched on Dunsinane, so there's even room on the dining room table to set it up.

In "Carcassonne: Hunters and Gatherers" you use tiles to create a world with forests, streams and meadows. The meadows have deer and tigers; the streams have fish; the forests have gems that earn you special tiles. You add up the number of fish as you go along; you get points for forests; at the end you tally the deer and subtract one per tiger.

Bucky always thrashes me, but I haven't come up with a better game that's "angelable." He can't play a game that requires holding cards ("nonangelable").

---

* Bucky hates it when I call it 'pestering.' He prefers 'encouraging.' I always shoot back that I could substitute 'nagging.' He replies that if it bothers me so much, he could just go away, and then I call it encouraging.

Scrabble takes forever because although he has no problem coming up with a word, getting it on the board is a challenge. *Take this tile and this one and this one and that one...of course that's a word! Now reach into the bag and grab that tile...no, the other one...*

We can play Monopoly if I roll the dice for him, except he's horrified at its depiction of capitalism. And he won't charge me rent. *"Can you imagine if God charged us rent?"*

Without going into details, let me just say you never want to duel an angel in chess. Just, don't.

Carcassonne he enjoys because it's angelable, it's cooperative, and we're creating. *"God didn't do it this way,"* he commented the first time we played. *"But this is fun too."* And then he creamed me.

He promises he's not checking out the tiles beforehand. He just strategizes well enough that every tile looks like the best tile he could have drawn.

I shuffle the tiles, position the counters, and set aside the special pieces. I'm red because "red always wins." He lets me go first because the rules say *the youngest player should go first.* I build a river and set down a hut. He tells me to draw from the third stack of tiles; after he studies it, a light-image of the tile appears where I should place it, along with a ghostly image of where to stand his little blue guy.

"She's driving me nuts," I say after a couple of turns.

"She means well," Bucky says. "No, don't protest. She wants you to be happy. Get me a tile from the second stack."

Next it's my turn. Yippee—fish. Four points for me. "Cower in terror before my Carcassonne prowess."

"Quite impressive," says Bucky. "First stack. Put it there."

"Nice." I award him six points. "She defines happiness so narrowly. Can you imagine if Jesus showed up at her door? She'd try to set him up with someone."

"She'd try to set him up with *you*. Your move." Bucky has already doubled my score. "Then you'd tell Jesus you work at a bakery."

I huff. "I said I was sorry."

"Don't knock it. You can make a lot of dough that way."

I throw my next tile at him, and he laughs.

I pout. "Biblical angels don't make puns."

He folds his arms, and my tile reappears in my hand. "They're polylingual puns. If you spoke ancient Mesopotamian, you'd be in stitches when Michael wrestles Jacob."

I lay down my tile. No points.

"Hey!" Bucky's wings spread. "You put a tiger in my meadow!"

I smirk. "Poor baby."

"Oh sure. I'm trying to usher your immortal soul into Paradise, and you put a tiger in my meadow."

"Are you going to take your turn or just whine forever?"

"Fourth stack," Bucky says. "Put it there." Two points to him, and—

I gasp. "You're cutting off my fish system?"

"Poor baby," Bucky says.

I say, "You're only sore because I'm winning. Oh, wait. I'm not."

Bucky snickers.

"But you're okay with me not being married." I make my next turn. "You always said it's not an immutable law of the universe that everyone get married and have kids."

Bucky points to the first stack, and while I place his tile, I add, "So why is she on my case about marriage? She never re-married after Dad died."

Bucky has heard this before, but he's not looking bored. He simply doesn't answer while I draw a tile. I get two points. His turn. He gets six.

I say, "You'd tell me if I were jeopardizing my soul."

"Absolutely."

"Am I jeopardizing my soul by not marrying?"

"No."

"Am I unhappy not being married?"

"No."

"Am I engaging in risky, harmful or illegal acts without a legitimized partner to let off tension?"

"No."

I lay down a tile. "Then why should I get married?"

His wings flex. "Tell her that."

I tilt my head. "Oh, sure. *Mom, Bucky said—*"

"Not *Bucky said,* but what you just told me. You're content. Your soul isn't in jeopardy. You've considered it, and right now you don't need to make a permanent commitment."

I shake my head while I move for him. "She won't listen. She thinks I'm a kid."

Bucky says, "Because you're acting like a kid."

I stare open-mouthed.

He shrugs. "You're an unattached kid in the world's biggest playground. You're making friends, building sand castles, and enjoying yourself. That's fine: it makes you a better advocate for Avery. The juvenile part is that you're griping to your buddies rather than facing your accuser with a clear, non-emotional case."

I frown. "Go on."

"What more is there?" Bucky considers a moment. "Figure out what needs she thinks a man would fulfill that you either provide for yourself or don't think you lack. Stability—is that overrated? Someone to be with—is marriage a guarantee? It wasn't for her. A second income—money is overrated. Make a list."

He drifts to the window to gaze down at the dormant cherry tree. At nighttime, lights dot the buildings, both window lights and street lamps from Garfield Place. "Present it to her as a matter you've pondered, not a lark." He rests his head against the glass panes.

"Do you think I'd be better off married?"

Bucky says, "I'm not a spirit-guide."

I huff. "I'm not looking for revelations of the apocalypse. I want your *opinion*."

"I'll tell you what worries me." Bucky faces into the apartment, leaning against the window frame. "You don't plan long-term. I worry you'll rabbit-trail your life into a blind alley and end up without income, without a home, and without a safety net."

Bucky is big on safety nets.

He adds, "If things continue as they are now, I figure that in five years, you and Bill will look at each other and get married because everyone expects you to, not because you love each other."

I bite my lip. "That would make Mom happy, at least."

"That said," and Bucky fusses with his outermost feathers, "much as I appreciate stability, I'm of the opinion it would be worse for you to be married and restless than single and restless."

I swallow. "I wouldn't walk off if I committed."

Bucky's voice is so soft: "I'm not sure."

I'm not sure.

He's returned to looking outside, but his gaze is higher, either at the rooftops on Garfield Place or level to the light-dimmed stars while Park Slope dives toward the river.

He's not sure of me. He's not sure what I'd do, trapped. And now I'm thinking, I've never been committed. Not for life. Schooling ended. I left my family, and in the back of my head I've always known if could land a job building space shuttles in Fiji, I'd be on the next plane. Every job I've walked into on a probationary note: I'd stay as long as it challenged me. No boyfriends longer than a year. Apartments rather than houses, and I could have told you at any moment how many months remained on my lease.

There's only one: "What about you? I'm committed to you."

His mouth twitches. "You have no choice. You could ask for a new guardian, but unless you were beyond all hope, you'd always have someone. That's not commitment. That's acceptance."

I blink rapidly, and he turns to me. "I didn't mean to hurt your feelings."

My voice cracks as I leave the room. "I'm not sure how else I'm supposed to take that. *You're completely unreliable* isn't commonly considered a compliment."

In my heart: *I didn't say that!*

"Then what did you say? That you're not important to me?"

I stalk through France to my own room and slam the door. Way to impress him with my maturity, huh? As if doors keep out angels. But when he doesn't reappear, I have at least the illusion of being able to sulk in private.

I dial my iPod to ABBA because it annoys him, and I put in my earbuds so maybe he'll stay out of my head.

I have never not honored a commitment. I might need an extra cup of coffee after staying up all night— well, an extra pot of coffee—actually, a vat of coffee that doubles as a Jacuzzi—but I always show up for work. I'm on time for my mother's parties. I've never blown off a date for something better except the night I spent in the ER getting stitches, which even my stood-up date agreed was the acceptable choice.

So where does Bucky get off saying he's not sure I wouldn't walk? Doesn't nearly three decades count as a track record?

The thought pops into my head, *Goodbye, Stranger.* And then, *Built-in obsolescence.*

Ooh. He's braving ABBA to talk to me. I shut off the iPod.

I hear, *You always have an exit strategy.*

There are no exit strategies in a marriage, I think. *That's why I don't want to get married.*

But <u>aren't</u> there exit strategies in a marriage? replies Bucky.

My eyes fly open. *I would never, never have an affair.*

I'm not talking about an affair, Lee. I'm talking about the thousand ways to run away from your husband while standing right at his side.

I'm cold all over. *Go on.*

He replies, *You go on.*

There's television. Beth has her origami to escape into; Stuart has his music; Hal has cooking. I would have my Mustang, my tools, the constant search for a new pastime. The way I could run off into my own head if life got bland.

When you see someone fleetingly attractive, says Bucky, *and you know you can't play with him, whom will you blame? Will you blame the man for representing freedom? Will you blame your husband for limiting your choices? Or will you blame yourself for locking yourself into only one track for the rest of your life?*

Lying on my back, silent earbuds still in place, I fold my arms over my chest. "So I shouldn't ever get married." The words ring with finality.

Bucky says. *You could get married. But before you think about it seriously, you'll need to consider what it means to be committed, every day, to the same person, for the rest of your life.*

I shudder.

I open my eyes to find he's sitting at the foot of my bed, his knees against his chest, his wings curved and his head aslant as he speaks. "If you were to marry, you'd have to figure out how to make your commitment to him new every day. You'd never be able to promise a lifetime because that's not how you're built." He forces a smile. "I couldn't do it that way. I have to understand a relationship as organic. But it would work for you if you disciplined yourself in advance to look at every day as its own commitment."

Maybe. Eternity is a long time. *Tomorrow* isn't.

Bucky says, "Can we finish the game?"

I give a mock pout. "You know who's going to win."

He rests his chin on his folded arms. "I know a lot of things. I just enjoy doing things together."

Three hours later, I've got extra blankets spread out, pajamas on, teeth brushed, brain fuzzy. My head hits the pillow, and I think, *Good night, Bucky.*

Bucky sits alongside my bed, one hand on my head.

I close my eyes, but my mind keeps returning to my mother, to the backhanded disownment, the scorn.

I sigh as I tighten the blankets around my shoulders. And then, I get a great idea. A splendid idea. An idea even Bucky would love.

Hey, God? I think out into the stratosphere, *I need you to give me some patience.*

Wings flared, Bucky bolts to his feet. "Oh, no—you didn't!"

Chapter Ten:

Never pray for patience

"I still can't believe you did that," Bucky says for the fiftieth time.

Even on a bicycle, I'm going to be late to work. Me, whom Max says "is only late if the light is red." This morning, that would be all of them.

Bucky spreads his wings and glares Heavenward, but we can't unsay last night's prayer. Usually the lights are in synch so if you look up any avenue they're all red or all green. Not today. Today they're alternating.

"I told you never, never pray for patience." Bucky has said this ten times today, and that's not counting how often he said it last night. "God *will* answer."

No, dear. An edge comes into my thoughts. *You never told me. I'd have remembered.*

"Are you sure?"

Very.

Bucky puts his face in his hands. "I am the worst guardian in the world."

You're one of the best. My jaw aches from keeping my teeth clenched. *But right now you're getting on my nerves.*

"It's the effect of the prayer." Bucky's shoulders sag, making his wings droop. "You'll be lucky if I'm the only thing that wears on your nerves."

No one notices I'm five minutes late because the other three mechanics and Max are all clustered around the computer making suggestions. The waiting room is fuller than it should be, at least four people seated and three more on line.

One more mechanic can't help in a situation like this, so I vanish into the garage. The coffee machine stands empty. Aha. Something will go right today—I'll make the coffee, and it won't taste like twenty-weight.

Except the on-button glows red, and when I pull out the filter, it's got dry coffee grounds, and there's water in the reservoir.

This isn't just a Coffee Bootstrap problem. We're doomed.

I mutter, "Patience until I can make a run for coffee at ten?"

Bucky flinches. "It'll be at least ten-thirty."

"Aren't you a ray of sunshine this morning?"

Ari pokes his head into the bay. "You know anything about computers?"

"Only that they're our friends, and we don't drop our friends off the BQE overpass."

His nose wrinkles. "We can't access the appointments or the customer histories, and Max thinks we can't run credit cards."

I sigh. "And let me guess—we're double-booked?"

I dart into the waiting room long enough to grab the open tickets. Two state inspections, an oil change, a brake job, a tune-up, an undiagnosed front-end vibration, and two cars towed in for the mysterious "won't go." I should get the fastest ones out of the way, so I grab a state inspection, then think twice.

If Bucky is correct, I'll find five red-flag problems and the customer will become belligerent. No one needs patience that badly. I take the oil change.

Ten minutes later, I've drained the oil out of the bottom and can't get the cap off the top to replace it. So concludes the first lesson in patience training.

It's eleven o'clock when Max calls all four mechanics into his office.

This day is torture. The credit card system is still down. One customer accused me of overcharging her, and another couldn't believe a female changed his oil. Half an hour ago I overheard Bucky telling another angel, "I'm terribly sorry—she prayed for patience."

Max shuts the door. With deep gravity he looks us, one at a time, in the face. Finally, he sighs.

"Okay. Which of you jokers prayed for patience?"

I gasp.

Max stares into me like a spotlight on an escaping prisoner. "Well, Lee, here's your ticket out of here. My grandmother needs a ride to the doctor, and you're it."

Ari and Carlos bust up laughing. I frown at Max. "What?"

"You get paid for the rest of the day, but I want you somewhere else. Let the universe teach you patience on someone else's nickel."

"Don't do it, Lee," says Carlos. "Save yourself."

Is he nuts? Everything's screwed up at the shop—this is my golden parachute! I might get stuck in traffic, but that's a painless way of learning patience. Max's granny must be ninety-nine years old! If we idle on the highway long enough, she can teach me to knit or sing songs from the old country or whatever it is old people do.

Max says, "She's legally blind, and she uses a walker."

Ari adds, "And you don't have to worry about her keeling over because Satan's afraid to take her when she dies."

Max pelts Ari in the head with his optical mouse.

I say, "We're kind of swamped—"

Max holds out the hand that has 93% of its fingers intact, into which Ari dutifully replaces the mouse. "I'll take your repairs. You take her."

"Why can't you—"

Max strides toward me. "You're the fool who prayed for patience. If I go and you stay, I'll return to find I have no more business. You're leaving for the rest of the day regardless. It's your call whether you want to get paid for it."

Carlos says, "And you don't."

Ari rubs the side of his head where the mouse whacked him. "No amount of money is worth it."

I glance at Tim, but his face is like stone.

Hesitation blossoms within. *Bucky?*

Bucky only replies, *Maybe this is the wages of sin I keep hearing about.*

My mouth twitches. *Either that or the wages of Max.*

Five minutes later, armed with directions to a house in Floral Park, I place a phone call.

"Is this Mrs. Beatrice Lockhardt?"

A gravely voice: "Put me on your no-call list."

"Max told me to call. He said you needed a ride to the doctor for a 1:30 appointment."

Again that barking voice: "You got a name?"

"I'm one of Max's mechanics, Lee Singer."

The woman laughs. "Are you a man or a woman?"

Bucky's eyes widen.

I steel myself. "When should I pick you up?"

"Quarter to one."

The appointment is 1:30. Forty-five minutes leaves us sitting for a half hour in a waiting room...although I could work on patience there, reclining on plastic chairs while browsing *Sports Illustrated*. And maybe with a walker, she needs extra time to get into the car. Patience again!

"Right." I jot down the time. "I'll see you then."

"I'm not home. Pick me up here."

I turn over the sheet of paper. "Where are you?"

"You have to get off the highway and head toward the fire station."

I blink. "Which highway?"

"The one that lets you off near the fire station."

Mentally I run through the entire Belt, the BQE, the Prospect Expressway, the LIE and the Grand Central, and every exit off every highway fits that description. "Which fire station?"

She huffs. "The one near the school. There's a fire station and a school."

I rub my temples. "Which borough are you in?"

"Queens." She sounds exasperated, but that narrows the number of parkways I can wander. "When you get off the highway, there's a fire station and a school on the same street, and there's a traffic light."

I've stopped taking notes. "Okay. After I pass the fire station and the school, then what?"

"Make a right at the traffic light and go past the houses."

I throw my pencil at the desk, put up my feet, and rock back on the chair. G*o find her, Bucky.*

Um...no.

I glare at him.

He avoids my eyes. *Not allowed. Sorry.*

Right. Patience.

"At the corner there used to be a fire pull-box and a mailbox. Are you writing this down?"

"Mm-hmm."

"That's a dangerous corner. Make a right and go a couple of blocks to the house with a chain-link fence. There's also a pizzeria and a bagel shop."

"Uh-huh."

"Make a left where you see the convenience store, and we're on the corner. The house is beige. There will be a car in the driveway."

After two years working for lawyers and three years as a mechanic, I've gotten expert at saying, "Of course," instead of "You have *got* to be kidding."

After a moment I say, "Do you have a phone number for where you are?"

"You've got my number."

Yeah, but then I can't call anyone else at the house for directions. I shut my eyes. How about MapQuest? "What's the address?"

"Why do you need an address? I just told you how to get here." She adopts a third-grade teacher tone. "Get off the highway and head down that road until you pass the fire station and the school. At the light you make a right and head to that intersection with the three-way stop—"

I bolt upright. I've been there once, maybe a year ago...the three-way stop—that was the "dangerous" intersection! "Wait—I know where you're talking about! The street without the stop sign is coming up the exit ramp, just over the overpass, past the fire station and the school—"

"That's what I told you!" She huffs. "Then you make a right and make a left at the chain link fence and the telephone pole."

I jot a few directions from memory. "Okay, fine. I'll be there at twelve forty-five sharp."

"Good. And Leslie," she says, "try to be less annoying. I'm an old woman."

After I manage to find a house with a mailbox in front and a roof on top, I knock. The fact is, I've done this too often. Max offers pick-up service to our customers, and some of their directions haven't been quite as clear as Mrs. Lockhardt's.

I glance at the loaner car. It's a real gem, if lumps of coal are pre-diamonds: a 1989 Dodge Ares (no, really) which has over time settled backward on its shocks so the nose points skyward, bespeaking dreams of reincarnation as a Saturn V missile. When you step on the gas, it's the same feeling (and rate of acceleration) as if you stood behind the car propelling it with your foot on the bumper. It's a New York shade of sky-blue (ie, filthy) except for the right rear quarter panel which gleams a tasteful black. The radio doesn't have a jack for my iPod. I'm lucky it has buttons for FM.

"Of course we have a loaner car," Max will croon into the phone, eyes agleam as he woos a potential customer. "It's our service to you."

Our true service is revealing just how many friends you can call for a ride home from the mechanic. Over a dozen times I've hiked to the corner to retrieve the car when clients abandon it, preferring to walk three miles. There's a trick to not stalling. The trick involves driving a different car.

Driving for Max's customers (yet another *service*— have a mechanic shuttle you home while she test-drives a car with brake troubles*)* has also provided the following guidelines:

• Expect directions such as "This exit!" blared out with fifteen yards' clearance.

• Also expect a shoulder-grab while the passenger shrieks, "There's a sharp right in six miles!"

• Once a client says "But I don't complain," the remainder of the trip will consist of nothing but complaints.

So really, I'm good. I've done all this before. I'll bring her there and back, like Bilbo and the Ring—or was it Frodo?—and then I'll be patient.

After I knock a second time, I wonder if I haven't gotten the wrong house after all (*But there's a fence and a telephone pole, Bucky. That would be a stunning coincidence!)* On the third try, a white-haired woman in a brown coat bangs open the door, knocking me into the stair rail as she carries her walker onto the stoop.

"We're late, Layla." She lifts the walker and carries it down the steps, down the walkway, right to the car. She's a head shorter than I, and I'm by no means tall. Fighting a grin, I let her into the front seat, then fold the walker to stash in the trunk. Mrs. Lockhardt clutches her shiny purse on her knees as I start the engine.

She peers at me through wire-rimmed glasses, then purses her red-lipsticked mouth. "Do you even own a mirror, Lenore? Or are you one of those lesbians?"

It's possible that Max and his grandmother are playing a joke on me to get revenge for the patience fiasco, but a sideways glance at the woman reveals no sign of a sense of humor. She plants her feet squarely on the floor, then adjusts the rear-view mirror to her liking.

I offer to help her buckle up.

"Why? You're a bad driver?"

I pull out wondering if maybe this woman doesn't know something I don't—like she really did sell her soul in return for being too mean to die.

That's ridiculous, of course. If she's too mean to die, why visit the doctor?

As I'm getting ready to pull onto the main road, Mrs. Lockhardt huffs. "I've got a doctor for this and a doctor for that. Makes me sick just thinking about the money they're getting from one old woman. But I don't complain."

My eyes go huge. An involuntary glance at the clock.

"Oh, and I'm not going to Elmhurst Hospital anymore. That doctor canceled. I'm going to a different place."

On the wheel, my hands tighten. "Where is it?"

"I'll direct you. It's on Simon Street. You know where Simon is?"

Simon Says, do I look like a street map of Queens?

"I'm afraid I don't, Mrs. Lockhardt."

"Well, take a left here."

Like most drivers, I prefer to have the entire route laid out. Mrs. Lockhardt, on the other hand, keeps a clenched fist on her knowledge, as if imparting it will leave her ignorant for all eternity. We navigate a maze of one-way streets running exactly parallel to Roosevelt Avenue. This ensures I can stall at a hundred stop signs in a row.

In between directions, I receive a rundown of her various illnesses. I find out about her diabetes, her heart condition, her thyroid, and the proper care of something called a "pessary" *(I don't want to know what it is—I will resist asking)* to which I am treated an explicit definition of three blocks later.

At a four-way stop intersection, Mrs. Lockhardt breaks her litany of medical jargon with, "You'll be going left."

I put on my left turn signal. "Left here."

I turn left.

Mrs. Lockhardt sits up in the seat. "Why'd you turn?"

"You said to turn left!"

"I meant the road curved left."

"So what you meant was that I should go straight."

"I meant that the road would curve and you should—"

"—should follow the curve of the road rather than plowing into a house because *that* was what was directly in front of the car?" I glance at her sidelong. "Give me a little credit."

She points urgently to a side street. "Make a right here!"

Three orange sawhorses declare "ROAD CLOSED" across the neck of the street. There is no pavement visible behind the flashing yellow lights. "I think I know a better route."

I've long since deduced Mrs. Lockhardt is directing us toward Elmhurst Hospital, even though a grand jury subpoena couldn't make her admit it. Maybe she fears that once I have the reins, I'll never take instruction from her again and we'll circle the medical buildings like a satellite, orbiting with tantalizing closeness but never locating the Optimal Parking Space nor the Closest Entrance. I get on a main road and sail toward the hospital while she mutters, "I guess you could do that too. But I hate this road. Too fast. Too many lights."

Right now, I'd run every one of them if it got me out of this car.

A word about Elmhurst Hospital: a police officer I dated three years ago says that without a doubt, Elmhurst Hospital has the best trauma unit in Queens. "If you have an emergency, no matter how bad, their emergency room will pull you through. They're top-notch. Then ER sends you upstairs, and they kill you." That officer has left explicit instructions with his partner, "I don't care if I'm shot in the Elmhurst Hospital waiting room. Take me to Boothe."

Max's granny tells me, "You're taking advantage of me, trying to butter up Max for your job."

My hands tighten on the wheel.

"I'm going to tell him how you made me miss my appointment."

By now, I have flattened the accelerator. Mrs. Lockhardt continues, "Just because you're young and have a good car and your health, you think you can treat an old woman like dirt. Have I told you how sick I am?"

Hold tight, Bucky. I'm going to plow into the nearest tree.

Please don't, Bucky says. *If the patience thing isn't finished yet, you'll have to wait fifty years for your judgment.*

The speed limit on most New York City streets is thirty, but there's a de-facto speed limit simply because of how many cars are trying to use them. You can't really do better than sixty on the major roads. At least not usually.

Mrs. Lockhardt has a wrinkle around her mouth. "It's a crying shame what these doctors charge. I'm an old woman. Where do they think I'm getting my money from, anyhow? They want nothing better than to take an old woman for everything she has. The doctor inserted a pessary last June, but do you think—"

Breaking the speed limit—it's a K-car or I'd be breaking the sound barrier—I should have been pulled over long since. But fate won't smile on me today. If I were pulled over, I could get out of the car. I could make a nuisance and get myself arrested. Jail sounds enticing. Solitary confinement: I'd appreciate learning patience under those conditions. Solitary. Confined.

Shortly thereafter, Elmhurst comes into view. Beside it I find a Simon Street, and Simon obliges us by having a medical arts building. I cruise to the door Mrs. Lockhardt indicates (repeatedly) and pull up as close as I can.

"Why are you stopping here? I've got a handicapped placard."

"I can drop you off and then go park."

Hell has a special spot for perfectly healthy individuals who park in handicapped spaces—ironically, the spot closest to the furnace. Mrs. Lockhardt hangs her placard on my window and assures me that very special spot.

I swing over to the handicapped spaces to find they're all taken (so now Satan will have to learn patience too). The next space over is free, and we park there. Mrs. Lockhardt insists I not help her out of the car, then tells me this car is too low and the door closes too easily. I bring out her walker.

Next she criticizes how far the handicapped spaces are from the entrance, how there aren't enough of them, and how I was rude to park so far from the door. She's an old woman, after all, with a walker, and it isn't easy like when she was young. When she was a young person, she'd never have dreamed of making her elders walk all the way across a parking lot.

Looking worriedly at me, Bucky says, "Very few acts of real heroism get acknowledged by society as a whole."

I've clenched my jaw so tight my head throbs.

Mrs. Lockhardt lifts her walker and carries it past the five occupied handicapped spaces and up to the entrance. "Are you coming with me?"

I wish I could do this without sounding sarcastic, but why exert the effort? "Wouldn't miss it. I hear they've got the best waiting rooms in New York."

Mrs. Lockhardt fumbles with her purse for sixty-eight seconds before pressing either the up or down buttons for the elevator. We've arrived ten minutes early, but when she checks in with the receptionist, she apologizes for being late because her driver got her lost. I pull a four week-old *Sports Illustrated* from the side table. It's an extension of the time machine that is today: way back then, the Giants still had a shot at the Super Bowl.

Mrs. Lockhardt asks for directions to the bathroom, and she returns with a paper cup the size of a shot glass, filled with water. She drinks it, then gets some more. She educates me: every few months she needs to have her urine tested. She resumes the monologue about her diabetes, her heart, her blood pressure, her pessary, and I might actually need to look up from the magazine and pay attention except the nurse asks Mrs. Lockhardt to step inside the office.

Bucky? Am I patient yet?

Bucky flinches.

Max's grandmother returns. "They said there's not enough."

Behind the magazine, my eyebrows raise. Way, way too much information.

"I'll have to drink more water and try again." She returns to the bathroom and emerges with the tiny cup filled.

As an intelligent human being, I have by now determined a couple of points of fact: the first is that if she's really got three doctor appointments a week, she can piggyback this test onto another. She's taken advantage of the free ride to relieve boredom by tormenting someone.

Secondly, if there "wasn't enough" for a urine test, she isn't doing anything about it. One ounce of fluid is hardly going to satisfy the requirement for whatever it is she's having tested.

When I find I'm fantasizing about hurling furniture, I claim I need to make a phone call. I hike from the doctor's office to the lobby.

The air is cooler here, and the long line of windows affords a view of overcast skies. Maybe someone is enjoying the day somewhere, but it isn't me.

I phone Max. It shouldn't be him either.

I use the pay phone because I don't want the skunk to avoid my call.

"Hi, Lee."

Huh? "And you knew it was me because—?"

"Because caller ID showed the same number I've seen whenever anyone takes Grandma to the doctor."

"You're such a jerk."

"More of an opportunist. I'd rather lose my best mechanic than drive Grandma to the doctor ever again."

I can hear my blood pressure escalating.

"But I meant it about paying you for the rest of the day."

It must have pained him to say that. "Don't bother. I want you in my debt."

The trouble is, although wise in the ways of the world and no pauper in my endowment of imagination, I can't think of anything horrible enough for true repayment.

I click the receiver but keep the phone to my ear listening to the dial tone. Time to go back to hell. Well, maybe in a minute. I can stand here in the empty corridor and enjoy the white noise for a few more minutes.

There's no reason the world shouldn't end now. Now. As in, right this second. As in, legions of angels could erupt out of Heaven and set things right with the world. Come on—now would be just fine. Maybe Michael the Archangel is just about to order the Seven Archangels to blow their trumpets—and I'd have to go to with them. Please?

Back in the waiting room, I choke on the same stifling air, squint in the same buzzing fluorescent lights, and flinch to the sound of Mrs. Lockhardt in the midst of saying, "—but I don't complain" to a middle-aged woman unfortunate enough to be waiting for the same doctor.

Mrs. Lockhardt stares at me and declares, "I'm sorry it's taking so long, Lenore. I don't know why they're not taking me in again!"

That sentence has nothing to do with me and everything to do with the receptionist. I give my warmest smile, and I make sure the receptionist can both see and hear me. "It's no trouble, Ma'am. I have nothing scheduled for the rest of the day." I settle into a seat as if content to move all my belongings into this very waiting room and live here forever.

Mrs. Lockhardt gives a huff. "I just have no idea what they expect from an old woman! I already drank *three glasses* of water!"

The other patient shakes her head in commiseration.

"And they're making this poor young lesbian stay here waiting for them too!"

Never one to be used as a weapon without my permission, I chime in, "I told you, Mrs. Lockhardt, I'm fine. As long as it takes is fine."

As long as it takes spirals into another hour. Mrs. Lockhardt condescends to drink one additional half-paper-cup of water (*Leave some for the fishies, Ma'am*) but after the nurse escorts her back for a second attempt, it's decided she should try again later in the week when she returns for one of her other appointments.

I have already turned down any availability for any time in the next several years, not with "hah, no" but with a Bucky-approved "I'll check my calendar," which makes it seem as if I agree with her noble purpose but doesn't commit me to anything.

I pick her up at the curb to make sure I have the radio on before she gets in. At least I should have something to listen to other than the details of prolapses and serial organ failures.

Mrs. Lockhardt demands to sit in the back because my driving made her sick—or was it the car? I've gone beyond the point of listening.

I return the way we came. Mrs. Lockhardt asks how on earth we're going to get to Floral Park by going *this* way. Really, it's the same street. She insists it isn't, and that I'm taking advantage of an old woman's poor eyesight.

She finds a week-old copy of the *New York Post* in the back and calls it nothing more than a blatant scandal-sheet of the right wing. The sports report comes on, and she says it's a crime how much those guys get paid. She hates the overcast weather, it goes without saying, although she says it anyhow. *Oh, but I don't complain.* I inquire what she thinks of the new public library hours, and she promptly (and undisappointingly) returns with it's a crying shame that young people today don't know how to read. (*You mean other than blatant scandal sheets of the right, don't you, Ma'am?*) The radio, at least, seems to be on my side; after one song Mrs. Lockhardt mutters, "What the hell was that?"

Nearly back in Floral Park, we pass an auto parts store, and I pull into a space. Actually, it's a bus stop, but she'll be in the car, so I shouldn't get ticketed.

"I'll be right back," I say. "There's a tool Max keeps forgetting to get me at the shop."

"Open a window before you go. It's stuffy."

I crack the windows and then take my time finding whatever I need for my Mustang *(they sell brakes, but I need a break—can I get that here too?)* and joking with the guys behind the counter. Hey, wild, a female who uses tools. No, really, you don't need a Y chromosome to operate a ratchet.

Bucky appears as the cashier hands over my change. "Traffic enforcement."

I shove the five dollar bill into my pocket and dart outside, jump into the car, and peel out of the bus stop. "Sorry about that, Mrs. Lockhardt—but you don't want to mess with parking enforcement." I merge into traffic and head toward her home using Max's hand-drawn map. "They get paid to do nothing but write tickets, so they're going to write them."

At the red light, I check the map, close my eyes, and determine I have only ten minutes until it's over. But at least she's quiet now. Four blocks later, at the next red light, I glance in the rear view mirror and realize why.

"Oh, crap. I lost Max's grandmother." I bang the u-turn in the middle of Jamaica Avenue and head back to the auto parts store. "Bucky, why didn't you tell me?"

Bucky's speaking in my heart: not allowed.

"Then what good are you?"

His reply: sometimes he's not sure.

Minutes later, there's Mrs. Lockhardt, sitting on a bench with her mouth a line and her purse on her knees.

Flashers on, I stall to a halt in the bus stop even though Traffic Enforcement is right there. In every other city in the nation, hazard lights indicate a car has broken down: in New York, they mean, "I put it here."

Mrs. Lockhardt's drone greets me as I step out of the car. "—have ten grandchildren, but do you think even one of them would have the decency—"

Traffic Enforcement gestures to the car. "Oh, look, she's back."

I fold my arms. "No ticket."

"You were illegally parked."

I smile. "You can keep having this dazzling conversation while you fill out the form."

Traffic Enforcement frowns. "Just get the hell out of here."

Mrs. Lockhardt wants the back seat again, and I help her in, the whole time fielding off terrified comments that I'm about to drop her into the curb.

As an act of mercy, every light is green on the way home. Max's map, with quaint landmarks like street names and house numbers, brings us directly to Mrs. Lockhardt's house. Could it be? Am I finally patient?

She hefts the walker and marches up her front steps. Then she turns. "Here."

She hands me a dollar.

My brain drones into a high wine, and instead of saying what I've been thinking all day, I whip the five out of my pocket. "I couldn't possibly. The pleasure was all mine."

She takes the money.

Back at Mack's, I stall the loaner car halfway in a space. The cold has surrendered to a pattering drizzle, perfect weather for the bike ride home.

Max edges toward me in the lot, as if nearing a leper.

I call, "It's safe. I'm patient now."

He gives a contented huff, then comes closer. "I thought she'd do the trick for you. We got the computer and the credit card system working right after you left, and a few people didn't show in the afternoon, so we're caught up." Max slides his hands into his jeans pockets. "I know you're off the clock, but would you mind one more thing? A customer needs a ride to Tenth Avenue and Carol Street."

It will keep me from getting wet on my bike. "Sure, why not?"

Behind me, Bucky groans.

Five minutes later, I meet another old woman with soft wrinkles, a fur coat, and all thankfulness for my help: the anti-Lockhardt.

I settle her into the car, where she takes a look at the vehicle's condition and opens her umbrella in the front seat.

"The roof's going to drip on my coat," she croons while I stare slack-jawed. She rides all the way home with her umbrella over her head.

Chapter Eleven:

Overdressed

Ready for either suicide or homicide, I sit in the loaner wondering what to do next.

There's no way I should see Avery right now. I'd influence her all right, but not the way Randy wants. Hal won't be home. Beth would say something pacifying. Bill would listen. I should call Bill.

In the passenger seat, Bucky runs his fingers along a rip in the vinyl. "Are you going to be okay?"

I'm not sure. "The next time I pray for patience, you're under orders to slit my throat."

"It might surprise you to learn I don't follow your orders." Bucky frowns. "I'd bet you never do it again."

"Good, because I'd slit my own throat."

"Hey." He touches me, and although I can't feel it like a real touch, my skin tingles. "It's done."

I start the engine. "Can you do me a favor? Is Bill at the gym?"

Bucky vanishes, and a moment afterward I feel agreement. The loaner starts on the second attempt, and shortly we're in motion. We're also in luck: it's all downhill from Tenth Avenue to Fourth, so when the car stalls, I can drop into neutral to keep rolling while restarting. In front of the gym, I overshoot the handicapped space so the car will die for good in the bus stop, and I leave it where it stalled.

Bucky studies the "No Parking" placard. "What could this mean? Could it be—a sign?"

I ignore him. It costs a hundred fifty bucks to free your car from the impound lot, twice the book value. The City of New York can have a free car if they want it.

He follows me into the gym. "Oh well. I hear it's a wicked generation that asks for a sign."

I find Bill filling out a form. I hug him from behind, probably making a ball-point line across someone's insanely important data. "Hey, guy. Are you busy?"

His smile broadens as he turns. "I don't have to be."

"Grab your coat. My treat."

First I show off the car. "It's a loaner," I say, and he laughs out loud: "Who was the generous soul that loaned it?"

I suggest ice skating, but he nixes that because it's raining. He thinks paintball might take too long since he's got to go back to work, and I don't think the car could reach there anyhow.

"We could use my car," Bill says.

"But where would be the fun?"

Rain sheets down the windows, so no one can see when Bill leans across the seat and kisses me once, then twice. Before he gets a third, I push him away. "Let's play video games."

We end up at Pino's Pizza again on Seventh and First, feeding a roll of quarters into an upright video game machine with:

• unbelievable loudness
• graphic violence
• sheer stress-relief

I am not blowing up buildings: I am blowing up Mrs. Lockhardt's home, with her inside, along with her pessary and her diabetes and her 15th century opinions. It is worth fifty cents to kill her in assorted horrible ways.

Bucky passes his wings between me and the screen, startling me. "Maybe you remember something about harboring anger in your heart?"

"Psychotic...inhuman...unfeeling...spawn of Satan!" I punctuate every word by firing a different weapon.

Inside I hear a tiny voice. I fire a bomb to drown it out.

Bill smirks. "I've had those days too. Politician?"

"Grandparent." Boom!

Bill fires on a bad guy. "I think if you kill your own grandparent, the lawyers don't let you inherit anything."

"Not my own." There's that inner conscience twinge again. Boom! "I don't want to talk about it."

A monster emerges from nowhere and devours me— or rather, my little guy—and then Bill. I reach in my pocket for more quarters, but Bucky sends a warning.

This time I look up at him.

Bill says, "Let's grab something to eat. I have to get back soon."

I sigh. "The Stairmaster gets lonely?"

"My employer gets lonely. Before five isn't an issue, but commuters arrive after that."

I trail Bill to the counter where he orders zeppoli (what Bucky calls "deep-fried golf balls coated with powdered sugar") and a couple of sodas (because zeppoli aren't sweet enough). The high-schooler behind the counter remarks that he added extra sugar because he wouldn't want to annoy me.

I eat only one. My stomach remains in knots.

Bill talks about his clients, but even though I love the stories, I'm tense. Every so often I feel Bucky prompt me: don't I feel ridiculous staying this angry at someone who doesn't care if I'm mad?

Leave me alone.

Bucky slips into the booth alongside Bill, leaning across the table. "Not even a smidgen?"

I look only at Bill. Bucky leans all the way forward so his eyes are right in my own, and then he says, "She's just a lonely old woman."

I burst out laughing, but Bucky had timed that remark with a funny part in Bill's story.

Bucky vanishes. Now I do feel ridiculous, but he had to have been joking.

I was, kind of. But think of her overworked guardian.

She still has one?

He stays to minimize the damage. It would have to be hopeless to make us abandon our posts.

I shiver. He said he'd leave if I lied to him: am I hopeless?

Ten minutes later, Bill sneaks a kiss before heading out the door. "I'll walk. As often as that thing stalls, I'll get there faster."

"It's downhill," I protest, but he's gone.

I'm not the only customer, but I feel alone. Two quarters remain in one pocket, so I head for the game machine to administer Mrs. Lockhardt one more death.

Bucky sits atop the console. "Can I play?"

I shoot him a look. *Did you forget something?*

His eyes widen. "I'm not harboring anger in my heart!"

I meant you don't have a body.

"Oh, that. It's an electronic game, silly."

Which clearly makes all the difference in the world. He's never messed with my PlayStation...or has he? Maybe that's how he staves off boredom while I sleep.

I fish two more quarters from my wallet. Feeling like an idiot, I select the two-player game.

Bucky flares his wings so they fill half the wall. "Prepare to go down in flames."

I flex my hands on the joystick. *Let's see how smug you are after I finish kicking your tail-feathers.*

"I don't have tail-feathers." Bucky pitches forward so he's watching the screen upside-down, braced with his hands. A solid being couldn't maintain that position for longer than half a second before experiencing the joys of a concussion. "We'll see who's smug later."

This is, to some extent, a cooperative game when played as a two-player. You're battling the same bad guys, but every so often you might just take a pot-shot at the other player if he's about to nab a treasure, or maybe take the final shot at a monster, thus stealing his points.

It's loud. It's predictable. Bucky plays well, but he doesn't outdistance me (if you do that, the behind player dies) and he doesn't steal my monsters, so it's rude of me to shoot him and nab the life-giving chalice ("I'd have given it if you'd asked," he mutters) and I feel a teensie bit guilty when I rush into the next room and dust him.

Bucky huffs. "See if I keep the mosquitoes off you next June."

"What happens in the game stays in the game."

"I stand corrected. I just won't shoot this monster."

And blam, my character gets gnawed upon. Cue tragic music.

"Darn," Bucky says. "That looked painful."

My replacement character flashes up onto the screen, but it's not ready to move yet.

A delighted gasp from Bucky. "Hey, treasure! Too bad you're so far away. You could use that extra life right about now."

The end result is, we keep the game going for ten minutes, and afterward I enter my name as a top-ten scorer (just "Lee") while Bucky enters "angel."

You should put your real name.

Not enough space.

There's room for 14 letters. That's going to drive me nuts. *What's your real name? Nebuchadnezzar?*

That would fit.

Firing a dirty look at him, I gather my coat.

The loaner car sits awkwardly at the corner, seeming for all the world as if it's next in line for the Grim Wrecker.

I shove my hands in my pockets. "What time is it?"

"At the tone," Bucky says, "you'll remember I'm not a wrist-watch."

I grope for my cell phone and check the screen. Five after five. "O Exalted Angel," I intone, "might I, your unworthy charge, address a request to your magnificent self?"

Bucky's feathers fluff. "That's more like it!" and then he darts away when I look for something to throw. "You want to know where Hal is? He just got on the subway."

The closest station to the Ansonia Clockworks is at Seventh and Ninth. I check his business card, which says he works on 34th Street. Both of those are connected by the same subway line. Unless there's train trouble, he'll arrive in twenty minutes.

I abandon the loaner, imagining it's used to that kind of decision, and start hiking.

With time to kill, I gaze in shop windows on Seventh Avenue. I say hello to the old Korean woman putting out oranges at the little grocery. She'll wave to me in the mornings and sometimes toss an apple if I wait at the light. I pass the collectibles shop that changes its display every Monday; this week's theme is stuffed monkeys. Next is the Obscenely Priced Clothing Boutique.

Bucky hums. "That would look good on you."

I stop. "That yellow thing?"

"Not the color. You'd look like a wraith. But the cut of the dress, the way it would move." Bucky studies the dress, then me. "But not a print, and definitely not yellow."

"I'd look like a drowned canary. A bankrupt drowned canary."

At the next shop entrance (actually, a *shoppe* entrance) I turn in to the kitschy gift store with everything locked behind glass and a cashier armed with a can of compressed air.

I should mention I'm the only person I know to have been thrown out of a Hallmark.

I prowl aisles filled with what you'd predict: angel statuettes with flowing blonde hair, blue eyes and exalted expressions, all of them standing in a windstorm. No masculine angels; no non-Caucasians; in fact, no non-

Aryans. At least one product line envisions Heaven as a place of which Adolf Hitler would have approved.

Bucky gasps. "Lee! Look at this one!"

I shudder. Not again.

"Lee, come on! Lee! Lee-Lee-Lee-Lee-Lee-get-over-here!"

Resigned, I look. It's a female angel strategically draped with what might be gauze (but in that wind—I don't want to know what happens next!) She balances on one foot with her wings extended and her face rapturous.

Beside me, Bucky spreads his arms and wings, and by the time he starts balancing I'm engulfed in giggles, and then he puts on the rapturous face, and I've got tears streaking my cheeks.

It's a game we've played for two decades: Bucky imitates the statues, conjures props, laments the spinal issues in these angels' futures.

"Look at this violinist! She's doubled over because the stand is knee-high, and the violin's a half-size! Did the Heavenly Philharmonic get its budget slashed?"

I picture an angel at the chiropractor's, discussing lower back problems caused by heavy wings and bad posture. My shoulders are shaking. I've got a stitch in my side. "Bucky," I hiss, "quit it!"

"And why always the violin or the harp? How about the bassoon? And when was the last time they made an angel playing the saxophone? I happen to know some saxophonists—"

I smirk. "That's not in the Bible."

"Neither are violins. You know what they play in the Bible? Trumpets. Let's look for the trumpet section." He leans forward. "Hmm, not a single brass instrument. But look—more violins. For that matter, where are the cellists?"

My fingers press the hot pain in my ribs.

Bucky gasps. "I just realized—none of these angels are wearing shoes!" He looks at himself and then at me, his eyes dim. "I feel so overdressed."

I whisper, "No shoes, no service."

"It's like being caught between Scylla and Charybdis."

"Huh?"

He sighs. "Philistine."

A sharp voice: "May I help you?"

I point to something at random for the irritated clerk. "I was wondering if I could see that figure."

The woman pulls the correct key from a ring of fifty before fitting it into the lock as if she's the mayor at a ribbon-cutting ceremony. She hands over an angel holding a baby angel, which as far as I know can't happen. The Bible says angels don't get married, and I can't envision single mom angels.

Bucky says, "I wonder how you toilet-train something that flies."

Wow, I didn't need to think about that. I hand it back to the clerk and thank her, then move on.

The next case draws an exclamation of disgust from Bucky: half a dozen dog breeds, all with wings and halos. "I'm out of here. I need to present myself before the Almighty Court and beg God to end the world now. Like, today. Before any of those get sold and the manufacturer thinks it was a good idea."

Don't leave! I send to him. *They frighten me!*

The clerk hasn't stopped following. This isn't even the Hallmark where I got ejected.

In the next aisle I spot a group of stained-glass angels. They're gasp-worthy, their lines clean and hinting at timelessness. Who am I kidding? I can't afford them.

And then, in the next case—

It's not Bucky. Not really. But a palm-sized angel statue looks out (not up) at the world with the eagerness of a child awaiting the whistle-blow for free swim. His wings are white, not brown with yellow bars, but he has Bucky's half-curly hair and dimpled smile.

A peek through the glass on which he stands reveals that this, the only realistic angel in the store, retails for ten bucks.

The clerk glowers behind me.

"I'll take him." I'm already removing my wallet from my belt pack.

Five minutes and one ten dollar bill plus tax later, nestled in his original box in a glossy bag, is my mini-Bucky.

When Hal climbs the subway steps, staring at the pavement with a visible exhaustion, I step directly in front of him. First he raises his head to tell me to get the heck out of his way, and then in the next moment— delight.

I push my umbrella toward him. "I didn't know if you had one."

He keeps his umbrella folded and steps beneath mine. I sidle away from the subway exit so we don't irritate the other passengers, keeping him sheltered with me. I love the rain. I didn't love the annoying, dousing, frigid rain five minutes ago, but right now, I love the rain.

He recovers his poise. "Do you come here often?"

"This is my favorite street corner." There's not much room beneath an umbrella, so I rest my hand on his arm. Have I mentioned I love the rain? "I see you're tired, but maybe we can go somewhere?"

He nods. "Lead on."

Believe it or not, I gave this some thought in the five minutes I waited. A "jazz bistro" two blocks from the station features live music during the dinner hour and has a menu like this:

Stefano's Salad: Mesclun, grilled zucchini squash, marinated baby bella mushrooms, artichokes, olives, feta, and couscous with balsamic vinaigrette.

In other words, this could be terrific, or it could make the Hindenburg look like a campfire.

I steer Hal in that direction, and before we're at the corner, he has his arm over my shoulders.

We don't match. He's got khakis and dress shoes and carries a laptop bag. I'm wearing jeans and a sweat-shirt under my jacket, but since he thinks I work as a personal trainer, he shouldn't mind.

When we're seated, Hal pronounces the menu satisfactory, then guides me toward an appetizer involving mushrooms, goat cheese, and roasted red peppers. We'll split that.

The entrée items are all pretentious, so I opt for a soup-and-salad combo involving French onion soup and a decipherable sandwich (tomato and arugula with fresh mozzarella on focaccia). Hal orders something with a name that would frighten me if I met it in a dark alley, except it involves chicken and roasted red peppers.

Next Issue: Superman Versus the Menacing Mesclun Monster!

I ask about his day, but he says I'd be bored. I disagree: anyone who chose his own career finds something about it exciting—and I'd love to hear him excited, so I ask him to tell the craziest story he can about his job.

It works. He describes a receipt jungle at his previous job, how he worked acrobatics to figure out what went with which account, and how by untangling that big bowl of spaghetti, he discovered one of the bosses siphoning money from one account to another. When faced with the ultimate question, he polished up his resume.

Hal gives a wicked smile. "I also learned secondhand the effectiveness of the *anonymous tip.*"

By the time the appetizer arrives, Hal has eased the Lockhardt-induced knots inside my brain. I compliment Hal on his choice, which gets him discussing unlikely food combinations.

I confess (while averting my eyes) that this *bistro* frightens me.

"The music alone outclasses me." I force myself to look up at him. "If you weren't here, I'd have fled."

He takes my hand. "I'll fight off the big bad menu if the waitress asks about dessert."

"Desserts don't usually involve five breeds of lettuce and balsamic anything."

He gives my fingers a squeeze. "You're not going to be quizzed, and you know how to use a fork."

"Nine times out of ten," I admit, and he laughs.

"I'm an uncultured freak." I bite my lip. "My mom told me to take my niece to a museum to get her some culture, but I won't know which end is up."

"See which way the fork falls when you drop it." Hal chuckles. "Right over by the library, the Brooklyn Museum is having an Autobahn exhibition."

Huh. That's weird. Why would they have pictures of German cars?

Bucky in my mind: *Philistine.*

I frown. "Would my niece like that?"

"It depends if she likes birds."

Oh, *Audubon,* not *Autobahn.*

As the waitress brings his entrée and my soup (and I just realized, she owns a Chevy Blazer with a rust problem) Hal says, "How was your day?"

With a shudder, I say, "I kidnapped you so I wouldn't keep thinking about my day."

Hal gestures to my shopping bag. "Is that retail therapy?"

While we eat, I unwrap the angel statue. Hal studies it and renders a verdict: "They paid attention to the face. Usually the expressions on these knick-knacks are blank."

I huff. "It's worst with the Michael statues. Half the time he looks bored, like he's sweeping the floor rather than driving a pike into the heart of Satan." The soup is oniony, not salty, but scalding. I open the bread to release the steam. "But I landed one five years ago where he's enraged, his armor dented and his cape not only torn but also smoke-damaged as if he got hit with a flame-thrower—and I imagine that's closer to how it really happened."

While cutting his chicken (it has spiral slices of lemon over the top—I'm relieved to see Hal pushes them to the side, because I wouldn't know if you were expected to eat them) Hal says, "You were going to tell me why you're so enthralled by angels."

Because we rock, Bucky says in my heart, and I grin.

I'm a walking textbook of a very few things. I know how to fix anything on your car, and I know everything anyone's ever written about angels.

I tell him angels are pure spirits with no bodies, that they were created all at the same time, before humans existed. I name all nine choirs in order (Seraphim, Cherubim, Thrones, Dominions, Virtues, Powers, Principalities, Archangels and Angels). I talk about how a third of the angels rebelled, and they want to hurt us. Because that's not a fair fight, every human being is assigned a guardian angel, and the overwhelming majority of personal guardians come from the choir of Angels.

The rusty Chevy waitress is hanging around the table beside us, listening. No one thinks about angels, but everyone is interested if you bring up the subject. Maybe I should write a book.

Hal shrugs. "A lot of this is conjecture. It's not as if we see angels on a regular basis."

I don't respond.

"If they're that far above us, think of the culture gap." He chuckles. "I can't imagine them being interested in clothes or how to parallel park."

Again, I don't reply.

He leans forward, gesturing with his fork. "I would guess that ninety-nine out of a hundred people will live their entire lives without seeing an angel, and that's the way it should be."

I recoil. "Why?"

"Because whenever you hear a story about angels, they do things for people that we couldn't do ourselves. They feed them in wastelands, tell them things they could never have figured out, or stop their cars from plummeting over a cliff." He opens his hands. "You wouldn't have an angel showing up to tell you the time of day."

My ears burn. "But...if they're looking out for us—"

"For the big stuff." He shrugs. "Seeing an angel would be a miracle, so there'd have to be a really important reason." He arches his eyebrows. "Well? Have you ever seen an angel?"

My ears ring.

He waits a beat. "If even you haven't seen one, then it's a good bet they don't show up without a grave reason." He glances up to locate the waitress. "So, are you thinking of dessert?"

Chapter Twelve:

Good Teeth

I've been able to see Bucky since I was three. People didn't understand why with three brothers I still needed an imaginary friend, but they thought it cute. Once I realized they didn't believe me, I stopped talking about him. Only Randy knows Bucky's real.

I should remember the first time I saw him, but it's unclear. Was it the smiling boy illuminated by moonlight over my bed? Or the time that same boy knocked my mother's keys from her hand right before a crazy-fast car zoomed down the street? Maybe it was when I saw him at the park on a swing after another kid had dismounted, rocking down with the loss of momentum.

A better person would remember. I remember my first kiss and my first driving lesson, the first time I ate kim chee and the first time I realized my mother wanted a different daughter. Not the first time I saw him, though, the way you can't pinpoint the moment night becomes day, only that you've awakened to discover it's happened, and you're so glad it has.

When Hal says goodbye, he kisses me without regard for any passers-by. It's a lingering kiss, as if he wishes more would follow.

I keep my arms around his shoulders. "I'm glad you had a good time."

"You're a fiendish kidnapper," he murmurs into my ear. "I'm suffering from Stockholm Syndrome."

I leave the loaner parked where it stalled rather than wrestling it back to Sixth Avenue. With the air a lot colder than it was at five-thirty, the rain has turned freezing, and eddies of slush appear on the hoods of cars. Two people pass in the opposite direction, discussing if it's only the weathermen sowing hysteria when they predicted a foot of snow for Thursday.

Half a block later, Bucky keeps pace at my side. "Okay, I'm confused. Most of the time you'd have said, *Bucky, are we getting snow?*"

I watch the pavement as I walk.

"Penny for your thoughts?" he says.

"You don't have a penny."

He gasps. "A pox on being bankrupt in a consumer society." His brows form an inverted V. "Would it be a capitalist crime to share your thoughts for free?"

I keep my hands jammed into my pockets. We're almost at the corner of Sixth Avenue, and once I make the turn, it's five blocks to home.

He drawls, "You're wondering about what Hal said?"

"Why can I see you?"

Bucky chuckles. "When you never asked why, I didn't know whether to be hurt or amused, but I opted for amused. You're not into existential questions."

"And?"

"You want the whole thing while we're walking, or do you want it back home?" He pauses. "Beth is there, so that rules out shared confidences over tea or whatever cozy images you'd have conjured."

I regard him sidewise. "Monologues in the freezing slush are fine."

"Eden was amazing," Bucky says.

I halt. "You really are starting from the beginning!"

"Not quite the beginning." He grins: he must have been preparing this story for as long as I've been alive. "Satan had already rebelled, and Adam and Eve were still new. The angels were fascinated with these creatures. We're completely different from you. Did you know," Bucky says, "that if an angel in human form stands with his eyes closed and arms extended, he's going to tip over? Every time. We used to compare how long it took to topple."

I bite my lip. "Did you try it too?"

"Down in ten seconds." He chuckles. "It's just not natural for us. If an angel takes human form for an assignment, you can tell because he watches his feet when he descends steps."

I resume walking. "Go on. So then I came along—"

"No, then Adam and Eve dined on their fateful Waldorf salad and your race got ejected from paradise, and Satan vowed destruction on humanity. As you told Hal, that's not a fair fight, so each human was assigned a guardian, and some important people got two."

"Good thing I'm not important. I'm not smart enough to deal with two of you."

Bucky swats me with his wing; my head tingles.

"Right away, I knew that's what I wanted."

"That's beyond me." I narrow my eyes. "How could it benefit you? I understand doing it once you've got orders, but actually wanting it?"

"Guarding is a chance to have an impact on a soul." Bucky's eyes are bright enough now that I squint. "Sure, there's no recognition for most of us, and the vigilance is constant. When a person's being attacked, it's because they got through us first. There's heartbreak when you give your charge every possible chance and he makes the wrong decision anyhow. But," Bucky adds, "a human soul is so diamond-brilliant when it's pure. I watched civilization develop, and I studied families, and I wanted to be a guardian."

That's odd. "Don't you all become guardians?"

He shakes his head. "Just as with humans, we have a variety of vocations. There are healers, messengers, angels who guard systems or countries... I wanted to guard a person."

I smile. "I'm glad."

"I'm glad you're glad." As he meets my gaze, warmth shoots through my stomach. "On the off-chance that I might get selected, I began praying for whichever soul I would guard."

That's too much like Bucky for me not to giggle.

"For a thousand years, I prayed for you every day, and I didn't even know for sure you'd exist."

"Honest and for true?"

"Honest and for true. One day I got summoned before God. That was scary: I had no idea if He'd tell me to knock it off already. Instead He took me for a walk through the North American prairie." Bucky rubs his chin. "That area is now a soy bean farm, but at the time there were buffalo trails through the waist-high grass, and prairie dogs, and hawks circling. And in the heat of noon, silence."

For a moment I sense the sky suspended like a bowl, a cloudless blue fading toward the apex, and plains flat enough to leave vision unimpeded for miles.

"God and I walked while I marveled at the world, and God delighted in what He'd made. And then He assured me that He'd noticed my desire to guard a person, and to my thrill, He promised I would."

There's the briefest sense that Bucky flung his arms around God, but then it dissipates and I'm standing at the corner of Third Street. We cross.

Bucky continues, "God then asked, if I could request any favor for my charge, what would it be."

It's all clear now. "And you asked that I should be able to see you!"

"Heavens no," Bucky says. "I asked that you should have good teeth."

Two minutes later, I'm still leaning against a lamppost, laughing with tears on my cheeks, trying to stop gasping. Anyone would think I'm a lunatic, but I can't stop.

Bucky looks horrified.

"Teeth?" A stitch forms in my side. "You could have asked for anything—and you asked about teeth?"

"They didn't have dentistry back then." Eyes downcast, Bucky folds his arms. "If you got a toothache, you couldn't just get it filled. Teeth rotted away, hurting the whole time, and that made people grumpy. It impacted their spiritual development."

I can't even breathe. You think you know someone—

Bucky sounds stung. "Have you ever had a cavity?"

I shake my head.

"And do you have dental insurance?"

"Well, no—"

"So I'd think you'd say thank you." Bucky has retreated a couple of steps, and he's faded around the edges.

Straightening, I struggle to avoid any thought that might set off more giggles. "I'm sorry. Thank you. That was...practical of you."

Bucky's image gets solid again. "God thought so. He said that would be fine, and He asked what else I wanted, so I asked that you'd live in a place and time where you would have the freedom to learn about Him."

I cock my head. "Then for the third thing, you asked if I could see you?"

"No, Lee. God isn't a genie who grants three wishes if you rub the lamp the right way." He sighs. "I asked that you wouldn't live dominated by fear, because fear is the opposite of love."

We're now at the corner of Sixth and Second. "Interesting. I wouldn't have put it that way."

"I had a list of requests, some of which He refused and some He said were up to you. Finally God said to me, 'Bucky, why don't you ask for what you want?'"

I shiver all over. "He really said 'Bucky'?"

"He said [insert my God-given name here] but I'm not going to tell you." Bucky's wings flex, and he spreads his feathers. "And I said to God, 'I don't want to anger my Lord with a frivolous request,' and He said to me, 'I made you, and I know what you want. And because I love you, I'm going to give it to you.'"

My hair stands on end. "Just like that?"

"I knelt," Bucky says, "and I said, 'Lord, my Sovereign and Creator, I want my charge to be able to see me and hear me, because if he can, I think I'll be able to bring him to you perfect and polished.' God rested His hands on my head, and He said, 'I will grant that to you.' And then our meeting ended, and I stayed on the darkening plain."

Corner of President Street now. Both of us remain silent. I pick up from Bucky's memory the waving of prairie grass, the plips of crickets and peeper frogs, the whirr of nighttime insects as they dart through the immaterial form of an angel. Tiny birds for which I have no name peck at seeds, and above his head as he kneels, the purplish grain heads sway with the breeze.

Corner of Garfield Place.

"Thank you for telling me," I whisper. "That's really sweet."

Bucky doesn't answer.

Home now. I fit my key into the lock and squeak up two flights of steps. Beth sits at the table folding dragons.

Without speaking, I unpack my miniature Bucky to set him on the china cabinet shelf, and there he gazes in wonderment over the creations in our dining room and the place he and I call home.

Chapter Thirteen:

What does a poem gain by being incomprehensible?

Maybe I'm done with patience, but Mrs. Zhou has returned to our waiting area, child in tow, and informed me she has another flat tire in her guillotine trunk.

"That other car," I say. "Do you park it on glass and bent nails?"

She shrugs. "We have no luck with tires."

We're again dealing with a crack in the sidewall (meaning she's not driving over anything bad) and again, it cannot be patched. I check in the computer, but it's not one of the ones we've replaced in the past twelve months. I find a new tire, put it on the rim, balance it, and roll it out to her Accord.

"This is getting to be a habit." By now I could input the numbers without looking them up: the code for the tire, the cost, the total. It's going to drive me nuts wondering what she's doing that keeps cracking the sidewalls. "You're a wonderful customer, but I wish you didn't have to see me so often."

The other thing I wish I didn't have to see so often is her trunk, which still wants to gobble me alive like the plant from *Little Shop of Horrors*.

Max meets us at the register. "Good news. I found a trunk piston. We'll get it here in the next few days."

Mrs. Zhou is pleased. Not nearly as pleased as I am, but pleased nonetheless.

As she's leaving, I turn to Max. "I still need to retrieve the loaner."

He looks at the crowded waiting room. "Is it on the right side of the street? Then take the next ticket. You can drive it back after lunch."

Because, you see, Max is smart. He knows I'm going to walk somewhere for lunch, and I also need to walk to get the loaner. Thus he can save paying the fifteen minutes it takes to drive the car back because, well, I was clocked out.

Having been made patient, I don't protest. Assuming a similar process, I'd rather not be made charitable or humble.

For my next customer, I have a Dodge needing a brake job and a Dodge owner asking if there's anyplace to grab lunch.

Dude, I want to say, we're in Brooklyn. I direct him toward Seventh Avenue where he's most likely to find edibles, and he leaves. I wouldn't mind lunch myself, but in general the fine purveyors of lunches want payment, and in order to be paid, I need to do my job. I get to work on the guy's brakes.

"See," I whisper to Bucky, "I'm being patient about waiting for lunch."

His reply comes: relief about not having to do that again, followed by a curious sensation. I look up to see him sitting on the lift controls.

What was that?

Nothing.

Nothing?

Bucky shrugs. *It could have been a lot worse.*

I'm about to raise the lift when I suddenly laugh out loud, helpless to stop. Carlos and Tim stare at me—even Bucky is staring. I smother it, but tears sting my eyes, and my throat aches.

Bucky's eyebrows raise. "What?"

You waited for me for four thousand years— No, this is too rich. *You prayed for patience, didn't you?*

Bucky inhales, squares his shoulders and turns his face away. *I'm not going to discuss the intricacies of my prayer life with you.*

That just sets me into worse giggles. He's blushing. He vanishes.

Okay, so maybe that wasn't fair of me, but it's perfect. It's perfect because I never thought before of Bucky as imperfect—or of having a life before me at all. And yet he went for a walk with God and apparently received a hard application of The Cluebat Of Virtue.

He's always so confident—and right—that I never thought of him as young, inexperienced—impulsive? From a practical standpoint, that means angels can learn. That they can be surprised or change their points of view, and that's not something I ever considered.

Considered that maybe, a few millennia ago, he was something like me.

Half an hour later, I'm done replacing the brakes. Bucky still hasn't reappeared.

"Check the CV boots," Max calls from across the shop.

"Already checked them." The CV boots are fine. The brake pads had reached the squeal-zone, but there's no damage.

Max says, "Check for hairline fissures."

The only fissure around here will be in the driver's wallet, and I know this. Still, I double-check the CV boots. They are fine. The axle is fine too. Everything is fine other than the brake pads, which I'm already being paid to change.

Max pokes around under the car. "Find something else. A 2009 Dodge Durango is bound to have something else failing."

Bucky? I hate myself for this, but it's easier than fighting. *Is the owner back in the waiting area?*

It's an easier call if the guy is waiting. Bucky tells me he's not, so I dutifully examine the car for problems that will require the application of hundred dollar bills to resolve. Other than it's being a Dodge, there are no problems. Max gives the stink-eye whenever he passes, but I'm not going to trump something up.

Verdict: the owner's in luck, and I'm out.

In the waiting room, I ticket out the car. I call, "Mr. Davis? I have your vehicle."

As soon as he's within arm's reach, I smell alcohol.

It takes me by surprise enough that I drop his credit card. He doesn't look drunk. But he doesn't smell sober.

Forcing a smile as I pick up the card, I say, "Were you able to find lunch?"

Back in college we'd have called it a malted barley salad.

The man says he did, and thank you, his voice sounding only a little bit off. I stand corrected: this isn't barley salad. It smells stronger than beer.

I can't give a drunk man his car keys. "Did you drive here yourself?" He did.

Well, this is a pickle. Let's see: I can aid and abet a drunken driver. Or...what?

Bucky hates when I lie, but I can't see another way. "Oh!" I try to sound breezy. "There's a note about something we found. Let me check it out and be right back."

The man says, "What is it?"

I fight nausea. "A potential problem between the front seat and the steering wheel that could result in an accident."

And proving me right that he's drunk, he accepts this.

I return to the garage to look again at the Taurus. I have no idea how much the guy drank, but I might be able to keep him waiting long enough to sober up.

Max stalks over. "What's going on?"

"I can't give him the keys. He's drunk."

Max says, "Hand them over."

"I'm not doing that."

Max glowers. "What the hell do you care?"

I say, "I think we're supposed to care about other people dying."

Max holds out his 93% hand for the keys. "I'm not getting involved. Give him back his car."

"I'm going to find some other problem and fix it while he waits."

Max turns away. "I want the guy out of my shop before someone else realizes. Back the car out of the garage, park it on the street so it's not our problem, and then get the hell back inside. I'm ticketing him out right now."

Max stalks to the front. I call after him, "We'd be liable."

"Not if you didn't notice anything," Max says.

Just for a moment, I want you to imagine Bucky's face were I to swear to God before a judge to tell the truth, and then assure a jury I had no idea this guy was a danger on the road.

Despite my fervent desire, the car refuses to stall. I think, *Bucky, can you put a sword through the transmission?*

A refusal: this one I need to handle myself.

Some guardian you are.

He shoots back that I know what Max wants me to do is wrong.

But I need you to tell me what's right.

On the street, I find the narrowest space in the heretofore known universe, two inches longer than the car itself. It may actually be two inches shorter. No drunk guy will be able to get out without hitting the parked cars in front and behind, and better to hit a parked car than a moving one. After all this time, I have a black belt in parking, but it's going to take even me a while to maneuver it in.

I'm at the "thinking point" part of reversing the car when I realize, *Bucky? I don't have to handle this. It's not my job to keep drunks off the road.*

Before Bucky reacts, I have my cell phone in my hands. I dial 911.

I know you're not supposed to use the phone and drive simultaneously. Despite that, I find in the police dispatcher a very interested listener who wants to know exactly where I am, the make and model of the vehicle, the license plate number, and the driver's name. All of which are documented on the intake form beside me on the passenger seat.

I'm assured that two of New York's Finest will be pleased to make the gentleman's acquaintance within five minutes.

Max awaits at the desk, hand extended. I present unto him the keys to the Deathmobile, and he returns them to the customer with the encouragement to have a nice day. I issue directions, perhaps a tad confusing because I need to repeat them three times, to the spot fifty feet down the street. As the customer wanders through our lot, Max says, "Good girl. Never get involved in that kind of crap. Here, take an oil change."

By the time I have the car in the bay, Max is bellowing again, and this time, it means my job.

Anyone who can make Max turn that shade of purple without actually blowing an aneurysm must have a certain degree of skill: that much I'll admit. But the dressing-down I received, at a volume that should have involved a megaphone—that stings.

I didn't get fired. If Max didn't want the hassle of telling the cops a guy got drunk, he was even less enamored of explaining to the labor board that he fired me because I did it. Instead he'll make me wish I got fired.

Max told me in no uncertain terms to get out of his sight, then thought better of it. Reminiscent of yesterday, he scrawled an address on a scrap of paper and sent me into Manhattan to fetch that trunk piston.

To make matters worse, he also ordered me to drive the loaner back to the shop tomorrow morning. It's the automotive equivalent of crawling back on your hands and knees. With a trunk piston between your legs.

Bucky joked that if these workday errands continued, I'll forget what a screwdriver looks like. I couldn't laugh.

My inadequacies follow me onto the subway like a cloud of gnats, the other passengers looking away at the last second so I can't catch them staring. Half these people must have heard Max chewing me out.

Leaning against the train door, I turn on my iPod and pretend I'm not there.

At the next stop, Bucky says in my heart, *Would you like to meet someone?*

Be more specific. But he's so enthusiastic I know I'll say yes.

A sensation breaks over me, a welcome and a mild amusement: the presence of a second angel. I gasp. My iPod shuts itself off. I scan the train car, lips half-parted in a smile, only no one else can tell what's happening.

The presence checks me over with a promise of protection. It projects strength, confidence, good-humor.

I sense the moment before the doors close. I anticipate the jerk of the car as it rolls into motion. I read the rightness in the rocking of the train.

Who are you?

In my heart: the angel charged with guarding the New York City Metropolitan Transit Authority, holding dominion over the trains and the buses, alerting the conductors and engineers to hazards, safeguarding travelers, helping the lost find their way between departure and destination.

Wow, I send. *Thank you for everything you're doing.*

Amusement in response. A sense of complexity, enjoyment, machinery fitting together, tenderness for the millions relying on these machines but never considering the ones keeping them running.

Keeping them on track? I suggest, and in return, laughter.

I'm spinning inside. I sense a warning, and I grab the pole just before the train lurches.

I thank him again, and there's a sense of deference, "you're welcome" and "farewell" mingled.

The presence departs. I swallow compulsively.

Bucky?

I'm here. His reassurance clings like a hug, but I still feel empty after the other one has gone. *He was passing through, and I thought an introduction might cheer you up.*

Keeping my eyes closed, I try to hold onto the warmth. *Thank you.*

Max could have shipped a trunk piston direct from the dealer for three figures and passed the nonsavings along to the customer. But he also knew she was happy with a free broom handle, so in the interests of making money, he determined that a junk yard under the West Side Highway was the very best source on earth for this part.

"You're sure about this?" Bucky says as we walk from the C-train toward Eleventh Avenue.

I stop. "Do I have the address wrong?"

Bucky scans the street like the Secret Service. "I'm concerned about the neighborhood."

"You'll protect me. You're an angel."

Bucky frowns. "Remember that thing about fools rushing in?"

I pause. "I'm not rushing."

There's a long silence as Bucky turns this over. When he doesn't reply, I figure that means it's all right.

On Tenth Avenue, I stop by a guy selling five dollar "Rolexes" to peruse the goods on the folding table. I haven't worn a watch since 2001. He also sells hair gear that would fall off my head. The guy ceases his hateful stare long enough to blank-facedly take money from a woman who picks up a handbag.

From Bucky: *There's 'not rushing in,' and there's 'never getting there.'*

I think, *You actually want to do this?*

I want to get it over with.

That's what I like: a guardian who fills me with confidence.

Between Eleventh and Twelfth Avenues, I reach a lot enclosed in a fourteen-foot double chain link fence topped with coiled razor wire. The fence is filled with broken bottles and other trash. On the opposite side, a Rottweiler barks in a frenzy, and on the gate itself is a sign that reads "WELCOME."

I turn to Bucky. "That's hospitable, right?"

The gate slides on wheels just enough for me to pass through. The hellhound is on a chain which, I'm relieved to note, doesn't quite allow it to grasp my throat in its jaws.

It takes a moment to locate the trailer in the middle of a hundred cars being parted out. No bets on how many of these are stolen. Hubcaps line the fence, on display as if this were The Metropolitan Museum of Modern Rust. Bumpers lie in one corner, trunks in another. I'm paying my respects at an automotive cemetery.

Threading between piles of parts and wondering if I should have brought flowers, I make my way to the trailer. I'm halfway there when a man in a denim jacket emerges from the corrugated iron car port alongside the trailer and lights up a cigarette.

"Hey," I call. "I'm here for a trunk piston."

He points toward the trailer, then resumes smoking.

Welcome, indeed.

At the trailer, I knock on the door. No answer. I push it open and step inside.

The door bumps into a stack of tires. I peek around the door frame to find the room crammed with parts, and parts, and more parts. Cars demolished in the worst ways imaginable still have one or two pieces salvageable: here's a rear-view mirror. There's a glove compartment door. That's a radio. The chaos resembles what would happen if a GM factory vomited in your living room.

Still no one around. "Hello?" I wonder if I haven't wandered into a sci-fi flick, where all these parts will draw themselves together into a hundred-foot robot named Zod.

I locate a path through the clutter to the only other room in the trailer. And there I find—

A library: slender books line the walls on mahogany shelves, accompanied by a stack of *The New Yorker*, and on the desk is a leather-bound blank book. Behind the desk sits a man wearing a suit, oxford shirt, and tie who runs slender fingers through his graying hair as he stares, face furrowed, at a list on the creamy page. Woven through his fingers is one of those fat pens with a marbled blue veneer. After a moment, I realize it's a fountain pen.

He crosses out three of the entries in his list, then writes two words in the margin, crosses out one, then frames words with his thin lips until he pauses to write another line entry.

Finally he looks up, eyes tortured. "May I help you?"

My brain blanks. Eventually I come up with my own name. "I'm Lee Singer. My boss sent me for a trunk piston for a 2009 Accord."

"Oh, yes." He caps the pen, lays it crosswise on the journal, and pushes to a stand. On his feet, he's a head taller than I am. "Accompany me, please."

He speaks in a light tenor with a clipped manner. It's almost pleasant against the welder's torch next door as it screams through aluminum quarter-panels.

While we're walking, he says, "Do you read poetry?"

Oh, I bet that was a poem he was writing, not a list. "I don't really get it."

He huffs. "And you can thank e. e. cummings for that, wrenching poetry from the hands of the masses and rendering it into contorted jumbles that none but the most highly-educated literati purport to understand. Tell me, and don't spare my feelings: what does a poem gain by being incomprehensible?"

Behind me, Bucky says, "Some critics would assert that the imprecise nature of language frees the mind to paint its inner visions on the canvas of your verbal construction."

This I repeat. The poet pivots, eyes alive against the rusted tableau at his back. "Deconstructionism devalues the authority of the writer."

Bucky says, and I repeat, "Once the piece is written, the writer stands in the same relationship to it as any other reader. The text alone generates its meaning in the consciousness of the beholder."

Bucky and I played this game in college when I dated one of the theater arts guys. He could "talk the talk" and either would put keywords in my head or else just would just talk while I parroted it verbatim, maybe three words behind. Half the time, I couldn't even understand what they were saying, but Bucky could sling phrases like "ontological significance" and "thematic recurrence" without breaking a sweat,* and he had fun talking the other guy into a corner. That relationship didn't last long enough.

Since he's talking literature too, Bucky must have paid more attention than I did in my core courses. For five minutes in the cold, while I wonder why I haven't

---

* Strictly speaking, he can't sweat. But you get the point.

been handed a trunk piston, I listen to myself arguing about poetry.

Finally, with a disgusted exclamation about how a multi-thousand year tradition of poetic creativity has been kidnapped from the very hands of the people, the man leads me into the garage. There we wait for the previous jean-jacketed man with the cigarette to finish cutting the trunk off a Lexus with a smashed front end. Poetry Man gestures to Cigarette Guy, and they walk among the dead cars until we come to a crunched-up silver Accord (a Honda Accordion?) with the top sliced off.

Hands clasped behind his back, Poetry Man circles the car, then points to the trunk. Cigarette Guy forces open the trunk, and Poetry Man leans in, studies the interior from several directions, and again points with his immaculate finger. Cigarette Guy pulls a ratchet screwdriver out of his tool belt, then jams up the lid with a rusted tail-pipe to remove the piston assembly.

Cigarette Guy cradles the part in his palms like an offering. This he presents to Poetry Man, who examines it (still with his hands clasped at the base of his spine) and nods: it is acceptable unto him.

Cigarette Guy thrusts me the trunk piston, then stalks back to the shed.

While I'm shoving the part into a canvas tote bag, Poetry Man says, "We're having open mike night on Thursday at The Grey Goose. Would you care to attend one of my readings?"

I would rather put my head in that open trunk and have Cigarette Guy yank out the tail-pipe. Instead I accept his business card with the date, time and place printed in tiny letters on the back. It can go in the file with all the similar cards my mother has handed me. In fact, he may already have a card there. *"Oh, honey, he owns his own business—and he's a poet too!"*

I turn over the card: Porter Brothers Salvage. I exclaim, "You're brothers?"

He nods. "It's hard to believe, I know. But he's made it clear he's only staying until his cheese-making business takes off."

Chapter Fourteen:

Camel thieves

As I head back to the subway, I find Eighth Avenue choked by a hundred people on line.

What on earth...? Looking up gives no clue: they appear to be queuing up outside one of the TV station offices.

This could be fun. I get on the end of the line.

Bucky appears beside me. "What are we waiting for?"

I flash him a smile. "Let's find out."

"I could find out for you."

"Don't you dare." I hunch my shoulders. "This day's been awful enough. I need a surprise."

"Suit yourself," and Bucky proceeds to sit on a parked car looking at something in his hands.

After five minutes, as more people file onto the line behind me, I turn to him. *What are you doing?*

He raises the paper, and I laugh, drawing dirty looks. Bucky's holding a *Heavenly Times*.

"I only get it for the Sudoku." He returns his attention to the puzzle.

The line inches forward. By now I've determined it involves a movie version of a novel called The Camel Thief. We're nowhere near a theater, but if it's new, maybe we're trying for tickets to a premiere.

"Darn. I've done this one before." The paper vanishes. "At least the line is moving."

Shortly we're adjacent to a magazine stand. My toes tell me they're frozen, but not frozen enough to trump my curiosity. My breath frosts away from me, but hiding in my pockets, my hands are warm. I've got the canvas bag with the auto part under my right arm, tucked down: the native New Yorker stance.

While I scan the crowd, Bucky scans magazine headlines. "Hey, ten things you can do to spice up your evenings! Oh, wait, they don't mean chili powder. Five things that will drive him crazy! Oh, wait, they don't mean leaving your socks on the floor. Hey, they asked two hundred guys what lights their fire! Oh, wait, they don't mean charcoal briquettes."

I let off a long sigh. Bucky peers at me. "Are you still worried? I doubt Max would fire you. You're here because he doesn't want to do something he'll regret. This will relax you: pictures of chocolate cake on three different covers." Bucky zips in front of me. "Did you know chocolate cake on a cover instantly sells twenty percent more magazines? If they could, editors would put a picture of chocolate cake on every one."

I force a smile. "Even *US News*?"

"Especially *US News*. Ten ways chocolate cake is patriotic: five ways to drive your congressman crazy by lighting his fire." Wings spread, he glides to the roof of the newsstand. "If I asked for a pretzel, would you get me one?"

I'm very sensible. "You don't eat."

"But they're warm and soft, and they make you feel like a kid." He puts into my head a picture of me holding a steaming pretzel wrapped in a paper napkin.

I muster a smile. "Thanks."

When we get to the window, a woman takes my name and hands me a pamphlet and two tickets. Free. I step aside to remedy my ignorance.

"Oh, cool! Bucky, we get to be extras!"

The pamphlet explains: *The Camel Thief* will be released next Christmas, and today they're filming a scene during which a guy on a talk show tries to convince the host about an international ring of camel thieves. They need three hundred extras for the audience. We'll watch them film the same scene five or ten or fifty times (or one time if they nail it) and applaud or gasp or otherwise follow directions.

I bounce in place. "They want us at seven. Let's go grab dinner and—"

Bucky takes half a step back. "Have you forgotten something?"

I blink, then think hard. "If I have, I've forgotten what I forgot."

"I don't need a ticket." He arches his brows. "And I can't be captured on film."

I frown. "You can't, or you don't want to?"

"I might if I tried." Bucky fidgets. "It never seemed important to find out. But my point is, you have two tickets and you only occupy one seat."

Not a big deal. Out comes my phone. I dial Corinne. "Hey, put Avery on a train to Times Square. I've got tickets for us to be extras in a movie!"

The conversation that follows can be summed up with: over her dead body. She has all sorts of things to say about it being a school night, not wanting to send Avery alone on the subway, and how would the kid get to school tomorrow? Arguing proves futile. I need a plan B.

"What about Bill?" We maneuver through the crowd, my trunk part in the bag on my shoulder. "He'd love it, but I'd never be able to get him to play hooky two days in a row. There's Beth—"

I stop in place and someone bumps me from behind. Wait a minute—Hal works on 34th Street, and his number is in my cell.

A few moments later, I have Hal on line one. "If you're not doing anything tonight, are you up to helping me foil an international ring of camel thieves?"

At five PM I meet Hal waiting by a newsstand at 34th and Fifth Avenue, where first he verifies that we have time for dinner, then suggests an Afghan restaurant on 26th and Third. "You claimed you were adventuresome," he says, "and I'm going to take you up on that."

It turns out no one Hal knows is willing to eat at this place. I settle on the cushioned seating and low tables, and squint in the low lighting at a menu incomprehensible other than the word "kabob."

He gestures to my bag. "Isn't your retail therapy getting out of hand?"

I shake my head. "I had to pick up a part for my job."

That was dumb. Now he looks intrigued. "What part?"

"Something terribly scary." I put gravity in my voice and pull the bag close. "Something we don't show the uninitiated."

Taking it for a game, Hal lifts the bag from my lap and removes the piston. "What on earth is this?"

"Be careful—it's got grease on it." I take it from his hands and hold it up in the dim light, then shove it back in the bag. "It's a piston. It holds up a lot of weight so it doesn't all come down on your head, but the one they're using now doesn't hold up anything. I'd rather not get my head chopped off, wouldn't you?.."

"You work in one scary place." Hal gestures to our exotic surroundings. "Speaking of scary, how is it that a jazz bistro terrifies you, but a completely foreign menu is a thrill?"

I push the bag back out of sight. "But I'm not supposed to know this style of food, right? My mother would be just as confused, which makes it kind of like climbing Mt. Everest."

Looking over the menu, Hal starts making suggestions, but I interrupt. "You know what? I trust you. Order for me."

His eyes widened. "You want it to be a surprise?"

I nod.

Disappointingly, he asks the waiter for "a traditional Afghan dinner for two" which are all words I understand.

Disappointing until the food arrives, that is. That's when I learn that a "kadu" is a pumpkin turnover with a yogurt dip. I enjoy a salad made of cucumbers, onions and tomatoes. We split a pot of jasmine tea. Every new plate requires an explanation, and by the end, Hal declares me, indeed, adventuresome.

While we're eating, he tells me he's thought more about Avery and my mentorship. Although I brace for a declaration that my mentorship is every bit as seaworthy as the *Andrea Doria*, he only says, "You should take an art class. They offer them through Brooklyn College, and I know a number of smaller shops offer classes like sculpture or beading. They teach the basic techniques because they're also selling you the materials."

I gasp. If you have to learn a new skill, you need tools for it, by God! "That's a good idea! Maybe woodworking."

I never learned to use a jigsaw because the last time I suggested it, Bucky got on his knees and begged me not to. But I bet now it would be okay. I could get a lathe and a chisel and one of those planer tools. Then I could sit in Randy's living room with branches from the park and whittle things with a pen knife like in the Westerns.

In the back of my head, I feel Bucky in urgent prayer. Thanks. Thanks a lot.

While waiting for the dessert, which I'm betting will be a fruit dumpling, I steel myself. "It's that very special time." Hal looks puzzled. "I need to ask why you're thirty and single."

He forces a laugh. "Oh, that."

"Yeah, that." I lean forward. "You aren't gay, and you don't live in your mother's basement, and you haven't mentioned running a World of Warcraft guild. I figure there has to be something."

"Perceptive, are you?"

At that point, the waitress arrives with bowls of something liquefied. Hal tells me it's "phirnee," a rice pudding made with rose water and pistachios. None of that sounds as if it blends, but at the same time, none of those ingredients will kill me (unlike, say, the ingredients in my Froot Loops) so I try it. Again I'm surprised because it's odd, but tasty.

Halfway through, Hal says, "I dated a woman named Annabelle for two years. We were engaged."

When he stops, I prompt, "And she was cheating?"

"I wish to God she'd been cheating." His eyes sharpen. "No, instead I kept hearing about how much better I was than her loser ex-boyfriend, the guy who'd been through five jobs in two years and whose idea of the good life was watching football with a Budweiser rather than Milwaukee's Best."

Not that he's bitter or anything.

Hal jabs his spoon into the bowl. "So two years later, we were writing out wedding invitations, and I found one addressed to the Loser. I said, 'Why are you inviting him?' and she gave me some head-space crap about how he helped make her the person she was."

Really? If I did that, I'd have to invite fifty people to my wedding.

He rolls his eyes. "I removed it from the stack. Later I found it included again, and I was about to rip it up without telling her, but then I noticed it had an extra stamp. So I opened it, and I found a letter inside where she bragged that I was going to do more with my life than he ever was, and he was going to rue the day he dumped her—and I—"

He stops. He just stops cold.

My heart stills. "You don't try to hurt someone like that if you're not carrying a torch for them."

He looks away.

I shouldn't have asked. She did something worse than lying about her job. I've never done it, but I can't imagine making love to one man and thinking about another. He's right: at least if she'd been cheating on him, he'd have felt he could compete. But to start dating someone with the intent to win back someone else—he never had a chance. It didn't matter who he was.

His shoulders fall. "Eventually she admitted she'd been emailing and texting him all along, trying to make him jealous. But—" He shrugs. "Fine, then. Let him have her."

He sounds defeated, but I haven't the heart to tell him he was right: if he hadn't cut her loose, she'd have run anyhow at the first signal that the other guy wanted her again. "Did she get back together with him after?"

He shrugs. "I don't know. I don't really fucking care."

My mouth twitches. "I'm sorry. That sucks."

"How well I remember that." With an irritated look, he runs his spoon through his bowl. "She made it all look real. Maybe she even told herself it was real, but it didn't matter to her *who* she was dating, as long as she was dating someone to make the Loser jealous, even if it meant marrying someone to get back at him." His jaw tightens. "We even took a wedding-cake baking class."

I chuckle, trying to change the subject. "You would make your own? Five tiers of white fluffy sweetness?" When he nods, I stare. He's serious? "Really? Five tiers?"

"She had two hundred fifty people on her guest list. It would have been huge."

I put a hand over my heart. "You had a narrow escape in two ways."

He looks startled. "What do you mean?"

"I mean that if I ever have a party with two hundred fifty people, I won't be one of them." I shake my head. "My brother Randy had an extravaganza. It left me traumatized for months."

What a day. My mother suggested tying an elastic band from my wrist to Corinne's bouquet to make sure it went straight to me. I was fifteen.

"A big wedding would have been fine by me, if the bride hadn't been thinking of a different groom." Hal stares away. "Why do you even have an opinion about that? You're never going to get married."

Wow, his voice got sharp. "My life is full. It wouldn't be all that nice to a husband to try wedging him in."

He still sounds snippy as he folds up his napkin. "Fair enough."

After the meal, we walk to the studio where we'll launch our international career of stardom. Our tickets admit entrance to all of us, even Bucky, and we're ushered into seats, then shifted a few times in order to make sure the audience looks sufficiently diverse. (I love New York. If life evolves on another planet, they still couldn't have a gathering more diverse than any random subway car.)

A director explains our role: we are to applaud at this prompt, murmur at this other prompt, look incredulous here, laugh there. For the especially dense, a sign overhead will remind us.

Hal turns to me. "Tell me again how you come up with these things?"

"We're in New York." I grin. "It'd be a shame not to do them."

Watching the preparation makes me homesick for the theater work I did in college. I tell Hal how I started as a bit part (I had one line, which to this day I cherish: "May I take your order?" Encore! Encore!) then switched to stage crew for two more productions.

Hal gives a chuckle. "How did you go from actress to physical trainer?"

I'm about to say "What—?" when I remember, oh yeah, right, that little bit. "That story involves a stop over at nursing school and a few years as a legal secretary."

Before Hal can recover from his double-take, the director spares me. He explains yet again how to applaud for the applause sign and murmur for the murmur sign. By now I could direct this scene if I had to.

Here's the gist: the set-up is a popular talk show, the Larry Bronson Hour. When it starts, one guest will already be on stage, a blue-haired Indian violinist talking about her string quartet. Then Bronson will thank her and introduce one Doctor Gregory Snyder. We will get the applause sign as Dr. Snyder shakes Bronson's hand. Bronson will ask about a recent archaeological find, and Snyder will launch into a monologue about an international ring of camel thieves, with a trail of perfidy going through the Boy Scouts all the way back to the Dalai Lama, who is trying to cover it up.

This sounds like an awesome movie! I bet it'll have at least one chase through a network of caves, and maybe someone climbing a pyramid.

The first time the sign says "Murmur," Hal dutifully murmurs, "What a bunch of garbage."

"Have you ever ridden a camel?" I ask. "It sounds like fun."

The sign goes off, and Bucky says, *Camels don't look comfortable to ride.*

You're supposed to stop talking now, I think. *The sign says silence.*

Bucky straightens. *I'm not making any sound!*

I can hear you, so doesn't that make you disobedient?

I'd ask God, Bucky replies, *but you just told me to stop talking.*

Again the sign flashes "murmur." Hal leans closer. "Can you even follow the plot? Did he just say Jesus was killed by the Romans for suspected camel thievery?"

I won't bother defending the movie. It is what it is. Instead I kiss Hal lightly on the lips.

The sign goes off. Hal's eyes are wide.

There is no sign for "hold hands," but we spend most of the next three takes doing that (except for when it says "applause" because, well, think about it.) Hal mocks the dialogue. I ask if he and Stuart will read this for book club, and he informs me: No. There's plenty of eye-candy between Bronson and Snyder, but not as nice as the eye-candy at my side. At the scene's end, the final guest to come on stage is the author doing a cameo.

We're out of there by ten o'clock. "I'm going to regret this." Hal shifts his laptop bag to his opposite shoulder so the hand closer to mine is unoccupied. I switch my motor vehicle part around and do the same so our hands can find one another. The temperature has plummeted since we went inside; we hold hands inside his jacket pocket to prevent frostbite. "I was supposed to be working from home."

"That's why I like my job." I squeeze his hand. "I can't bring my work home."

Bucky says, "What's in the bag?"

Oh, yeah. Today I kind of did.

Hal sounds tired. "Try being an accountant during tax season. Sometime during the end of March I'll bolt up in bed because I dreamed my boss forgot to tell me the company bought property in the Alps three years ago."

The night has picked up the kind of quiet you get when the air is so painfully cold even sound doesn't want to travel through it. I slip closer so I can wrap my arm around his waist. "Poor you."

He puts his arm over my shoulder and pulls me near. "No. Right now, I think I've got it pretty good."

Chapter Fifteen:

You're cute when you're delirious

Drenched in sweat, I wake up on my back, arms flung away, blankets cast to the floor. I can't breathe. Do I have pneumonia?

My second though, more accurate, is far worse: Mrs. Goretti has realized it's winter.

As I lie gasping, I piece together the most likely sequence. Hearing a frigid forecast on the late-night news, Mrs. Goretti must have been double-assaulted by her conscience: first that she must not awaken us with a phone call, but secondly that in order to prevent the formation of tenantsicles, she had to turn up the heat to a level that would stop Satan in his tracks. ("Wow, that's hot."*)

Heat rises. We're on the top floor. Mrs. Goretti and Mrs. Goretti's thermostat are on the bottom floor. Due to low blood pressure, Mrs. Goretti feels the cold acutely. She also has a good old-fashioned sense of guilt: it would inconvenience her tenants to put on a sweater, so she cranks the heat to eighty-five.

Brownstones are sturdy. In addition to the eponymous brown stone, the walls are made with plaster

---

* *Bucky was probably kidding that a demon popped into the living room and said, "Would you have a map handy? I was looking for Bartel Pritchard Circle in Park Slope, not the Ninth Circle of Hell." Probably.*

rather than plaster-board. Supporting the real plaster is real brick. Plywood? Hah! An acre of old growth hardwood forest died for every house. I'm not sure the Apocalypse will take us down.

God: Didn't I send you to obliterate Park Slope?

Michael: Uh—we had a little trouble there.

Gabriel: You're going to have to handle that yourself.

My point being, they retain heat like a Thermos. Our first winter here, I tore downstairs, convinced the boiler was going supernova. It couldn't really be a hundred ten degrees in our apartment, could it? Mrs. Goretti insisted we were freezing. I begged her to show me the freezing parts. Protests to turn down the heat only convinced her that we must always be cold, only we were too polite to say anything. And up went the red bar another notch.

For the record, a window air conditioning unit will not work when outside temperatures are below thirty degrees.

In France, the temperature bulbs in the Galileo thermometer have collapsed to the bottom, I assume from heat-prostration.

Opening the window is the first step of the temperature dance; the next is to remain beside the window to breathe, and the third to scurry from the window when the first blast of cold air hits my sweaty skin. I retreat to the house's interior until I'm too hot again, then dash for the dining room where the first three steps are repeated. Next the bathroom. Then the second window in the dining room. The second French window. Finally the window in my bedroom.

When the phone rings, I need neither Bucky nor caller ID to tell me it's Mrs. Goretti.

Even the phone is hot. "Good morning."

"Lee, dear, it's Mrs. Goretti." When I acknowledge, she continues, "I heard it was going to snow—"

I turn to find Beth stripping off her fleece pajamas without regard for the open windows.

"—and I'm worried you might get cold."

Not unless we drop dead, and even then, our body temperatures will rise rather than fall to reach room temperature. "We'll be fine. Don't trouble yourself."

Beth pops the freezer door and inhales deeply of the frost within.

"It's no trouble at all." She gives a heartfelt, "You're such a good girl."

Hanging up the phone after I thank her, I turn to Beth, beside the freezer in her underwear. "Did you oversleep?"

"Snow day. No school."

I just opened six windows and never looked outside? When I do, the view draws a gasp: it's blinding. It's untouched. It's the worst thing that could have happened when I still have to return the loaner to Mack's.

I dress like a mountaineer, in layers and with two pairs of socks. I pack a change of jeans and socks in my back pack. First I shovel Mrs. Goretti's sidewalk and steps, and then I head to work.

But on second thought, seeing the icy road, I wonder how hard it is to stop a K-car with no brakes. Yeah. I don't turn toward Seventh Avenue.

"Smart call," Bucky says. "I'm a good guardian, but not great."

I queue up the *Rumours* album in my iPod. After a while I've achieved the too-hot-too-cold state of someone working out in zero degrees. It's too hot beneath my coat, but my hands feel numb and my cheeks sting. The slush seeps through my supposedly waterproof boots. Cars make slucking sounds as they drive a shade slower than normal. At the corners, I clamber over mounds pushed up by the plows.

At the shop door, Max meets me, and I thrust a trunk piston at him.

Nothing's said about the cops. Nothing about a drunk man's car still sitting at the curb. The only admission that he even remembers yesterday's threat to can me is a glance over my shoulder as he takes the piston.

I brush past without taking off my jacket. "No dice. Tow it home."

His voice ticks up. "It's not in a snow emergency lane, is it?"

"I wish." I write the intersection for him with clumsy fingers, then stand shivering near the space heater until I feel more alive than a corpse. Perhaps I shouldn't have complained about Mrs. Goretti's overenthusiastic thermostat.

We get a stream of walk-in parents taking advantage of the snow day for an oil change. By eleven-thirty, I've done so many that I only stare stupidly at the following words, as if they're in hieroglyphics: "Tire Rotation."

You know how you're supposed to mark the tires as they come off so you remember where to replace them? If not for Bucky, some gentleman might not have had his tires rotated, even though they all spent time off the vehicle.

At lunch, Max orders pizza for everyone (then collects five bucks apiece). In a chair beside his desk, I nibble half a slice of pepperoni before realizing I can't stomach the rest.

Max kicks my ankle. "Did my grandmother put a hex on you?"

Bucky?

No hex.

"No hex."

Fever, though.

Max's wife Allison puts her wrist against my forehead. "You're burning."

"It's the weather," says Ari. "My mother got knocked flat by something."

Carlos adds, "You were at a doctor's office Wednesday, too. No telling what you picked up."

Max frowns. "Go home."

My eyes flare. "I can't be sick. It's Friday." Tonight I have a date with Bill.

"You're right. What was I thinking?" He turns to Allison. "Get the loaner car with the wrecker and drive her home, okay?"

I should protest. I lost a half day yesterday, and Max doesn't pay sick time. But especially after the drunk driver garbage, I don't want to lose my job if I forget to replace the oil after I drain it. Home I go.

Oddly enough, the apartment doesn't feel warm anymore, but the Galileo thermometer still reads the same. I crawl into bed.

Two hours later, I awaken long enough to realize Max was right. A sweat leaves me clammy, and only extra blankets will satisfy. Bucky says something in my head, but it's too hard to figure out what, so with closed eyes I again fade.

At four o'clock I hear Beth, and I stumble out to meet her.

"Gah! Get away!" Beth covers her mouth with her scarf and throws out her hands as if warding off a vampire. "What makes you think I want what you have?"

"I need to call Bill. I was supposed to see him tonight."

Beth backs up to the wall. "Don't you dare touch the phone. I'll have to bleach it." She shoos me with her hand. "Get! Out! Back to bed!"

I print Bill's number on a piece of paper, which Beth takes with tongs. Afterward, it will make a burnt offering to the health deities, no longer worthy of becoming origami.

My social obligations fulfilled, I stumble back to bed. Maybe I'm fading in and out of reality, but it doesn't seem long before Beth's voice calls around the corner of my door frame:

"You awake?"

I push onto my elbows. The room spins. The pillow crashes against my head. What's wrong with gravity?

Beth pushes open the door. "It's okay—I remembered I had a surgical mask from school."

I'm not sure whom she wants to wear it, but when I look up, she resembles a muzzled dog.

"Bill says it's fine, and call him when you can." The blue fiber muffles her voice. She gives me two Advil in a paper cup, and the pills don't want to pass through my throat. "Is there anything else you want?"

I deflate into the mattress. "I want my mother."

"Don't we all?" Beth twitches my heel. "If you need anything, give me a holler."

That's the last I hear before I realize the room has been empty for some time.

I manage to get to a stand even though the floor is tilted; leaning against the wall, I work my way across France, through Beth's room, across the dining room, and into the bathroom. I hear Beth cooking in the kitchen.

When I peer into the bathroom mirror, I'm marshmallow-white except for my cheeks, which look slapped. It'd be no use taking my temperature. I'm an oven.

Bucky's invisible, but he's worried.

Back in the dining room, I turn my head toward Beth in the kitchen, only I'm seeing Hal.

That's weird.

"Hey." He sets down a knife as long as my forearm. "How are you doing?"

I rasp, "He should have warned me you were here."

"You'd better sit down before you fall down." He guides me to the table and into a chair. I'm sitting sideways so my elbow is against the back. "I thought you might need some Jewish penicillin." I stare blankly. "Chicken soup? Real chicken. Fresh garlic. Celery. Leeks, God's own soup onion."

He lifts his jacket off the other chair to drape it around my shoulders. It smells like him. I tighten it by the arms. "How'd you get in?"

"Beth let me. I said I'd stay until she got back from buying a Hazmat suit."

I squint. "I hear violins."

"Vivaldi. My iPod is in your speakers."

"You'll corrupt them." I lean sideways. "They won't play ABBA any longer."

He touches my hair. "I'll have to lend you my music."

"You'll have to explain it to me." The apartment smells cozy. I'm dizzy. As he gets up, I turn toward the table, then rest my head on folded arms. The weight of his jacket. The sounds of things moving in the kitchen. The idea that Hal is in my apartment and somehow I'm here in the dining room. Wasn't I in bed?

A touch on my shoulder. "Have some tea." As I raise my head, he crouches so he's at eye-level. "When did you take any Advil or Tylenol?"

I can't remember. Inside I hear Bucky says, *Two hours ago. Advil.*

I'm a row-boat bobbing on ocean waves. "Bucky says two hours ago. Advil."

Hal sighs. "You need something else. You're about two hundred degrees." He returns from the bathroom with a clacking plastic bottle. "Bucky, huh?"

My head is back on my arms. The boat must have sunk: I'm five feet under water. "He remembers things like that. Responsible."

"Take these." Hal puts two Tylenol beside the mug. "Should I be worried that you're hearing someone I can't see?"

Hal's not making sense. "Why should you be able to see my guardian angel? I can't see yours." Hot but not scalding, the tea relaxes my throat. The apartment is still cold, so why does Hal have his sleeves rolled up? His jacket makes a nice burrow.

Hal chuckles. "You're absolutely delirious. Did you call the gym to tell them you won't be there?"

Weird that he's concerned about his rival. "Beth called Bill."

Hal says, "He'll take your clients?"

He's making no sense. "I don't think Bill can change the oil."

Hal brushes the hair from my forehead. "You're cute when you're delirious, but you need to get back to bed."

"You're sweet." With my arms around his neck, I press my face in the hollow of his shoulders. "You came here and made soup."

"I noticed that myself."

I wrap my arms all the way around him. "I think I love you."

"What an amazing coincidence." He lifts me to my feet. "But you need more sleep. You're talking about oil changes and seeing angels, and if I buttered you I could fry an omelet."

I'm breathing hard by the time we make it to my room. He tucks me in, but I don't let go of his jacket. The world is all twisted—if I have a fever, shouldn't I feel hot? I think I'll ask Hal instead of sleeping because it's stupid to have a guest and take a nap, but then Bucky puts his hand over my eyes.

I ache all over when I awaken. Every swallow is a knife in my throat. I reach a hand to find Bucky, like pressing my hand against a window. He puts his fingers up against mine, but of course I can't feel him because it's just pretend-touch, the way when we were kids we used to do this mirror-thing, and he'd laugh because I'd try to fool him by moving suddenly, only I never could, and I used to think he could read my thoughts, but then he said he couldn't but that people are easy to predict after you've studied them for a few thousand years, and I'm always going to be transparent to him, which I think is okay.

"This isn't good." Even the dim glow of Bucky's eyes hurts mine. "You're not thinking straight."

He dissolves around me like a mist, and I let the warmth break over me like a storm cloud of holy water, and there I am at the center like a silver lining, and here I am wishing I wasn't quite so cold or that my body didn't ache everywhere so I don't even want to move.

I feel my warmth slipping away, and I clutch it tighter.

"Lee, give the nice man back his jacket."

I look up to see a figure. Oh, cool: *Lo, though I wake in the valley of the shadow of Beth, the flu is at my side...*

Beth tugs again. "You have his jacket in a death grip, and he won't fit into yours."

Framed in the light of the door, Hal says, "Your jacket doesn't have my keys in the pocket, either."

I sit up. The room isn't tilty. "You're leaving?"

Beth finishes extracting me from Hal's jacket. "He's trying to."

"It's nine," Hal says. "You were sleeping." He pauses. "If you're getting up, I'll stay while you have some soup."

I venture to my feet with care, and when the floor obliges by not being made of ball bearings, Hal takes my arm. Shortly I'm outfitted with a bowl of soup, and the microwave vibrates as it heats water for tea.

I nod toward him. "Did you eat?"

He rests his hand on mine. "I had some when it became clear you were down for the count."

"I'm sorry you lowered yourself." My throat still hurts. "It's a two-bit kitchen."

He smiles. "It worked fine."

The soup doesn't scald, but it soothes the sore spots. The more I awaken, the more delicious it is, hardly the salt-in-a-can-plus-yellow-number-five I expected. Hal made it with chunks of chicken, slivers of carrot, quartered mushrooms, and sliced celery. The broth has an onion essence. He sprinkled parmesan cheese over the top. The Queen of England doesn't recuperate this deliciously.

Beth brings tea. I haven't eaten since those three bites of pizza, and it strikes me I that I'm hungry.

Hal turns to Beth. "Do you think she's got some color back?"

"Don't ask me." Beth sets down some buttered toast, which I accept gratefully. "You white people turn all sorts of colors. I can't keep track."

"When did I pick up an entourage?"

Hal laughs. "About the time you started seeing angels."

My heart stops. "What?"

His eyes sparkle at what must seem the world's best joke. "The Archangel Bucky-el revealed your last Advil was at five."

The spoon slips from my fingers into my lap.

"Bucky's no archangel," Beth calls from the kitchen. "Bucky's a friend from grade school."

"Well, she was seeing him in the apartment about three hours ago, and he had wings." Looking back at me, Hal folds his arms and leans against the table. "Keep eating. You're hardly the first person to babble when you're running a fever. You were going on about fixing cars, too."

I want to die. As in, right now.

You don't get an out, Bucky puts into my head. *You're recovering, so you're going to have to deal with the consequences.*

Over Hal's shoulder, Beth shoots me a look. I lower my eyes.

Hal rubs my shoulder. "You're supposed to feed a fever."

Beth says, "You're supposed to eat what you want. The body knows what it needs."

Hal and Beth get into an argument about holistic medicine, and the only thing they agree is that chicken soup has enough natural health-producing effects that I must consume gallons of it, only then they begin jockeying about the best reason. Hal claims it's the fresh vegetables; Beth argues for the added water vapor in the air; Hal counters with the increased fluids, which Beth returns with a discussion of how chicken soup hearkens back to childhood memories of being cared for.

They're having a great time. I feel threadbare.

"Keep eating." Bucky sits atop the china cabinet. "You can't fight this off if you have nothing to fight it with."

I finish the soup while Hal comes up behind me. "You're incredibly tense." He massages my shoulders, then works his way down my back, and I lean forward. Beth pulls away the bowl, and I drop my forehead to rest on my wrists. He works his way back up along my neck with pressure under my jaw and then up into my hairline.

My eyes close as he steps away to check something in the kitchen. How can I sleep twenty hours in one day and still be tired?

I hear clean-up noises. "I'm going to leave my knives and cutting board."

Don't worry," Beth says. "I bought more bleach."

He returns. I try to get to my feet as he puts on his jacket, but he leans over me and kisses my cheek. "Tomorrow you can walk me to the door. Tonight you rest."

Well, that's a plus. "I'll see you tomorrow?"

"Someone has to teach you how to reheat soup." He gives my nose a nudge with the back of one bent finger. "I can't leave that to amateurs."

I find myself smiling. "I still have your whisk."

"There you go. A chef always returns for his whisk. Sleep tight." He gets his coat, and Beth walks him out the door.

Down-down-down: it's easy to follow their descent, and then a slam of the heavy door simultaneous with the groans of the steps as Beth makes her way back up-up-up.

"You've got to tell him." She heads into the kitchen, and even as she continues talking, the smell of bleach suffuses the apartment. "The guy is over the moon for you, but he's going to flip when he finds out you're lying."

Bucky isn't visible, but he's emitting a *Listen to her* aura.

Beth reappears in the doorway wielding a sponge and elbow-length yellow gloves. "Think about how his last girlfriend treated him. You're going to get the backlash from that in addition to everything you deserve."

"Tomorrow." I bite my lip. "I'll tell him then."

"If you don't tell him, I will." She rolls her eyes. "Maybe you could practice. *Hal, I was afraid you'd laugh at me, but I'm really an auto mechanic.* It's not so hard."

I rub my temples. "I like the way you said that."

"It sounds so vulnerable. If you say, *I lied to you,* he's going to think of you as a liar, but if you tell him *I was afraid you'd leave me,* he'll probably prove he wouldn't have, and he'll do that by staying." Beth shakes her head as she returns to the kitchen. "It's a classic manipulator tactic, but it should work. By the time he's figured out you're telling him you lied, he'll already have told you it doesn't matter."

That way he can carry the resentment for years. What an alternative. Not that I have many alternatives at this point, short of taking whatever job I told him I had in the first place. Maybe Bill could hook me up over at the gym—

Don't be an idiot. Bucky appears in the chair across, so stern I jump. His eyes burn, and I feel him speaking without words: Beth has a good idea. Use it. She'll back me up. Bucky will help me. Hal's guardian will help me too. But I've got to do it.

"Okay." I put my face in my hands. *Hal, I'm sorry, but I was scared of what you'd think of me.* "I'll do it."

Chapter Sixteen:

A special ingredient

I awaken after ten, able to swallow without pain and blessedly undizzy. I don't need to reorient myself every time I move. Our apartment again feels like an Easy-Bake Oven. How out of it was I yesterday, that it felt normal?

Good news: I'm hungry.

Even better: Hal said he'd stop over.

With care in case I'm about to be visited by Vertigo and her cousin Gravity, I push myself upright. I ought to shower and change. It's okay to look like death warmed over when you're dying, but I'm not anymore.

Abruptly Bucky appears, dressed in white and holding a lily. "For behold," he intones, "I bring you tidings of hot coffee, for unto you this morning in the kitchen is brewed Green Mountain Coffee Roasters cinnamon hazelnut."

I can only stare at his expectant smile that says *I'll look cute so you won't hit me.*

My groggy brain can't come up with a good retort. The best I can manage is to make a face. "You're still bummed that you didn't get picked for that job?"

His resolve cracks. While he laughs, I add, "I hope your audition was better than that."

"Hey!" He whaps me on the head with the lily. "This will be a sign to you: you will find a bagel wrapped in a paper bag and lying on the counter."

"Well then." I edge my legs out of bed. "Let's go into the kitchen and see this thing that has happened, which Bucky has told me about."

I make my way across the apartment, but before I can hunt down the bagel, I realize the plagues have struck Egypt again, only they got misdirected to our dining room table. Beth sits with piles of frogs and locusts, a sea of red paper, and things that look like snakes.

The plague-master keeps folding frogs. "You feeling better?"

"Somewhat." I glance into the kitchen to see a paper bag on the counter. "You bought me a bagel?"

"Consider it a bribe." Beth doesn't look up. "Don't scare me like that again."

I lean against the door frame. "You were scared?"

"Hal wanted to bring you to the ER, and I wasn't sure he didn't have the right idea. I told him no because I didn't want to have to answer questions about your insurance. Like, say, who you worked for." Beth bites her lip. "I'm dead serious about the mechanic thing. Tell him today."

In the shower, I let the hot water sweep away the sweat and the residual aching.

Bucky, you there?

Do you want me to appear?

Do it and die. I lather up, letting the steam work its magic so breathing comes easier. *I can't believe I told Hal about you. Thank goodness he didn't believe anything I said last night.*

There's a hesitation from Bucky.

Did he believe me?

Well, Bucky begins, but then nothing for a long time. I wash my hair. While I'm rinsing, Bucky says, *That wasn't all you said.*

I told him I worked on cars.

You told him you loved him.

Standing under the stream of water, I stare at nothing. The water, the ceramic, the suds racing for the drain.

I cannot remember saying that to Hal. Shadows inhabit my head: him in the kitchen; his coat. But no words.

I reach for the faucet to turn off the water. *What did he answer?*

I'm not sure I should—

BUCKY!

I yank my towel off the rack, then wrap myself around. "You coward," I hiss. "What did he say?"

Bucky appears, looking stung. "It's hardly cowardice. I'm not sure it wouldn't be violating a confidence."

"How could it be breaking a confidence?" I keep my voice low so Beth won't hear. "Wasn't I there?"

"You weren't really, no." Bucky closes his eyes, and delight flits across his features. Then, normal again, he focuses on me looking cheerful. "I'm allowed."

I'm going to kill him. "And?"

"You said, 'I think I love you,' and he said, 'What an amazing coincidence.' But then he made you go back to bed because he realized you were two eggs short of an omelet."

I sit on the edge of the tub breathing the steamy air, rubbing my temples.

The floor is white hexagonal tile with the occasional black thrown in, but scuffed. Maybe a hundred years ago they gleamed in the narrow sunlight penetrating the rectangular window over the toilet. Through time, nicks and dirt have worn away the shine, removed the slipperiness, and rendered the whites grey and the blacks dull. In some places the grout crumbles. But who ever looks at these things? Who would notice one more shiny thing gone flat?

Water drips from my hair down the back of my neck until the towel drinks the droplets at the base of my spine.

Hal thinks he loves me. I said I loved him.

"Do I love him?" Chin in my hands, I look at my bare toes, at the bath mat, at the curved feet of the tub.

It's been so long since I've been "in love." I'd written the rest of my life as a single woman, or like Bucky said as a kid on a big playground. Being in love—that would be huge. It would mean... It would change everything. Loving someone means making plans, directing your life, asking someone's opinion. It means thinking for two.

Loving means nakedness—the worst kind of nakedness, not the kind where you stand with your clothes off. It means you can't run when you cry. It means when someone hurts you, even if you joke it off, he knows it.

Beth is going to wonder if I've collapsed, so I towel dry. I slip my t-shirt over my head. I brush my teeth. I comb my hair while avoiding my own eyes in the mirror.

In the dining room, Beth's hands slip over paper with a whispering sound. Flat squares morph into amphibians while I prepare my coffee and my bagel. The liquid slurps into the cup, and as the porcelain warms against my palm, I stare at the dented refrigerator. The narrow stove. The chipped porcelain of a sink overhung by cabinets that have shifted off-level during a hundred years.

Hal.

Later today, he'll see me. Maybe he'll want to know whether I remember my words from last night. Maybe he'll set the scene to say it again. A man I lied to. An admission I have to make. Maybe two admissions. Only right now, I'm not sure if I can admit either one, or what I'll lose if I do.

When the doorbell rings, Beth both spares and condemns me by hiking downstairs. Alfred Hitchcock would have filmed five movies in this house just for the effect of hearing two sets of feet climbing past the third floor to the fourth, and me.

Hal, I was afraid you'd laugh at me, but I need to tell you something.

Beth pushes open the door, and Hal enters at her back. "Behold! She lives again."

"Thanks to you and the restorative powers of soup." My stomach lurches. "Beth tells me I wasn't quite in my right mind."

I'm seated at the table, and he joins me without removing his jacket. For an instant Hal's face is haunted. "You had us worried until the fever came down."

I hear creaks in the hallway: the third floor neighbors? A better person would know who lives there. I fetch their mail but I don't know their names.

Hal finally unzips his jacket. I ask if he wants coffee, and when he follows me into the kitchen, I apologize that not only did I not roast the beans myself, but I didn't grow them in pots on the fire escape either.

Beth has remained in the dining room. Now would be as good a time as any: *Hal, I was afraid to tell you this.*

The hallway is still creaking, and just when I think to ask Beth if she's expecting Stuart, there's a knock on the door.

Beth opens, and I hear, "Oh, hello, Mrs. Singer."

Once when I attended summer camp, we made ice cream, filling the outside of the machine with ice and rock salt. After the cream had condensed into sweet fatty goodness, the camp director pulled out the inner container, and my best friend doused me with the superchilled water. This is the same feeling, minus the screaming.

I take a step toward the dining room in time to bump into my mother carrying grocery bags. "Oh, sweetie, I was so worried. Beth said—"

And then she stops. Staring over my shoulder. In the next moment: delight.

My mother thrusts a bag at me so she can shake Hal's hand. "I don't believe we've met." Her voice is sweeter than summer camp ice cream. "You can call me Lacey."

"I'm Hal Baxter." He keeps me between them. "I wanted to make sure Lee was doing better this morning."

Beth comes into view behind my mother. "I guess I forgot to tell you that your mom phoned."

I fire her a dark look as I set the grocery bag on the countertop. "I guess you did."

Mom hands me the other bag. "Mrs. Goretti let me in. She's very concerned." She studies Hal again, allowing her eyes to travel over him from hair to shoes.

In an attempt to spare him, I say, "We were just having coffee. Want some?"

"Absolutely." My mother hands me her coat. "If it's no trouble."

I carry my mother's coat and purse to my room where I drop the coat on my bed, then chuck her purse at the wall.

Bucky, I can't tell him with her here!

Assent.

Make her leave!

Negation.

Did I accidentally pray for patience while I was delirious?

Negation. But a sense of reaping the whirlwind.

I return to the kitchen to hear Hal telling my mother about his job. I can detect her brain going cha-ching as she computes his income with more accuracy than a forensic accountant on the trail of a mafia don.

The door slams. Beth has fled. This will prevent me from killing her.

I unpack the groceries. Cans of chicken broth, saltine crackers, bottles of Gatorade, instant macaroni and cheese (it's Kraft Organic, too!—only the best for her daughter) plus a bottle of vitamin C hidden at the bottom. My mother thinks of everything.

Hers is not a conversation with Hal so much as an interrogation: how long has he known me? Where does he live? Where does he work? How did we meet?

I could throttle her. Instead I guide her to the dining room with a trail of words following behind like the smoke of a steam train. This isn't a job interview—Hal didn't show up in his best suit and carrying a laptop bag. Although come to think of it, he's wearing a long-sleeve polo shirt and khakis. Does he even wear those to paint the house?

I need to change the subject. "How are my brothers doing?"

"I spoke to Morgan last night," my mom begins.

Hal excuses himself to the kitchen to check on the coffee. I can hear the coffee maker is still spitting, so I know that was an escape.

As soon as he's out of the room, my mother leans close. "He's a great catch!"

"I haven't caught a thing." It's tough keeping my voice low when I want to scream. "He cared that I was in danger of death last night, and he made sure I had something to eat."

My mother's eyes widen. "He cooked for you?"

I forgot. Food = love.

"He's a gourmet chef." Hal emerges from the kitchen as I say that. "He made the best soup I've ever had in my life. No offense." My mom always bought the store-brand concentrated glop.

Hal offers, "I'm teaching Lee to cook too."

My mother startles. "It's about time."

I roll my eyes. "Don't listen to her. I can microwave a pizza with the best of them."

"I don't doubt it. I've seen you push the buttons." He takes a seat on the far side of the table.

Silence lingers between us.

I want to tell him I'm sorry. I want to apologize that my mother views everything with a Y chromosome and at least 90% of the same DNA as my potential husband. I want to tell my mother to get out of my apartment and quit acting as if she cares I'm alive at all.

Instead I meet Hal's gaze across the table—and he knows. It's in the relaxed lines around his eyes, the way he holds his shoulders, the amusement ghosting his lips. He has his fingers knit, and when he reclines in his chair, I detect momentary regret.

He wanted me alone. If my mom really wanted me to marry someone, she'd get out of here now.

"Hey, mom," I could say in an imaginary universe, *"Hal and I were going to dance around the question of how we feel about one another, never getting near what he's afraid to ask and I'm afraid to answer. Somewhere in all that, I'd have to admit I didn't deserve his trust but I was asking for it anyhow. I'd probably kiss him. So if you don't mind, would you scram?"*

Seriously, she hasn't visited my apartment in two years.

My mother turns to Hal. "You made the soup from scratch?"

He glances at me, and the apartment is no longer as stifling. "Soup's easy."

My mom says, "How do you make it?"

"It changes every time." Again Hal meets my eyes. "Sometimes two ingredients that don't seem to be good partners blend really well when you throw them together."

I fight a giggle.

"Then you heat things up a bit." Hal looks at his hands. "Surprisingly, everything mixes perfectly, and you wonder why you ever thought they could be complete without each other."

He's such a tease. "It sounds highly experimental."

"I don't think you can plan it." Sitting forward, Hal adopts a serious expression. "But then one day when you're not even looking, you find a special ingredient."

I bet my mother has never heard a recipe like this. I smile wickedly. "Tell me more."

"You know it'll be a flavor you never experienced before." A mischievous light crosses his eyes. "But after the first taste, you can't live without it again."

I steeple my fingers and rest my chin against them. "Sounds delicious."

Hal says, "Did you know you can freeze eggs?"

Ooh, he's good.

My mother says, "You can't freeze an egg."

Hal breaks the spell by looking at her. "If you're blowing them out of the shells, say for a preschool project, you can whip them up, strain them, and freeze them in single-portion sizes. I'd use an ice cube tray."

That's hilarious. "Are frozen eggs as delicious as omelets?"

He arches his brows. "Not in my opinion."

My mother stays as long as Hal does. She must believe she's encouraging him, but after coffee, Hal abandons his usual rejoinders and seems off-balance.

He reheats last night's soup. It's still delicious, but about ten minutes after eating, my body shuts down. Nausea, chills, sluggish thinking.

My mother announces that I look pale and steers me toward my room.

Being of brilliant intelligence, Hal realizes this will leave him alone with her, so he has to take off. "It's tax season. I should have been in the office already."

Oh, God, how long was I asleep? "Isn't it Saturday?"

He nods. "Most people don't see me at all between January first and April fifteenth."

There's no kiss before he lets himself out of the house.

Two minutes later, my mother tucks me into bed. I close my eyes. "You haven't done this since I was five."

"I've done it since then." She kisses my cheek. "You need to sleep this off. I knew when Beth said you were sick that you needed someone to take care of you. I didn't realize you'd already found someone to do it."

I guess I had. There's Bucky, and there's Beth, and there was Hal when I didn't even expect him.

My mom puts the blankets closer around my shoulders. "I'll be in the living room if you need anything."

There's nothing else I need. It's cozy, and the taste of special ingredients lingers in my mind.

Chapter Seventeen:

Ping

I wake up after noon on Sunday. Beth has left a note on the table: my mom called; Hal called; Randy called; right after him, Avery called; Beth wants a raise because she's not paid enough to be my secretary. Ha-ha.

I wander into the kitchen and find the last of Hal's soup in the fridge. Special ingredients he hadn't thought would blend well.

Cheeks flushed, I smile as I remove the container.

By Sunday evening, I'm a thousand percent better. Hal has sent periodic emails from work, and I send periodic apologies. He's working late because he spent Saturday morning here.

He'd die if he knew what I did next: when I don't find a ready-made seven-course meal in the pantry, I grab a box of instant mashed potatoes. I eyeball the measurements, microwave the mix, throw on a dollop of butter in honor of Hal, and perch at the computer with the hot bowl on my knees.

"Let me tell you about a recent invention." Bucky sprawls along the couch with one wing draped to the floor. "It's called protein."

Oh, right, someone else can critique my menus. "Sounds intriguing. Someday you'll have to tell me about it."

"Keep eating that way and your body will tell you about it."

I make a face.

While checking for email from Hal, I get an instant message from Avery asking if I'm on. I reply.

A moment afterward, "You feeling better?"

I answer, "I'm upright."

The computer has different tones for IMs and email. Beth hates to hear "ping" every time she gets a message, so she disables the volume. I like it. It's thrilling, with a pathetic sort of lameness.

Ping "Will I see you this week?"

"I'm not sure," I type. "Depends how I feel."

Waiting for her reply, I surf to a Facebook forum for mechanics.

Ping "Everything sucks, Aunt Lee."

I sigh.

Ping "Could you come breathe on the whole volleyball team?"

I type, "Who knows what they'll do if they all have fevers of 104?"

While I'm typing, her reply comes, "Kerchoo—we're still better than you."

Ding I shift-tab and end up in my email program, where Hal has written to me, *Why is it that the person with five receipts feels the need to put each in a separate folder? Whereas the one with thousands puts a rubber band around everything from transcontinental travel to the purchase of a pink eraser?*

Ping "Maybe you should go breathe on the principal, too."

I type, "Only if you promise the other girls' parents will be with her."

Then I reply to Hal's email, *Along with receipts that have an office computer and a birthday gift for the grandchild purchased at the same time?*

Ping "Would it keep them out of school for a month?"

I reply to Avery, "The sun is going to extinguish in six million years. That means the popular girls will have to hassle the unpopular ones in the dark."

Bucky stretches full-length on the couch. "You know, it's two weeks until your birthday."

Oh, man, the clock's ticking. "And?"

He sits up. "When are we going to pick out my plant?"

On my birthday I buy Bucky a plant to celebrate that he was assigned to me, even though the actual anniversary of his assignment is late May—coincidentally the same time I have to throw away a desiccated plant which I forgot to water. The year the cactus died was a unique humiliation.

Bucky doesn't mind: it's a ritual, and he's pleased that I remember.

Ping from Avery: "You mean it'll never change?"

Bucky says, "Don't take too much trouble about it. You can just get one at the grocery store this year."

There's self-effacing, and then there's Bucky, their king.

"The grocery store plants are half-dead already."

Avery again. *Ping* "Maybe we can evolve."

I type back, "Humans will evolve into brains in jars, and some people will insist their jar is better than yours."

Bucky says, "But I don't want you to have to make a special trip."

"There's two weeks." My email makes a *ding*. "I'll get your plant."

The email is Hal's. He quotes my last message, adding, *I see you've met my supervisor.*

Ping "Can I put Ashley's brain in a jar now?"

Bucky says, "I thought maybe something that doesn't flower."

"That's boring." I check the mechanics forum again—more customer stories. "What else do plants do?"

"Spider plants remove toxins from the air."

I type to Avery, "Do they make jars small enough?" Then I say to Bucky, "Am I giving you a gift to benefit myself?"

He shrugs. "It benefits me too, if it keeps you healthy."

Ping

When I check the window, it's not a smart remark about brains in jars. Instead, it's Bill. "Are you still sick? You need any food?"

I type, "Someone came over and made soup."

Ping "Oh—the master chef?"

Startled, I type, "Yes, in fact."

He sends a winking smilie.

"Don't get any ideas," I type. "The only thing I did in bed was sleep."

Ping "But things are heating up?"

My hands tremble. "They seem to be."

There's a pause. Then, *Ping* "Congratulations!"

That's what I like about Bill: no strings.

Ping "But keep me in mind if things don't gel."

I type, "You don't deserve to be anyone's second-best."

Sitting on the couch, Bucky says, "You're really sweet sometimes."

I shoot him a puzzled look, but he offers nothing further.

Ping "Understood, Babe. But any time you're up for a movie, let me know."

I type back, "Thanks."

Ping "See you around."

"You too."

Then the connection closes, and I feel alone. Prickly.

Bucky says, "Maybe you won't forget a hanging plant as easily."

I turn to him. "Did I just break up with someone over IM?"

"That was a mutual parting of ways." Bucky points toward the kitchen. "If you use that old hook over the window, maybe Beth would water it."

"You're trying to drive me crazy, aren't you?"

Bucky grins. "It's amusing to see you juggle three conversations."

"Go jump in a lake."

As I'm shutting down chat, I find Avery's last PM, which reads, "Mom won't let me keep a collection of jars on the window." I head to bed without replying to Hal's last email, which says, *I need to tell my boss that cheesecake is not a business expense, even if she eats it to dispel work-related stress.*

Monday finds me well enough to head in to work. This is good. Sometimes it stinks to be paid hourly.

Everyone calls or emails on Monday night to check how I'm feeling. It's nice to be popular, but it's a pain to tell the same thing to everyone: I'm fine, thanks for checking, went to work, hope you didn't catch anything (that was to my mother and Hal. Beth, to no one's surprise, is healthier than last Thursday. She spent Sunday rebleaching the apartment.)

Tuesday afternoon at the garage, I check my email to find a note from Hal. He hints about dinner if I feel up to it, but nothing definite. In fact, he sounds cagey. I reply that I feel fine, but I don't hear from him again before clocking out at four-thirty.

If he might try to reach me later, I'll work out now and grab a shower so I won't smell like whatever it is my mother thinks cars smell like. I'm glad Hal works in

Manhattan: he can't kidnap me on the way home from work the way I kidnapped him.

As I step into the gym, I see it—a nightmare.

Bill and Hal, together. Bill grins as he sees me, and when Hal turns, his face is a pleasant frozen wasteland.

I'm cold all through. Don't believe Hal's smile. Believe his eyes.

He steps forward. "Lee." Am I the only one who can hear the strain behind my name? "Bill and I had the most interesting conversation."

Bill shoots me a wink. "I'll leave the two of you alone."

Bill isn't faking it. He thinks Hal is thrilled to see me.

I want to bring Bill back to stop the next conversation from happening, but I can't do that any more than I could stop the R train by grabbing the third rail.

Hal comes close. "Maybe you'll step outside with me a moment."

He walks out the door.

My brain screams to hide, to run, to put miles between us.

As if wearing a bridle, I follow.

Hal says nothing as we walk beyond the glass front of the health club and around the corner, but then he plants himself in place and locks onto me with his blue, blue eyes. "Bill tells me," he says in a voice tight as piano wire, "that you work for a political action committee."

I hunch my shoulders, shoving my hands way down my jacket pocket.

"He didn't know what political action your committee is pursuing. I'll also note you never talk politics." His breath comes up like clouds. "So on a hunch, I asked Bill if he'd told you about the man launching himself over the top of the Stairmaster, and he was proud to say he was. Even added some details."

My eyes burn.

"But it gets more interesting. Last week, Stuart said you teach preschool." He gets right up in my face. "Did you lie to all of us?"

Oh my God. Of course Stuart would have said something.

"What in blazes is going on?"

Shouldn't he be shouting instead of keeping his voice low?

"For God's sake, Lee! What job do you have that's so vile you can't tell anyone?" Okay, now he's shouting. "Are you a rich heiress? A telemarketer? A drug dealer?"

Bucky's urging breaks over me like a wave: why don't I answer? But here I stand, my throat closed completely. I stare at the crack bisecting two squares of the sidewalk.

"Are you a hooker?" Hal is so close I feel his breath on my forehead. "Someone's giving you rent money every month—who?"

At this point, I'd have to show him my tax return, and even that might not be enough. I know this. I turn aside, and the next moment I choke on a sob.

"Don't you dare pull that on me." He jerks away. "Is that how you shut people up when they realize you've played them for a fool?"

Bucky in my heart is like facing into a windstorm. I've never felt him like this, not even when I've defied him. Inside, I'm a stake driven into the ground.

Hal folds his arms while I try not to fall apart. "Don't bother calling with an explanation. I wouldn't trust you anyhow."

He stalks away uphill.

I fold my arms, tuck my chin, and slump against the brick wall of someone's garage.

I don't know how long I'm there. I don't want to watch Hal turn the corner, the last time I'll ever see him. He won't look back. He's gone. It's my fault.

Eventually I grope in my pocket for a tissue, only there's just a little shredded one. I do my best on my nose and press my wool gloves against my eyes.

Inside me, Bucky speaks to my heart in a hush: you really couldn't say it.

I don't reply. I just struggle to breathe, hearing cars on Fourth Avenue, and knowing I've just broken two hearts.

Chapter Eighteen:

Cheetos

Rule number one of break-ups is, *Don't call your ex.*

Bucky knows this rule. Come to think about it, due to angelic practicality, he may have been its creator. *"What's this fascination with closure? Don't call your ex."*

I've evolved an elaborate ritual for the aftermath of being dumped. Among other things, it incorporates angry music and a bag of Cheetos. But as the slam of the front door rattles the mirror, I remember I have no Cheetos.

O Dilemma. I'm not fit for dealing with human beings right now. But...Cheetos. The ritual demands Cheetos.

Bucky, could I send you to Key Food?

Have you ever seen an angel stare in disbelief?

Just lift a bag off the shelf and bring it here, and next time, I'll give them five bucks and say I found an error on my receipt.

Bucky says, "You're lucky I didn't just hear that."

I sigh. "Listen—"

"No, you listen. You're asking me to steal for you so you can commit the sin of gluttony and then improve the situation by lying."

"Are you saying I'd go to Hell over a bag of Cheetos?"

Bucky's shoulders square. "It's my job to make sure you don't."

"Key Food doesn't care when they get paid. They'd make money on the deal!"

His eyes should be casting shadows, they're that bright. "Just walk the block to Key Food if you want Cheetos."

"It's up on Seventh Avenue."

"It's hardly a pilgrimage to Mecca—"

"—and that'll take twenty minutes—"

"—which compared to eternity—"

I open my wallet. "Put five bucks in their stupid register and call it even!"

From downstairs: "Lee, dear?"

Bucky's eyes are sparking, and his arms are folded. I let out a long breath and call down the steps, "Yes, Mrs. Goretti?"

When she doesn't answer, I take the stairway to her apartment. She's standing in the doorframe seeming pale.

"Are you better? Your mother told me how sick you were." She pats my arm. "It must have been the chill in your apartment."

"I'm fine." I squint to make the most of all fifteen watts. "You're looking tired yourself."

"Just a little." She smiles. "If you're going shopping tonight, I need some milk."

Angels never seem smug in the Bible. Although I like to think Gabriel looked a tad smug after he told Zachariah to shut up for nine months, that would be a holy smugness, and it doesn't actually say he looked smug.

Bucky, however, looks smug.

I take Mrs. Goretti's two dollars. I guess I'm going to get some Cheetos.

Beth looks at my face, says, "Uh oh," and takes a salutary handful of Cheetos to indicate solidarity.

You never phone your ex.

I'm not sure he was my boyfriend—how can he be my ex?

He told me not to call him.

Never, never phone your ex.

Two minutes later, I'm sprawled on pillows in France with earbuds blaring The Clash's *Combat Rock*. The Clash goes really, really well with Cheetos.

Bucky's voiceless concern: I'm going to deafen myself.

Glaring in Bucky's direction, I dial it louder.

Liar. I'm a liar, and I got caught. I had chances to make things right, only I didn't take them.

The pieces fall together in my mind like a 24-piece cardboard puzzle with only twelve shapes remaining: Hal liked it when I kidnapped him; wanting to return the favor, he tried to figure out which gym was mine; remembering I walk to work, he took the R to Union Street and checked out the gym closest to my apartment; he asked for me; someone asked around, and Bill volunteered that I usually show up after work; an interesting conversation ensued.

Idiot. Idiot and liar. I've hurt everyone I love, right from day one. I should have been a boy. Even Bucky wanted me to be a boy. I've failed everyone.

Hey! A tingle as Bucky touches my arm. Beyond that I can't hear him through the music, only his shock.

I turn off the iPod. *What?*

Bucky bites his lip, his brows an inverted V. "You just implicated me in whatever abuse you were heaping on yourself."

I'm well aware whose fault this is. I turn it back on.

"No!" Bucky moves in front of me. "Lee—"

I pause it again. "You wanted a boy."

He recoils. "What?"

"You wanted a boy." I blink four times in succession. "When God asked what you really wanted, you said you wanted *him* to be able to see you. I disappointed you just by existing."

Eyes shining, Bucky shakes his head. "I never thought that."

"You're too nice to think that." Again with the earbuds.

Bucky gets right in front of me. I close my eyes, but my legs tingle where he's sitting through them. A moment later my shoulders prickle.

Get off me!

Urgency in return. My iPod shuts off.

I turn it back on again.

It stops a second time.

I rip out the earbuds and scramble to my feet. *Leave me alone.*

"I'm not letting you dump that in my lap and leaving it uncontested!" Bucky follows me into my room. "I told that story in translation, and English has no sufficiently personal neuter pronoun. It never occurred to me to prefer either gender because your soul would be a perfect fit to mine. I haven't spent the last thirty years grappling with the thought that perfection would be improved if only you had a Y chromosome."

I slam the door. "Not once you overcame the initial crushing blow."

"I wasn't disappointed!" Bucky extends his hands palm-forward. "I realize you're mad at yourself and you're mad at Hal, but don't take it out on me."

"Why am I this anti-female, if you haven't spent thirty-one years wishing I were a guy?"

"You have your own preferences." Bucky curves in the air with his wings cupped, hands clasping my shoulders. "You're in rebellion against your mother. You look better in dark colors. None of that is from me."

He drifts to the corner of my bed, hugs his knees to his chest, and rests his chin on his forearms. A moment after that he closes his eyes. "It may be my fault that you're cynical about romance. A guardian shouldn't be able to harm his charge, but I've wondered."

"Yeah, you ruined me for a real guy." I throw myself on the mattress. "You listen when I talk, you don't bring flowers, and you never leave the toilet seat up."

He waves me off. "The *Rumours* album." His wings droop. "Your brother played it a hundred and eight times after I got assigned, and even though it's cynical about romance, it reminds me of when you were very new. I'm not sure how much of my enjoyment backed up the pipeline from me to you."

"Don't go dumping your guilt on me." I toss a balled-up pair of socks from hand to hand. "Maybe I'm cynical because I've never seen a couple that stayed happy longer than two hours."

Bucky raises his head. "Your parents were happy."

"Bucky," I whisper, "I don't remember them together." His face softens. "And Mom never remarried. How good could it have been if she didn't want to try again?"

"Maybe she thought it didn't get any better." He shrugs. "How about Randy and Corinne?"

"And their ostracized daughter and years of money woes?"

Bucky opens his hands. "That's *devotion*. Love is an act of the will, not an emotion or a hormonal surge. Those are designed to be short-lived. Devotion takes willpower. Look at how Randy protects her and that tells you how much he loves Corinne. And watch for the ways she apologizes to him without ever apologizing for the fact that they don't have all the comforts they dreamed of."

I let off a hard breath.

"Love is struggle," Bucky says. "It's supposed to be. Even if this weren't a broken world, it's supposed to be hard to set aside parts of yourself in order to minister to the ones you love. That's what makes it worthwhile."

I toss the socks at him. "We're philosophers tonight?"

"It looks bad now," Bucky says. "But don't take it out on me. Nor on God. Nor on Key Food."

I offer him the bag of Cheetos.

"Sure, take it out on the Cheetos." He still holds his wings tucked about him like a shield. "I'm sorry."

He could be apologizing for any one of thirteen things. Who cares which one it is? I sit on the bed and munch Cheetos. "It's okay." Meeting his eyes, I offer a smile. "You haven't done anything to be sorry about."

Chapter Nineteen:

Don't ogle it—shoot it!

I love my job. Have I mentioned that lately? Maybe I need to remind myself.

The guy on the customer side of the counter says, "I'm only saying I want to improve my gas mileage."

I point the web browser to a page I've bookmarked for precisely this kind of conversation. "And I'm saying, if you want to improve your gas mileage, remove the spoiler."

I've had this conversation twenty times with guys flush with the joy of a new car and simultaneously flush with the embarrassment of only having money to put three gallons in the tank.

The young man glances over his shoulder with a compulsion born of fear: are the other mechanics removing his spoiler already? Will he find himself driving a boring car?

Poor kid. Life is full of disappointment: don't I know it? "I agree it looks cool, but here's a trade secret: spoilers don't produce downforce unless you're driving a 700 hp Firehawk at speeds nearing 200 mph. On a normal car, they only create drag."

He frowns. "I don't want to do surgery. I just want to spend less on gas. Maybe with an additive or something."

"*Car & Driver* did a track test with a Mustang with and without spoiler, and the spoiler hurt. Deal with it." I pivot the monitor so he can see the article. He turns away. If he were a cartoon, steam would pour from his ears.

On his way out, he stalks past Mrs. Zhou and her five-year-old. I experience a moment of "Huh?" followed by, "Oh! You're here for the trunk piston!"

She hands me her key, then opens a canvas bag big enough for Santa and begins removing a rainbow: toys and books for the child.

While I'm removing the dead piston, my head in the jaws of a trunk lid propped by a broom handle, I feel Bucky laughing.

Thanks, I think toward him. *At least my imminent decapitation amuses you.*

I wasn't laughing at you. Someone just gave me this.

He appears holding a sheet of angelic scrawl.

"I'm illiterate in Angel, remember?"

"Philistine." But he's beaming. "I'll read it to you."

I expect to hear it, but instead the whole thing pours into my head as if I'm reading it myself.

10 Signs You've Been A Guardian Angel:
- You repeat everything eight times.
- When you hear "A day is as a thousand years," you immediately think, "That's about right."
- When Michael heads off to fight Satan, you warn him to be careful.
- You try to deliver your friends' prayers to Heaven.
- You try to fix them first.
- And you're surprised when they're for worthwhile things.
- You find yourself explaining basic theology to a Cherub.
- You get shaky without someone to follow around.
- You move linearly through space to go somewhere.
- Sometimes you even calculate travel time.
- God tells you His plans, and you catch yourself just before saying, "Have you thought that through?"

- A friend visits and you're stunned when he listens to you
- You know 25 ways to alleviate the common cold, but you've never had one

Bucky's doing that thing where you're laughing silently, shoulders shaking, tears streaming down your face.

I loosen the piston from the body of the trunk. "Are we that bad?"

He gathers himself together, then breaks up laughing again. "Do you want to see me do an impression of a guardian angel?"

I look up, eyebrows arched.

Bucky points to a chair beside him. "They're *here!* Your car keys are *here!* Hello? Your car keys? Here on the chair! No, don't go search your pockets again. *Your keys are right here!*"

I lower the screwdriver and stare.

His eyes grow ferocious. "Listen or you're never getting out of here—the keys are here! For the love of little green apples, *look on the chair!*"

With none of the other mechanics near, I speak in a normal voice. "You're scaring me."

Bucky stops on a dime. "You have no idea. After about half an hour, it goes to this." He looks back at the chair. "Listen, for once! You took off your coat. You tossed your keys *on the chair* while I said, *Don't put them there or you'll forget,* and you dropped your bag *on top of the keys.* Move the bag! I don't want to spend the rest of your earthly existence in this apartment— *look at the chair!*"

Carlos passes by carrying a muffler, so I swallow the laughter. *Aren't you glad I can see you?*

"It's a perk." Bucky frowns. "During training I saw an angel I thought might walk off the job."

I look up. *He wouldn't!*

"It would have to be a hopeless case," Bucky says.

Brr. I'll keep turning this screwdriver and try not to think about that. With the new piston half-installed, my cell phone vibrates, followed by Avery's special ringtone ("Never Going Back Again"). Because she's not supposed to be calling from school, I take it. I'm either rewarding bad behavior or saving her life, but until I pick up the phone, I won't know which.

"Avery, my love."

"Aunt Lee," she gasps, "they want me to kill myself."

"What? Slow down." She's crying, and I've got no idea what's going on. "Deep breaths. What did they do?"

"They put a note in my locker. It says, 'Take half a bottle of Advil and your mom's antidepressants and you'll be out of our misery.'"

Damn it. "Listen to me. I need you to listen carefully. First you pull yourself together. I'm going to pick you up in two hours. You can endure anything for two hours."

She gives her snuffling agreement.

"Next, is there a photocopy machine in the school? I need you to copy that note. You put the original in a safe place, and then you march yourself to the principal's office with the photocopy."

"What will they do?" she wails.

"I need you to memorize a magic phrase. Repeat after me: *hostile learning environment*." I picked that up from the lawyers because apparently it works as a magical incantation. "You tell them to protect your right to an adequate education and protect you from a hostile learning environment. I'll talk to your mom tonight and give her talking points."

"Okay. Okay." She draws a shuddering breath. "It's not that bad, right? I mean—I'm not that bad."

"You're not bad at all. Trust me." I sigh. "This isn't your fault."

Then she needs to get off the phone because she shouldn't have been talking to me during school in the first place. I finish installing the piston and when I remove the broom handle, it stays up. A tug brings it down.

The old part extends to its full length when I lift it from the floor. *Bucky, could you go find the girl who left that note for Avery and replace her trunk piston with this one?*

I could, he replies, *but I wouldn't have a broom handle to give them because I'd be using it to whack some sense into you.*

Darn. *Well, could you at least make sure Avery's okay?*

He vanishes. I head back to the front desk. "All done, Mrs. Zhou." While I ticket her out, she repacks her son's canvas bag. "This has been fun, but I hope you don't have to see us again."

Avery and I enter the Brooklyn Museum with our eyes peeled, our mouths tight, and me certain someone is about to eject us for breathing too loud.

"It's not a cathedral." Bucky has a relaxed arch to his wings. "Even if it was, that should be awe, not fear."

It's hardly fear.

Bucky puts into my head an image of a judge thundering to a jury, "The verdict?" and the lead juror standing to say, "Not Cultured."

My mouth twitches in a smile. Bucky chuckles. "Or is that too close to the truth?"

He's been worried since Hal dumped me. He's too nice to push the issue, but I know he's wondering why we came here even though it was Hal's suggestion.

I haven't called my ex. I will not call my ex.

The directory says the Audubon exhibit is on the fourth floor. In the silent elevator, Avery shifts her weight. She says with an uncharacteristic hush, "Why are we here? Aren't museums boring?"

"Grandma says it will give you culture." I pause. "Me too."

She blows her bangs out of her eyes. "What's culture?"

"An ingredient in yogurt."

Avery cracks up.

"What did the principal say about the note?" I ask.

"Nothing."

"Nothing?"

She shakes her head. "I ripped it up."

"Why?"

"I don't know. It's not a big deal."

"You were given instructions on how to kill yourself, but it's not a big deal?"

She shrugs. "It's not like I have to do it just because they said."

Terrific.

"Didn't you say not to let them know they got to me?" She shoves her hands in her pockets. "Well, if the principal talks to them, they'll know."

I guess she has a point. It doesn't sound right, but if she can handle it, more power to her.

The elevator doors open into a world of birds. We drift from painting to painting in the interlocking hallways of the gallery, the wall plaques giving the history of both the birds and the painter.

Except he wasn't just a painter. The signs say that at the turn of the century, there were more Audubon gun clubs than bird-watching clubs. He'd shoot a lovely bird, pose it, paint it, then hunt down another and continue painting. Audubon is quoted as saying, "Don't ogle it behind a glass case. Shoot it!"

Oh man—I have a new motto. I should have come to the museum sooner.

I show Avery the quote, and from then we're prone to decidedly uncultured giggles. I say to Avery, "I wonder how many of this endangered bird he had to shoot to paint the pictures to encourage preservation of the species?"

Avery raises her arms as if sighting a rifle. "Only about two hundred of these left in existence. What a catch," and she pretends to fire the gun.

Poor Bucky is reconsidering his earlier reassurances. Well, tough. We smother our giggles whenever we pass a security guard, but they've got to be radioing from station to station. "Two crazy women headed your way making quips about posing birds so as not to see the entry wounds."

"Don't shoot the chicks," Avery murmurs at my side. "Let them starve to death without their mother."

About to reply, I halt before one particular painting as if I were the one in the rifle sight.

It's Bucky.

This bird—it has Bucky's wings—this is Bucky's pattern! White and brown-speckled wings with yellow bars on the secondary feathers.

I had no idea he was designed after a bird—or a bird after him.

I step close enough to see the brush strokes. Why didn't he tell me?

"They're pretty," Avery says. "But kind of small to shoot."

I can't tell her to hush, not after I instigated the sniping. But by the same token, I don't want to walk away from this, my bird-angel, so I read the plaque. *Pine siskin*. Bucky has the wings of a pine siskin.

The sign describes the bird as highly social, a seed-feeder, only three inches long, migratory. Nothing astonishing, but by the same token, it's perfect. Not native to this part of the country, but occasionally it can be spotted if you're really lucky.

I'm really lucky. I never knew.

Bucky?

Warmth floods my heart.

You're gorgeous. I admire a bird on a slender shoot that bends under even its slightness. *You're just so gorgeous.*

Back at her apartment, Avery trots into her room, and I keep on my jacket. No idea why—it's not like anyone's waiting at home.

When I say I'll be going, Randy ushers me toward the kitchen. Corinne washes the dishes while Brennan dries and Susanne puts away. "Did you have dessert?"

I shrug. I didn't eat much dinner, for that matter. Randy guides me toward the table where I find myself outfitted with a bowl of ice cream.

Randy sits. "Who's this guy mom is gushing about?"

"He's not anyone anymore." I push at the ice cream with the back of my spoon. "Tell Mom not to pick out her mother of the bride dress yet."

Randy pauses. "You're upset?"

I shrug.

"I'm sorry. I wouldn't have asked." He glances at the kids, but they're loud as they fool around at the sink. "Did you want to be dating him?"

I nod.

"Was Mom hallucinating a grand tale of two lovers agog?"

"Hal wouldn't be agog." I try to remember a teasing conversation about special ingredients, but instead I remember eyes colder than a New York winter. "More like aghast. Leave it."

My ice cream will melt. I can't even eat successfully: how incompetent is that?

Randy frowns. "You didn't have to take Avery if you felt bad."

"It's not like I had anything else to do." I look up. "You want some ice cream?"

"You'd better eat it." He puts his hand on my shoulder, then gives in and pulls me into a hug. "It's okay."

"He's not the first guy who dumped me." I try a little ice cream, and it tastes the way you'd expect: sweet, cold. It's industrial peach rather than the real thing with chunks of fruit blended in. No interesting ingredients. I should never have expected anything better.

Randy says, "Well, then I can ask you after all. Do you want to come here for your birthday?"

I squint. "Why wouldn't you ask that?"

"You were inconveniently born on Valentine's Day, so if you had a boyfriend, I couldn't very well ask you to spend it with your aged brother and his screaming spawnlets."

From the sink, Corinne calls over her shoulder, "You forgot his glamorous wife!"

Randy bursts out laughing.

I grin. "I'd love to spend my birthday with you, silly, even if you do have one foot in the grave. And your glamorous wife."

Corinne turns. "Menu requests?"

I purse my lips. "I love your ziti and meatballs. Or—" I stop. "You know, how about upscale? Why don't I kidsit while you two go out for Valentine's Day?"

Corinne snorts. "You forgot something. It's your birthday."

My heart races: this is actually a good idea, if they'd listen to me. "Someone ought to have a romantic Valentine's Day, so why not you two? When was the last time you went out alone?"

Randy and Corinne exchange a look that translates as either "I don't know" or "We still owned the Cutlass Sierra, so it had to be 2004."

"Honest, Randy." I glance at Brennan and Susanne. "The kids and I can watch movies and eat popcorn, and you can visit a restaurant without crayons on the table. There's still time to get reservations."

Randy chuckles. "Yeah, because my repertoire of restaurants is so vast."

Corinne says, "Your mom took us to that place last year."

Randy's eyes widen, and I know I have him.

I push my ice cream with a slowness calculated to make him feel sorry for me. That trick works on big brothers as well as on boyfriends: I know because I perfected it on Randy. "It'd mean a lot to know I was doing something useful. And Mom would stay off the get-a-boyfriend nonsense for a little while."

Because in her mind, my thirtieth birthday was the deadline, after which I'd be forever unmarriageable. The last thing I'll need that night will be my mother's serial phone calls, text messages and singing telegrams urging me to cast my nets into the water one last time, hoping to pull in two hundred fifty-three eligible bachelors like Peter becoming a fisher of men.

Randy's brow furrows. "This is backward."

"Say yes." I look at Corinne. " My brother is being an idiot. Make him say yes."

Corinne chuckles. "Say yes, Randy."

Randy shrugs. "Eat your ice cream. And fine, I'll take out my wife on Valentine's Day while my kids stay home with their Wrench-head Aunt Lee."

It's going to be a perfect birthday as I set sail into perpetual singlehood. I need only one more thing.

Bucky looks forward to his plant every year, but I don't want him to become an afterthought: *Let's see—I've got the toilet paper and the cheese, I still need to pick up orange juice, and look, here's the plant section.* I bet I can find a print of that Audubon painting. And wouldn't it be even cooler to surprise him with it?

The tough part will be sneaking around behind an angel's back, particularly one charged with protecting me every second of my life. So keeping my face a mask, I plan. What if I send him somewhere? He heads out to gather data when I plan highway travel or to check on Avery, so he doesn't have an aversion to leaving me for a little while. The trick would be finding an errand that would take fifteen to twenty minutes.

Won't this be the neatest thing? I could be the first human to deliberately surprise an angel.[*]

Now, what kind of errand would take that long?

When I'm home, I turn on the computer and surf. Watch me be clever: I Google Hal's name. I Google his address and phone number. Nothing interesting turns up, which I expected. I search on his email address, which turns up a few posts on a cooking group, and I check some of them. Arguments about the best way to broil this or that.[†]

During these web searches, I check my email once every thirty seconds. I've set the stage. It's going to take three minutes maximum before—

Bucky says, "Don't call."

Awesome. I didn't even start looking in the direction of the phone.

I frown at him. In a whisper, "What if he changed his mind?"

"It didn't sound changeable to me." Bucky folds his arms. "You keep quoting Rule One. Follow it."

I glance at the phone. I'm going to regret this, but I need to get Bucky out of the house. "Could you check him out? You know, talk to his guardian and find out if he's still mad?"

Bucky's face tenses. "What more do you need? He has your phone number and your email address. If he wanted to contact you, he knows how to do it."

---

[*] I astonish him all the time. I meant surprise in a not-like-the-shower-scene-in-Psycho way.

[†] *Heated* arguments.

Bucky's too practical. I shake my head. "If you talked to his guardian, you'd find out if there was anything I could do to make amends." I look at my lap. "I know I hurt him."

Remember that "feel sorry for me" technique? I perfected it on Randy, but I worked out the basics on Bucky.

Beth calls across the apartment, "Lee? You're talking to yourself again!"

Oh, right—she's home. "Sorry! I just wanted to speak to someone of equal intelligence."

Beth shows in the doorway, balancing an origami crane on one fingertip. "And the zoo closed the monkey house?"

I blow her a raspberry.

Sagely, she nods. "I see your point about the intelligence." She sits cross-legged on the floor. "What's going on with Hal?"

"He dumped me?" I check my email again—for verisimilitude. "Before I could tell him I was a liar, he figured it out himself."

"Ouch. Was that when you became the Cheetos queen?" Beth tucks up her knees and nibbles at the edge of her finger. "You want me to get Stuart to talk to him?"

I'm about to decline when my devious brain twigs to what she's saying. Slowly I say, "Does it ever help to have a third party find out what a guy is thinking?"

Beth says, "It can't hurt. What's he going to do? Dump you twice as much?"

I shoot Bucky a significant glance. He folds his arms.

"Let me think about it." I cock my head. "I don't want to remind him if he'd just be better off forgetting. And guys don't really talk like that."

"Stuart found out about the ex-girlfriend during the book club, so it's not all car chases and bodies in bathtubs." Beth gets to her feet. "Stuart is a phone call away, and he could talk to Hal within twenty-four hours without it sounding like you sent him."

As she leaves, I focus on Bucky.

"Fine," he says.

Victory! I force myself to sound upbeat. "Take as long as you need to. Beth's guardian can call you if I need help."

He shrugs. "The guys downstairs and next door can, too. Walls aren't a barrier."

He vanishes.

Quick as a shot, I Google "Pine Siskin Audubon print," locate a reputable seller, rush through checkout, login to PayPal, and voila, one Pine Siskin print will arrive within seven days. I'll hide the package in the apartment until my birthday.

As I'm shutting down the browser, I feel Bucky arrive but can't see him.

Bad news? I think. *Good news?*

Don't call him yet, Bucky sends, *if ever.*

Rats.

Logically I knew that would be the outcome. I'm not any worse off than before, and sure, I'll have my surprise for Bucky, but still. I hate this.

Chapter Twenty:

There's no moral component to flossing

Friday night I spend exactly as a woman of my stature should: on her knees in front of her mother's toilet.

And I have Avery with me. Won't Randy be proud?

Actually, Randy will be proud. After Avery phoned me from school five times, I agreed to pick her up early. Just as I was about to leave, I got a call from my mom because maintenance couldn't stop her toilet from running continuously, and the plumber wouldn't come until Monday.

It says something about Avery's current social situation that repairing a toilet with her maiden aunt is the best game in town.

Mom hovers at the door, then leaves, then returns. Avery perches on the edge of the bathtub, churning out one unending sentence about girls who have nothing better to do than remind her of the ways in which she is their inferior.

"Hand me the wrench." I want to make sure the water supply is good and off before I start unscrewing nuts and washers.

Avery watches as I tighten the shutoff valve, and then I hold up the flush valve to release as much water as possible into the toilet. About an inch remains, so I use my mom's ratty Mickey Mouse towel to soak it up.

Avery stops her monologue. "Where'd you learn to do this?"

"One of the best things a woman can do for herself is learn to fix a toilet." I huff as I rummage in the tool box for the WD-40. "For your sixteenth birthday, ask for a set of Craftsman tools and learn to use them."

My mother has come in behind me with more ratty towels from the rag bin. "She'd be better off learning to apply makeup."

"You need the makeup to bat your eyes at a guy so he'll fix your toilet. Skip a step." The inside of the toilet tank is dry, and everything is as lubricated as possible. "This is the inlet supply for the tank. You watched how I turned off the water at the shutoff valve, right? Because that's very important. Otherwise we'd all get sprayed when I do this." I disconnect the inlet supply from the tank and am rewarded with no gush of water. Wouldn't that be embarrassing? I take care of the residual drippiness with the bucket.

Mom says, "A husband isn't good only for fixing toilets."

My mom was a single mom all those years. She got my uncles to do things maintenance wouldn't, like install a ceiling fan. I used sit by the wall listening to Uncle Mickey: "This is a circuit breaker," "You spread on the joint compound thin," "Let me tell you about the time I forgot to test to see if the wire was live," and all for an audience of one. He didn't realize I was deciphering how the world got put together, and that I could put together a world by myself when I didn't like the world my mother had ready-made for me.

I turn to Mom. "I need some more towels to set the toilet tank on," and she heads out.

Avery says, "Did you study mechanical engineering in college?"

I laugh. "Are you kidding? Most engineers can design a bridge but can't change their own oil." I know—I listen to their phone conversations while they're paying me to change it. "I squeaked out of college with a degree in *human development and family studies*, and your grandma found me a nurse's aide position. That's what she had done, and I hadn't thought beyond graduation."

Shocked, Avery says, "They tell us all the time to have a plan."

"No one told me that." No one but Bucky, who spouted enigmatic speeches like "You're graduating in a month. Have you thought about getting a job?"

"Grandma urged me to enter nursing school right away, but I'd had enough of schedules and classwork, so I lived with her for a while and worked at Brookdale Hospital."

I don't tell Avery that this lasted until my mother told me she was moving to a one-bedroom apartment unless I enrolled in nursing school.

"After a couple of years," I say, "I was pretty well done with emptying bed pans and being berated by doctors. The final straw was when a doctor screamed at me for questioning his illegible orders. I knew patients usually got one of this kind of pill, but he'd ordered three. I think I saved the woman's life, but he was so shaken he took it out on me."

That's what Bucky said. I wasn't nearly so charitable as the angel, but for Avery's sake, we'll go with Bucky's version.

Avery says, "Really?"

"The patient's son was, as it turned out, an attorney, and he found me sobbing in the break room."

Avery exclaims, "He made you cry?"

"You think the girls in high school are bad, but in some hospitals, it's like they never left tenth grade." I sigh. "Anyhow, the attorney asked me what I keep asking you: why stay in a place where if I made a mistake, the doctors would blame me, and yet if I double-checked to avoid making a mistake, the doctors blamed me anyhow?"

Avery's mouth twitches.

"I didn't have an answer for him either, by the way. After you get pushed around so long, you think it's normal." I sit back on my heels. "He asked if I could type. Who can't type? He told me which temp agency he used and said one of the secretaries was going on *yet another maternity leave*, and he wanted a replacement who had *integrity*." I lean into the words the same way the attorney did so long ago. "He told me to register with this agency, and he would request me."

I can't tell Avery what happened next because it involved a teensie bit of truth-laundering. Since the next day was my day off, I dressed in my black skirt and white blouse, donned make-up, and rode the subway into Manhattan. I let my mother think I was interviewing with Hunter College Nursing School. Instead I signed up with Temp Attempts, where they added 10 wpm to my typing score, assumed I knew every version of MS Word because I passed a test on the five-year-old version, and accidentally checked off that I knew PowerPoint and FileMakerPro. They said I'd be hearing from them. (Hell, after all that, I'd want to hire me too!)

That took two hours, so I looked up two more agencies. One needed a medical transcriptionist for a four-hour job, and since I had the time, I took it.

For a few weeks, while the temp jobs came sporadically, I worked either at the hospital on my regular shift (40 hours over three days) or else I ventured into Manhattan to answer phones, type, file, and look young at the front desks of various companies.

When the first agency asked for a three month block of time to cover a maternity leave, I finally had no choice but to tell my mother. Mom then told me I had two months to find a new place to live.

I did, but that's another story. I'm brought back to reality by Avery, who's saying, "So then what happened?"

"What do you think happened? I put in three months as secretary to five attorneys, and they liked me enough to make me permanent: I showed up on time; I spoke clearly; I didn't dress like a hooker. These were qualities their temps had lacked in the past." I smirk. "Before you apply for your first job, I'll go over that with you one more time."

Avery ticks off the words on her fingers. "Prompt, well-groomed, articulate, chaste. Got it."

I recoil. "Whoa, vocabulary words!"

Avery mutters, "I have to do something in school. I don't have friends to pass notes to."

Touché.

Before Avery can ask why I left a job that involved air-conditioning and padded chairs, Mom returns to spread more old towels on the tiles.

"Okay, pay attention." I wink at Avery as if we weren't talking. "Next we unbolt the toilet tank from the toilet." That's trickier than it sounds because the bolts have rusted, but with WD-40 and upper arm muscles primed by shifting a Mustang, I wrench them loose. Avery is impressed. My mother, for what it's worth, doesn't heckle while I'm getting it done.

Once the bolts loosen, I lift the toilet tank off the toilet (damn, it's heavy—maybe I need a husband to lift toilet tanks for me?) and lay it on the towels. I shift it until it's upside-down, then unscrew the flush valve nut that holds it to the tank.

Avery says, "Why do I need to know all this, though?"

"So you never have to say please or thank you. It's not just toilets. It's freedom. You'll have something to offer, not something to take away from everyone around you."

Mom says, "There's nothing wrong with asking for a favor."

I pick up my wrench again. "I'd rather not rely on anyone."

Avery watches as I remove the flush valve, the washer and the gasket. I take the new one from the package and show Avery how the gasket goes on the inside and the washer on the outside, then install it, making sure the gasket will be tight enough that it won't leak.

Mom folds her arms. "It's not about trading services. It's about being together."

"You did fine without Dad." I look at her. "You showed me I could cut it on my own, and I don't even have four kids I'm raising solo."

Mom stops, tries to speak, then stops again.

"If you could do all that, why the hell can't I do it too?"

Mom bites her lip. "Maybe I want better for you."

I reply, "Maybe I don't think it gets any better. I don't see how it could."

Mom helps me set the tank back onto the toilet. Then I use the new brass bolts (maintenance had everything except know-how) to tighten the tank to the toilet bowl. It takes a few tries before I feel as if the gasket is compressed just enough to keep water out, but not so tight the tank will crack. Especially with my mom watching, I'd like to get this right.

I replace the intake valve and turn on the water enough to cover the outlet. The water stays in the tank. I turn to Avery for a high-five, and she laughs. I turn to my mom, and she grudgingly offers me her high-five too.

"Thank you, ladies." I let the tank fill the rest of the way as I replace the ceramic top. "You're a wonderful audience."

Two hours later, I drop off Avery with her parents, and I head back home. My Acura starts without hesitation. It's ten years old, so soon it'll begin protesting the cold, the idling, the slave labor of a transmission in city traffic. I'm not sure if I'll be sad when I have to get rid of it. Unlike my Mustang, it's nothing more than a vehicle to take me places. It's not the end in itself.

"What's the end of marriage?" I say out loud.

Bucky behind me says, "Death."

Oh, sure, be practical about it. "The other kind of end. You know, *the end justifies the means*. If marriage is the means, what's the end?"

"Getting into Heaven. You should know that." Bucky coalesces in the passenger seat, leaning against the door. He has, it amuses me to see, a phantom seat belt over his shoulder and waist.

I roll my eyes. "You'd say that about everything."

"The end of eating is nourishing your body, not getting you into Heaven. The end of breathing is oxygenating your brain." Bucky arches his eyebrows. "*Your* final aim should be getting into Heaven. Marriage happens to be a path that makes it easier for some people to attain that. You're still figuring out whether you're one of them."

As I glide to a stop at a red light, I frown. "What about companionship?"

"You have plenty of companions. I'm your companion, but we aren't married. And before you say it, there are many acknowledged benefits and other purposes to marriage: partnership, financial stability, formation of the core social unit in a microcosm of the larger society, sexual gratification, and the production of children. But those all fall subservient to the primary goal, which is that a couple must work to forward one another's way into Heaven."

I'm quiet until the light changes, when I turn off the radio. "Some couples get in one another's way of Heaven."

Bucky sighs. "Some people eat and throw it up afterward, too. Any natural good can be diverted."

We're quiet until I reach the next light. Then I smirk. "You tossed in 'sexual gratification' as if it's just another ingredient from the store."

Bucky says, "If you're implying sexual intercourse ought to be the primary reason to get married, you're incorrect."

"I'm not."

In the next instant, I have a horrible thought.

I look out the corner of my eyes at Bucky, even as I feel myself flush. "Um...you know how you wanted me to be virgin until I get married, and then, uh, afterward, I'd be..."

Gee, there isn't really a word for that, is there?

"Not?" supplies Bucky.

"Right. But, uh..." My cheeks feel hotter right now than when I told Hal I was seeing angels. "What do the guardians do during the time in-between?"

No change in expression from him. "We critique."

"Bucky!"

"We grade your performance on a five-page form and submit it to the oversight committee." He sighs. "Why do you think so many religions and cultures discourage extramarital sex? The paperwork is a nightmare."

A car behind me honks, and I realize the light's been green for several seconds.

That's it. I am never getting married. I don't care what my mother says.

Shaking his head, Bucky looks out the window. "You know I'm not serious."

"But—"

"It's not a big deal. I've seen couples engaged in intercourse." He appears baffled. "I've also seen people eating and people using the toilet. The Bible is full of who lay with whom and who conceived whom. What's the problem?"

What's the problem? How about privacy?

"Bodies are clumsy in general." Bucky sits forward. "I'm glad I don't have one, but there's very little about your physical existence that I have an aversion to."

As we stop at the next light, near Prospect Park, I turn to him. "Okay, what?"

"Flossing." He shudders. "Seeing you sliding that bit of string between your teeth is as close as I can come to nausea."

I roll forward with the green. "Again with you and teeth."

"Dental floss and contact lenses are the two aspects of modern human existence I would change in a heartbeat, assuming I had a pulse." His wings pull tight around himself. "For one thing, if God wanted you to stick your finger in your eye, you wouldn't blink."

I shift my gaze. "Is this coming from God, or is this coming from you?"

Bucky's cheeks redden. "Just me. There's no moral component to flossing."

We're quiet for long enough that I want to put the radio back on. Then Bucky pulls himself back together. "We all acknowledge that people have complementary parts which fit together. Given the content of many of the songs you hear, why would you be embarrassed to be seen engaging in the activity with a spouse? It would be your right within a marital covenant. God said in Eden to be fruitful and multiply. Adam didn't have a Xerox machine."

No, they'd have mentioned that in Genesis. And instead of a snake, it'd be one of those guys who tries to sell you fake toner. *Of all the office supply stores in the mall you may shop, but of the telephone toner salesman, I tell you do not give your serial number, or you will surely buy.*

Still, don't angels have an equivalent experience? "Wouldn't you be embarrassed to have someone knowing your innermost desires and disappointments?"

Bucky says, "Why?"

"Because that's private."

Bucky says again, "Why?"

"Are you a toddler?"

His eyebrows raise. "I'm confused as to why I'd want to hide desire or disappointment."

"It's a weakness."

"There's nothing wrong with weakness. Creation is full of it." Bucky shifts in his seat to face me. "I want you to get into Heaven more than you want it for yourself. I'm not ashamed of that. If, and may God forbid it, I lost you, I would be devastated. But there would be no shame in grieving."

I can't even think how to respond. Maybe there's no shame, but does everyone have to know about it?

"This is a culture gap." Bucky shrugs. "Don't worry."

"But the privacy thing?"

"It'll be the same as when you're in the shower." He chuckles. "You won't see me. I imagine at the moment, you won't be looking for me."

I get upstairs to find Beth in France watching television, but she turns it off the instant I step into the room. "Sit."

Oh boy. This doesn't look good.

As I unzip my coat, Beth says, "It turns out I didn't have to talk to Stuart. He'd already gotten an earful from Hal."

Wide-eyed, I wait.

Beth's brow furrows. "Hal Googled you and found something else you lied about."

My heart skips. "I did? About what?"

"Maybe you lied to me too, but it's so trivial I can't see why you would." Beth looks at the floor. "He found a memorial to your father, and he didn't die the way you said."

I roll my eyes. "And everything on the internet is by definition correct?"

"I'm just repeating what he told Stuart."

I head to the computer without removing my jacket, and as I wake it up, Beth says, "Haven't you ever done a vanity Google?"

"It never even occurred to me." I type my name into the search engine, which turns up fifty million pages. Right: *Lee Singer*. Hah. Putting "Juliet Singer" in quotes yields only three screens of hits, mostly alumni lists, my name in my great-uncle's obituary, and then on the second page, a firefighter's memorial.

"Hey, look! My brother told me he was enrolling my father." I click, and when it loads, there's a thrill when my father's face—angular, dark-eyed, wearing a firefighter's helmet—looks back at me.

"Hey, Dad." I'm warm. "Good to see you again."

Randy resembles my mom, but I'm more my Dad's daughter.

Beneath his name and dates of service, Randy's given a brief description of him. This is neat.

With Beth leaning over my shoulder, I read the memorial paragraphs, stopping cold toward the bottom.

Beth says, "That's it."

I'm going to kill my mother.

Chapter Twenty-One:

The best way to keep something a secret is not to post it to the world wide web

"How could you do that to me?"

I don't care if the neighbors hear. I don't care if Hal is grilling portabellas on his window hibachi in the Ansonia Clockworks and the wind carries him the echoes of me bellowing at my mother.

"What on earth did you think you were gaining with that story?"

My mother sounds urgent. "Please listen to me. You were so young!"

I've paced the apartment throughout the conversation. "I stopped being five twenty-five years ago!"

"You were terrified of fire! Every night it was more nightmares and you waking up screaming. I couldn't take it anymore."

"But when I got older, then what?"

My mother says, "I didn't want you to be ashamed of him."

I plunk myself on the couch, breathing hard.

Beth has been following me from room to room. No amount of Cheetos in the world would calm me at this point, but she skirts the edge of my orbit. She's sorry she told me. I'm not. I'm sorry no one told me sooner.

"We did tell you at first," my mother says. "The morning afterward, you found me crying at the table with your grandparents, and my brother coming in with McDonalds for breakfast."

I remember. My mother had to tell me Daddy wouldn't come home from last night's fire. But then, only pieces. Sitting on my grandmother's lap while she brushed my hair and told me I was a good girl, that my father loved me and would have come home if he could. Uncle Mickey, pushing the paper-wrapped breakfast into my hands. Randy was beside me. He made me eat. I'd never had an Egg McMuffin before, and I hated the cheese. I still can't stand American cheese.

My mother continues. "We did tell you about the two kids your father was carrying, that he died holding them when the stairway collapsed."

This part I don't remember. Only the plastic taste of cheese. The way my hands and feet seemed so distant from the rest of my body, my lips numb. The way Bucky appeared in the midst of all those people with a double-light in his eyes, and I'd thought to him, *Please bring back my Dad,* only his eyes dimmed and he shook his head.

"For two months," my mother says, "you woke up screaming every night, and always with the same dreams. You refused to walk on staircases. I couldn't cook on the stovetop because of the fire. No one prepared me for that. I didn't know what to do."

I press my thumb and forefinger to my throbbing temples.

My mother sounds small. "Are you still there?"

"I'm listening."

"One morning I couldn't take it anymore. I could barely sleep myself, and then you'd awaken for an hour, and I wouldn't sleep again. So I told you there had been a terrible mistake, that your father was a hero, and we thought they'd died, but really, the children were fine."

The children were fine.

Just like that. They were fine.

My voice grows lower, more measured. "Why did you say I would be ashamed of my father?"

"You might think he failed."

He failed? Failed by walking into a death-trap, by doing his job and being the man God made him to be? Heroism isn't contingent on success: history is full of heroic failures. You only have one life to give for your country, or your cause, or your fire department.

My voice rises in pitch. "Do *you* think Dad was a failure?"

My mother says, "I wanted to protect you."

Beth has settled in the corner, and I close my eyes so I won't see her. "I don't think the firefighters who died in the World Trade Center were failures, do you? Five thousand people died, but the world sees them as heroes."

All my mother says is, "It's not about failure. I shouldn't have said that. I never knew what to do with you and your imagination—that was your father's thing— and then you had something terrible to imagine, and I didn't want you to keep imagining your father's last minutes being afraid or sad. I did my best."

I can't speak to that. I don't know anything any longer.

My mother's voice is urgent. "He loved you, Juliet. I didn't want you to forget him."

"I would never forget my father!" My voice is shrill. "Do you know how often I've wished those children would track us down and tell us they appreciated his sacrifice?"

"I'm sorry."

"You'll be sorrier when you hear that Hal, the guy you liked so much on Saturday, Googled me and read a different story than what I'd told him."

My mother is silenced.

"I lied to him first about something else, so I know it's my fault. But I can only believe he Googled me to

225

figure out what the hell was going on, and then he thought I'd also lied about my father the hero who saved two kids. And that's the end of that."

Long silence, this time.

Finally from Mom: "I don't know what to say."

I don't either. "I'll call you tomorrow."

"I love you, Sweetie."

I just want to get her off the phone, so I say, "I love you too."

As I hang up, Beth meets my eyes. I give a little shake of my head.

Within ten minutes, Randy calls. "Mom is in hysterics."

I walk to the other end of the apartment to glare out at Garfield Place. "Good. I'm not too pleased with you, either."

I would have let the phone roll to voicemail, but in the middle of sending Stuart an IM, Beth picked it up.

"I thought the whole deception was insane."

"Didn't it occur to you that the best way to keep something a secret is not to post it to the world wide web?"

"No, Lee, because I'm stupid."

When that surprises a laugh out of me, Randy continues, "I've been in favor of you finding out for years, but I knew Mom would have my head. Instead I put the information where you'd find it."

"Hal found it." Over at the table, I rearrange a stack of junk mail that Beth will transform into origami aardvarks offering a low interest rate. "The guy who dumped me now thinks that in addition to my other crimes, I lied about my father, the savior of children."

"Ouch." Silence for a moment. "Mom said something like that, but I couldn't make it out. Was that the reason he broke it off?"

"It was broken off already. Perhaps out of sick fascination, he Googled me. He told Beth's boyfriend, who told me. And you got your wish, because I found out."

"Hm." Randy waits a moment before adding, "That's not how I intended."

"If you want God to laugh," I say, "tell Him your plans."

Beth appears in the doorway. "Stuart says he believes you about the website, for what it's worth." She stares at the floor. "He'll talk again with Hal, but you know," and she looks up, "I wouldn't get my hopes up."

I nod. "There's still that pesky fact that I did lie to him."

Randy says, "Why'd you do a stupid thing like that?"

"Because I'm stupid."

"What did you tell him?"

I bite my lip.

"You know, I'm entrusting my daughter to you once a week. Maybe you need to reveal your sordid secrets."

I sigh. "I wish you were here so I could bop you on the head with a rolled-up newspaper."

Which Beth would then unroll and fold into a life-size pony, and maybe I could ride it into the sunset and forget all this nonsense.

He laughs, but nothing's funny anymore. "Fine, fine. Look, you know where I am. If you want to talk about Dad, even if it's the middle of the night, call."

"It's not that bad." I trace the wood grain of the table-top, trading off fingers so each one makes a circuit of its own. "Just one more lie in a city full of lies."

For the second hour straight, I'm squaring off against a Civic that vibrates only at highway speed. The shaking onsets suddenly at 50mph. It doesn't occur at low speeds at all. The vibrations don't intensify above 55. A trip up the BQE verified all this.

This is the fun part of my job. Changing spark plugs is only a matter of learning how, and a tune-up becomes routine after a while. The client doesn't (usually) drop off the car with a note saying "Guess which maintenance task needs to be performed." Cases like these provide spice. They require sleuthing.

I'd suspected bad tires, except another mechanic must have had a similar suspicion: the Civic's nubbly tires still wear rubber whiskers on the sidewalls. The customer verifies they've been balanced.

I've ruled out the transmission. Some Civics shift from first to second with a heart-jolting *thunk*, but not this peppy four-banger. I don't think it's the clutch. The vibrations start at the top of third gear and remain continuous during the shift to fourth, and it doesn't feel like a tranny shake. It's too knocky.

I already put the thing on the lift and ran the engine like crazy in mid-air. Even with the tires off the ground, it shook at fifty.

All four spark plugs check out fine. A misfiring spark plug would cause that about-to-stall feeling at low speeds but tend to correct at high speeds, but I ruled it out anyhow.

Okay, then. Clogged vacuum hoses? Brakes engaging at highway speeds? Loose heat-shield?

Wait a minute. The fuel mixture.

My heart hammers as I run for the Chilton's manual, and then I bolt to the computer for the technical service bulletins. Fuel mixture. Of course. Come on—where are you—

And there she is. The EGR valve.

I whoop out loud. "Victory!"

Carlos and Tim look up from their cars, and Allison sticks her head out Max's office door. "Would you mind not startling the customers?"

I skip back to the car, laughing. The exhaust gas recirculation valve mixes hot air from the exhaust back into the combustion chamber, reducing combustion temperatures and also reducing formation of nitrous oxides.

Alongside the Civic, which I may have scared (but who cares?—it was shaking anyhow) I croon "We Are The Champions" into my wrench as if I'm on American Idol in the final round.

Max heads to the repair bay. "Okay, Singer. What's the deal?"

Changing keys, I sing, "The EGR valve—is stuck open."

Max's jaw drops.

I stop singing and bounce in place. "It's getting too much air in the fuel, so at highway speed, the car bucks like a bronco because the mixture is too powerful."

"You're a genius." Arms folded, Max leans against the side of the Civic. "I'll get on the horn with the dealership and have a new valve out here by three."

I pop the hood again and stick my head into the engine. A moment later, Bucky sits on the engine block.

"Nice catch."

"Did you know all along?" I murmur.

Bucky shakes his head. "You do your job, and I'll do mine."

"Keep your feathers out of the engine."

Bucky obligingly lifts his wings. Sometimes when I say that, he sheds feathers through the metal like snowflakes melting in the air. It depends on his mood and mine.

This is the kind of problem-solving I never got to do for the lawyers or the nurses. There was the time I diagnosed why the photocopier reported a paper jam long after I had created a paper-free zone for twenty feet around. But no others.

"This job is perfect for you," Bucky says.

My head jerks up.

"I'm not reading your thoughts. You're grinning like you won the lottery." Bucky pauses. "If you enjoy solving huge problems, how about you figure out why you keep lying about this?"

I sigh.

"It might just save yourself another heartbreak if you diagnose yourself." Bucky shrugs. "Oh, and you don't have to go home for lunch. The mail came, but my print hasn't arrived yet."

I drop the wrench, which clatters through the engine to the concrete floor. *How did you know about that?*

"Oh—" His eyes flare. "You wanted to surprise me? I wouldn't have said anything."

I get on my knees to retrieve the wrench, fighting tears. I can't do anything right.

"I'm sorry," Bucky says. "Don't let me ruin your good mood."

The wrench is a little too far beneath the car for me to reach without lying down.

Max calls across the repair bay, "Lee, leave it. They'll send the part tomorrow. You want to call the owner with the good news?"

I shout back, "You think he'd take the answer from me?"

Don't get me wrong—it's nice to report you've solved a problem that stumped five other mechanics. But given the owner's repeated disappointment, do we really want a female voice on the phone? Usually I'd be able to take it, but after screwing things up with Bucky, I couldn't handle being yelled at. I'd end up puking in the bathroom.

Max says, "The owner's a woman."

"You take it."

The only thing worse than a fifty-five year old male seeing a woman fixing his car is a woman seeing a woman fixing her car. No thanks.

Max appears in his doorway. "At least listen in."

In his office, the owner voices her thrill through the speaker phone when he tells her what an EGR valve should do, and what hers does not. She asks for the name of the mechanic who worked these wonders, and when Max says, "Lee," she replies, "Tell him he did great." Then she adds, "I'll be sure to bring my car to Lee from now on."

I love finding a car with a note on it: "DO NOT TOUCH! ONLY LEE!"

While standing alongside Max's desk hearing my praises sung, I flip through the *New York Post*. Blood, mayhem, adultery, Fleetwood Mac.

I skim the quarter-page ad: they're in concert. February 19th. Tickets cost half the earth. Too bad— Bucky would love that.

I rip the ad out of the paper anyhow.

I didn't think a couple hours a week would cause problems, but I've lost time mentoring Avery, plus the added cost of eating out on those nights, plus the cost of kidnapping both Bill and Hal, plus lost days being sick— it kind-of added up. My bank account is sad. No concert.

My stoic guardian angel squares his shoulders. "It would have been fun, but you shouldn't venture quite that close to the edge."

I regard him with annoyance. I do have, as it turns out, a shiny nest-egg. Why? Because back when I got my first job as a cotton-candy maker at Coney Island, Bucky insisted with a straight face that I deposit $10 per paycheck in a savings account, then made me increase that every time I got a raise. I can't even suggest using my savings to take him to a concert because he'll say, "What savings? If you had savings, it would be for an emergency."

I toss the checkbook into my desk and head to the kitchen. "There's only one solution."

"You don't keep a jar of pennies in the freezer," Bucky says by way of illuminating me.

"I have something better than that in the freezer."

"A jar of nickels?"

When I turn around with the carton of ice cream, his eyes gleam. "Come on—when did binge eating ever help anything?"

"It's not a binge until I finish the carton."

His eyes widen. "I can't even begin to counter that or you might think your argument legitimate."

I turn on my iPod, and the *Rumours* album starts up. "We can't see them in concert, but hey, we've got music right here."

Then he and I dance while I eat ice cream from the carton, and there's giggling, and I splash him with soap suds from the sink and rat-tail him with the dish towel. By the time Beth comes home we've got the kitchen cleaned up and the carton cleaned out. I'm the luckiest woman alive.

Chapter Twenty-Two:

Leave her alone, you filthy pig!

My first thought on waking is the ruined surprise, and I groan.

Yes, it was futile (stupid?) to try surprising an angel. Of course he'd ask the other guardians what happened while I was alone. "Oh, she ordered something online, then surfed back to a Delphi forum." Bucky must have checked my email (don't ask how—but I know he does) and seen the receipt from the seller; why wouldn't I intend him to find out? I never hid anything from him before.

It would be impossible to surprise an angel.

Therefore only an idiot would try a second time, and that means Bucky would be really, really surprised if I succeeded. It'd be like a meta-surprise!

As I head to the kitchen, I'm stopped by the image of a revolving sword, its blade in flames.

Oh yeah, good omen.

An image of Bucky stands on either side of the door. One of them proclaims, "Of all the food in the kitchen you may eat, but of the blue Tupperware crammed behind the potatoes on the second shelf of the refrigerator you may not eat, or you will die."

I'm convinced Bucky does this in the mornings because he misses me when I'm asleep. He spends all night thinking of nice things to do, and then he can't wait any longer once I'm up. In my less charitable moments I also think he does it because it's easier to mess with my head pre-coffee.

My nose wrinkles. "I will not die. Maybe I'll just have knowledge of evil."

Bucky looks queasy as the revolving sword and one of himself disappear. "I'm not confident of that."

Using the oven-cleaning gloves, I unearth a blue container, mercifully fogged, although a little liquid laps the shores of whatever it used to contain. I shove it to the bottom of the trash unopened.

That done, I can coffee-bootstrap while manipulating my master plan to surprise Bucky. As evidenced by the Garden of Not Eatin', morning is the perfect time to fire random neurons, so why not plan when I'm least inhibited?

And thus, we stage Operation Sneakitude.

We coined *sneakitude* when Brennan used to slip away from Randy and Corinne. They'd be occupied, and he'd just...leave. He never looked behind as he toddled away, certain no one would notice his craftiness. Unfortunately, sometimes they didn't, and he'd get all the way to the elevator by himself. Because Brennan was so *sneakitudinous,* Randy installed a deadbolt on the door up right at the top that Brennan still can't release by himself. I can barely reach it.

My plan will require some cooperation from God, but I think He'll agree. I don't know much about God, but I bet God loves giving someone a good surprise.

First the setup: I talk to Bucky about Hal all morning and make myself seem mopier than I am.

At some point, I send Bucky into another room "to make sure I haven't forgotten something" and stuff the newspaper ad into an envelope.

On the way to work, I visit the ATM to withdraw the bi-weekly gob of cash.

I arrive at work and begin changing an EGR valve.

I ask Bucky if I should phone Hal. He says no.

I ask Bucky if I should email Hal. He says no.

On my coffee break, I Google Hal and find nothing new. Bucky sighs.

Now for phase II of Operation Sneakitude: while finishing the EGR replacement, I ask Bucky to check on Hal.

Bucky again refuses.

I say, "It's not as if Hal will find out. And Stuart may have already told him I was lied to myself."

He looks unconvinced.

When I follow that up with, "Maybe I can make it right," I sound more plaintive than I intended.

I would like to reconcile with him. I would. I just don't see how I can make it better, so the only thing I can give him is peace. It's not as if he invested a lot. Two weeks. Four meals, one kidnapping, one attempted kidnapping. One exposure to a Lee-eating virus. One morning with my mother. Give him time and he can forget. Forget me.

I hate that, but he needs to forget me.

A shadow crosses Bucky's eyes. He says nothing, but the sorrow trills through him the same way I feel it when Avery talks about having no friends.

Bucky folds his arms and shifts his weight. "You do understand it won't make a difference?"

I blow off a breath as I slam the hood of the Civic. *But if you talk to his guardian, then I won't call him myself.*

Bucky vanishes.

Phase III: begin.

Dear God, I think, *please tell the other angels not to tell Bucky what I'm doing while he's gone.*

I stuff six twenty dollar bills into the envelope with the ad for the concert.

At the front desk, Ari is surfing the web. I thrust the envelope into his hands, whispering that I want him to buy me one ticket on his credit card, email confirmation to go to his address. Leaving behind a wide-eyed mechanic, I hop into the Civic to give it a test drive.

The little red four-banger does not, for the record, buck again at fifty miles per hour. Surprising an angel and fixing a car: I am a freaking genius.

On returning to the garage, I hand Max the keys with a thumbs-up. Ari's on Ebay (oh, clever!) so I grab a Subaru Legacy in need of a tune-up.

As I pop the hood, Bucky appears, eyes black.

Tim's playing his radio, so no one will hear. "How is Hal?"

"The same. What did you do while I was gone?"

"He's still mad?"

"More like baffled and hurt. What did you do while I was gone?"

"I test drove the Civic. No more kicking at highway speeds. Yay me." I force a chuckle. "This one's a tune-up."

Frowning, he folds his arms. "That's it?"

"Did you expect me to fight a dragon?" I pause significantly. "Did his guardian think there was anything I could do?"

"I have no recommendations." He studies me while I hook up the diagnostics, but I pay attention to the numbers the computer spits out. The Legacy is in pretty good shape. There's carbon buildup on the intake valves, but it's something to watch rather than something needing repair. I make note of it, then replace the spark plugs, distributor cap and rotor, fuel filter, air filter and PCV valve. I check the ignition timing, idle speed and the idle mixture.

In the middle of this, Ari pulls into the garage with a Dodge Caravan, then on his way to the supply closet, hands me an envelope. "Done."

"Thanks." I halve the envelope before stuffing it in my back pocket.

"No problem. You owe me."

A moment after he leaves, Bucky stands before me with flames in his eyes.

I back away from the car.

Bucky's gaze drills into me. "What have you done?"

"It's nothing." Rationally, he can't ignite the car, but with him shedding sparks, my instincts scream to run for cover.

Bucky's wings flare. "What did you do while I was gone?"

I hiss, "I test-drove a car and nothing else, Bucky! Back off!"

He vanishes.

When I surprise him with the ticket he's going to be thrilled, but wow. He's not pleased.

An hour later, I'm finished with the Legacy's tune-up, and I feel a hard Bucky-impulse in my heart: Go home for lunch.

He's still furious. Terrific.

I want to tell him, but I've worked so hard that it'd be a shame to spill the secret now. He's been mad at me before. He'll get over it.

Usually when Bucky tells me to go home for lunch, it's either because a package arrived or Mrs. Goretti needs something. The print hasn't arrived yet, though, and Mrs. Goretti tells me she's fine. Great—maybe Bucky's presence near Hal's guardian got Hal thinking about me, and I've got a "Dear Wretch" email I shouldn't read at work.

As the door shuts behind me, Bucky appears in the middle of the dining room.

My coat zipper isn't more than halfway down when he says, "You lied to me."

And vanishes.

I stand stock still.

"Bucky?"

Nothing.

"Bucky? Where are you?"

Oh my God.

"Bucky! Get back here!" Hysteria in my voice. "It's not like that! You coward—get back over here!"

My ears ring, and in the next moment my vision goes spotty. I drop myself to the hardwood floor. There's no way I'd have made it to the table.

I can't breathe. *Bucky? You can't do this. I won't let you do this! Come back!*

There's no answering presence in my mind. I can't sense him. I can't track his movement. He's not anywhere.

"Listen to me!" I scream to the empty apartment. "Show yourself! I was doing something for you! I was doing something nice for you, you jerk!"

My voice echoes. The apartment goes silent.

Half an hour later, I uncurl myself from my bed, unhug my pillow from my chest, and put on my coat.

I go down the stairs. I get on my bike. I return to work.

The world is silent. New York is silent. Passing cars are silent. I neither see nor hear anyone else in the city, in Park Slope, on Sixth Avenue. I am going back to work.

Pedal. Pedal the bike. I forgot my gloves. My hands are cold. I remembered my hat.

My eyes sting. My head is heavy. I can't think.

At Ninth Street, as I make the turn, a horn blares, and my tires give way beneath me. Next thing I know, I'm on my side, bicycle jackknifed between my legs, slush soaking into my jeans.

Someone hauls me to my feet, and I register a crowd, a man in a blue uniform bellowing in my face: *are you crazy you lunatic you could have gotten yourself killed what about my job watch where you're going!*

Other voices: *Are you all right? He didn't hit you, did he? Should I call the cops? Get the hell away from her— it's your own fault for driving so fast—*

One of New York's ubiquitous little old ladies (she seems about four and a half feet tall) is asking if I'm all right. I try to rub the slush off my jeans.

I'm not all right. I'm never going to be all right.

The bus driver hollers so loud I can smell gyros on his breath. I haven't eaten since breakfast.

The little old lady shoves between us. "Leave her alone, you filthy pig! You nearly killed her, now you want to scare her? Get out of here! Go!"

The bus driver tells me to go to hell, and then the bus lurches away. The other pedestrians ask again if I'm sure I'm okay and then disperse, leaving me alone with my bicycle and the slush.

I'm back at Mack's, still numb.

"Oh my God, Lee," Ari says as I hang up my coat. "You look like you just got hit by a bus."

"Yeah, funny that." I force a smile but even I can tell it doesn't reach my eyes, which feel so heavy I can only stare at the floor.

Carlos sits behind the desk, eating a hero heavy with onions. "You okay to go back to work?"

"I'd better be. Panhandling doesn't have a good medical plan."

I take an oil change. One step at a time: remove the oil. Re-cap the bottom. Replace the oil. Replace the filters. Prepare to go back to the front desk. Return to the car and check the fluids. Top off the washer fluid. Head to the desk. Stop again to put the oil change sticker in the windshield. Finally get to the desk. Deal with customer complaining it took too long. Figure out how to charge the credit card. Get signature. Wish the day was over. Wish customer a nice day.

The only ticket in the queue reads "Check engine light is on." [If all else fails, Max once told me, open the dash and break the bulb. I've never done that.] Ari's noted it doesn't like to start in cold weather. Well, who does?

At the very least, it's a challenge. Maybe it'll make my day worthwhile.

"Hey!" The customer charges the counter. "You put that back and let one of the men take it."

Blinking, I can only stare at a refrigerator-sized man with narrow eyes and a hard frown.

"I don't want you messing up my car. Put it down and go type or something."

The two customers in the waiting room are staring. My stomach lurches.

In the past I've dropped the ticket on the counter, allowing the chauvinist to cool his jets until a male mechanic is ready (and, I would note, Carlos and Ari become very sluggish. "I'd get to it now, but it's my coffee break. And then I need to phone my great-grandmother in Pakistan.") On feistier days, I've explained that there are no tools in the shop that require a penis. In some cases I've made big eyes and chirped that I was merely helping the big strong men by driving the car into the repair bay. And then done it myself.

This time, my vision blurs.

The man tilts up his chin with a chill on his face, and I bolt for the back of the shop.

In the bathroom, I'm on my knees vomiting into the toilet when Max storms up behind me. "What the hell happened?"

I can't see past the tears. Carlos calls, "I thought she looked like death."

"Allison!" Max calls, then turns to me. "Are you sick?"

"Customer," I stammer. "Wouldn't let me— Wants a man—"

Max snorts. "Oh, one of those? Give me a minute."

I have no choice. It's dry heaves now, but I can't stop.

Allison rubs my back. "Max will fix him for you."

Why am I acting like this? I can't catch my breath.

When Allison hands me a wad of tissues, I realize I'm sobbing. She sits beside me on the vinyl-covered concrete, rubbing my back. It's quiet, but I can see Carlos and Ari's feet by the door. There's shouting from the waiting room, mostly Max. *Do you really think I'd hire someone who can't do her job? Then you can just back your lousy car out of my lot and take it somewhere else, and I hope your engine seizes in the middle of Seventh Avenue!*

Max is awesome, but I wish— I don't deserve—

"Shh," Allison murmurs. "We've all had days like this, honey."

I choke, "I really can't imagine you have."

Max returns. "I threatened to put a wrench in his skull if he comes back. But geez, don't let him get to you. So he's a jackass. The city's full of them."

Ari says, "It's something else."

My throat closes again.

"Allison," Max says.

"No." I push the tissues against my face. "I shouldn't be home right now. And I need the money."

"Allison," Max says, "bike in the truck. She goes home."

Ten minutes later, my bike has gone in the truck, and I've gone home.

Chapter Twenty-Three:

I'm done doing stupid things for now

In the apartment, I find Beth packaging origami in hundreds of cardboard boxes the size of a hardcover Bible.

"You're home early." She looks up. "Whoa! What happened?"

I'm beginning to hate being transparent.

"I don't want to talk about it."

I drag myself to the table. Beth returns to her system: she checks a list, then wraps origami pieces in bubble wrap, nestles them in packing peanuts, addresses the box, double-checks the contents against a slip of paper, inserts the paper, and seals it.

There are fifteen boxes. It only seemed like hundreds. Same with the frogs: not thousands, only dozens.

After five boxes, I frown. "What are you doing?"

"My Etsy sales go out on Tuesdays."

I squint. "Etsy?"

She looks up. "Yeah, Southebys doesn't want me yet." Then she laughs out loud. "Didn't it ever occur to you we'd be knee-deep in origami frogs if they weren't hopping away? Or that boxes appear and disappear in the hallway?"

"I figured it was preschool stuff."

She returns to printing an address. "Or how I pay the rent? Get with the program, Lee."

I put my face in my hands. "I'm sorry. I'm a lousy friend."

"Well, yeah, but not for this reason." She pauses. "Really, what's going on?"

"I'm never going to see Bucky again." It's a knife in my stomach, fire spreading from the entry wound. "I tried to do something nice, and it backfired."

"You've known him forever. He'll calm down eventually."

"He wasn't mad. Just—"

Cold. His eyes were cold.

I push away from the table to go look in the bathroom mirror. I can imitate Bucky: I open my eyes bigger and wear half a smile, as if on the razor's edge of delight. (That irritated him: *"I do not look like that!"* But he did.) From that expression I flatten my eyebrows, tilt my head forward and harden my mouth. That's how I saw him last.

That wasn't the flare of rage. *Go home for lunch.* The decision had been made. He was only following through.

You can't back down when you're in charge of someone. Corinne told me that a long time ago: even if Randy botches a punishment for one of the kids, she won't undermine his authority. Bucky wouldn't undermine his own. It's over.

Over.

Tears threaten, only I force myself to stop. I head to my room, avoiding looking at Beth when she asks if I'm going to be okay. I'm not.

Before I go into my room, I stand alongside the windows in France to look at Sixth Avenue, at St. Francis' church spire and the cars on the wet avenue. How can people drive right now? My world just ended.

Never see Bucky again.

I fold my arms and tuck my chin, still watching cars. I will see him again—after I die—and I can explain then. Assuming he'll listen. Assuming he's not right now before the throne of glory filling out an application for a different human.

And then the idea. Absolutely simple, completely foolproof. Just step outside. I'd see him in ten seconds.

I mean—he said guardians don't leave unless it's hopeless. And he left, so— So what's the point? If the angel's abandoned you, doesn't that mean God abandoned you too? And God would know.

I slip my fingers up to the window lock, but I don't click it open.

I can't breathe, and now I can't see either. But if I'm hopeless—if I can't get into Heaven no matter what at this point—then living longer will hardly make it worse, right? And what if he's wrong? My mom thought I was hopeless from the day I used my princess dollhouse as a hangar for my brother's Star Wars fighters, but I didn't believe her either.

I take my hand off the window lock. I can't give up. I hate this, but I can't give up. I like living too much. I have too many experiences I've never tasted. I'll have to do them alone now, but maybe— Maybe I can. Maybe I can make it work.

But for now I can only manage to lie on my bed, knees to my chest. It's less dramatic than dying, but also less permanent.

I want to ask God to tell Bucky I knew what I was doing, maybe get him to talk sense to Bucky. But there's the rub: assuming Bucky isn't gone, just invisible, talking to God is tantamount to talking to Bucky. He's going to listen, and if I'm really hopeless, God might not.

Don't contact your ex. Never, never contact your ex.

Maybe I can get him back. I can't devise a way to do it this second, but over time, maybe I can come up with a plan.

Just not now. Right now, I want to disappear.

Maybe Bucky will wonder what happened to me. Maybe he'll do some angelic thing where he'll forget he ever had me, then go back to being happy in Heaven with all the other angels. Maybe that would be for the best.

I smear a hand across my eyes, then tighten up again on the bed, teeth clenched. Don't think.

The landline rings. Beth yells across the apartment to pick it up, it's Randy.

I fumble in the semi-dark until I find a phone beneath this morning's discarded pajamas. "Hey, Randy."

"Now you've got me all confused because I didn't expect you to be home."

"At the beep," I monotone, "please leave a message. Beep."

He chuckles. "Hey, Lee, this is Randy. Volleyball is going to run late tomorrow due to a basketball game, so we need to adjust when you take her. Bye."

I don't want to go to a basketball game without Bucky. Who's going to shout nasty things at the refs if he's not there? "You want me to pick her up late?"

"Or you could skip. Corinne could go."

"With the kids?"

"They've been to basketball before. Brennan likes it. Susanne does her homework."

I don't answer. Randy says, "You don't have to decide until tomorrow."

I mm-hmm him.

"Are you okay? You didn't lose your job, did you?"

This time I can't even give that much.

"What's going on?"

My voice cracks. "Bucky."

"Oh no! What happened?"

"He's gone."

"Are you sure?"

I can't speak.

"Stay right where you are," Randy says. "I'll be there in half an hour."

"You can't." I swallow. "You're at work."

"I'll tell them the truth: this is a family emergency. Promise me you won't do anything stupid."

"No," I murmur into the phone. "I'm done doing stupid things for now."

Corinne returns from putting Susanne back to bed. She refills my mug with hot chocolate, then pushes it beneath my face while I cradle my head in my hands.

"I'm still not sure I follow." That's to Randy, to verify I'm not insane. "She's been able to see angels for years?"

With an implied, "You entrusted our daughter to someone who's nuts?"

"Just one angel, and she doesn't tell people because it sounds whacked," Randy says, "but he's legit. I made her test him once."

Huh? "I don't remember that."

"I made you pray with him, remember? Maybe you don't. You were tiny." Randy shrugs. "You could repeat entire psalms after him, verse by verse, and not just *The Lord is my shepherd*. Things you hadn't heard yet. Then I got him to do the soliloquies from Hamlet."

Bucky must have loved that.

Corinne's voice rises a notch. "How did you know to do that?"

"Because I'm smart?" Randy chuckles. "My point is, Bucky is legit."

"Was legit."

"But what's even crazier," Corinne says, her voice marginally louder as she turns toward me, "is he said he'd leave if you lied to him, and you lied to him." She pauses. "Why didn't it occur to you that was exactly the stupidest thing you could have done?"

I grab a tissue. "Because I'm not smart?"

Randy says, "You still can't feel him around?"

I've been working at it like crazy. It's all a big echoing empty.

Corinne says, "He's not gone. And you're going to see him again."

"But he was so cold."

"Right now, I'm betting he's ruing that open-ended threat thing." She sighs. "You've got to follow through, but then you realize it's no good because there's no reward for changing the behavior. *If you don't eat those fries, we're never coming to McDonalds again.* How long is 'never?' If I kicked Avery out for using drugs, and she returned two years later begging for help to clean up, what would I do?" She opens her hands. "I'd take her back because she's my daughter, and I love her."

Randy says, "But speaking as a parent, you have to follow through at first."

I close my eyes.

"He prayed for you for thousands of years," Corinne says. "Do you really think he'd stay away from you forever—over a misunderstanding?"

"He didn't let me explain."

Randy says, "You've got to admit, it looked bad."

Did it? I sent him on a spurious errand. When he returned, he must have asked the other guardians if anything happened, and maybe they got uneasy but didn't tell him. Then Ari handed me an envelope full of cash and said I owed him. And I said I hadn't done anything other than test-drive a car.

Randy says, "Can you see why he might assume you ripped off a customer? Or Max?"

My eyes widen: I was complaining about money last night.

Corinne turns to Randy. "Can't an angel read your heart?"

Randy snorts. "Like I know what an angel can do."

"He can't read my thoughts." I bite my lip. "But my body language—he knew I was hiding something."

"My patented maternal NoGood Meter would have gone off the scale. I have to assume the same of his." Corinne leans toward me. "You need to talk to him."

247

I take a new tissue. "And if he's not here anymore?"

"Then ask another angel to send the message."

I begin trembling again. "I've never seen another angel."

Corinne's so damn practical. "Then ask God. If God assigned Bucky to guard you, then before Bucky could leave, God would have to release him. You don't want God to do that, so you'd better get God on your side."

Randy says, "That's such bad theology, I can't even begin to critique it."

Oh, God, why'd he have to sound just like Bucky right now? It's like swallowing a razor blade. "She's right about the assignment thing. If Bucky isn't here, it means he called in a temp or got replaced."

Randy sounds gentle. "At least you're not alone."

I slam my hand on the table. "I don't want another angel!"

Then I need another tissue.

Corinne puts her arm over my shoulder. "I know. For right now, though, you don't know what you have."

She's right. I guess I never did.

Chapter Twenty-Four:

A toast to the mighty "check engine" light

On Wednesday morning I drive across the city to report for duty.

Max leads me directly to his office and shuts the door. "What in blazes happened yesterday?"

"My life fell apart." I shift my feet and stare at the ground. "I'm okay to work today."

"You scared the crap out of me, and Ari was convinced you wouldn't come back." Max folds his arms. "Boyfriend dumped you?"

I swallow. "Best friend."

"That stinks. You could always get a new boyfriend. But hey, you're not pregnant, so Allison owes me five bucks." Max chews on a pen cap, then says around the mangled blue plastic, "All the same, you can't be messing up somebody's car because your head's in the clouds. The first thing that goes wrong, I send you home."

"You're all heart and a mile wide, Max."

He grins. "I knew you'd see it my way. This isn't a charity. Keep my customers happy, and if anyone gives you any crap, just roll over."

I huff.

"What do you care if you're getting paid to drink coffee while some guy waits an hour for a man to jump his battery?" Max picks up a gadget from his desk. "Get out of here. I don't pay you to look miserable in my office."

"What's that? New diagnostic tool?"

Before Max can tell me kiss off, I've plucked the playing-card sized unit from his hands. It's black with directional arrows beneath a blank screen, plus a menu button. I tap the screen, and up pops a map of Park Slope.

"Hey, a handheld GPS unit! Cool!" I've always wanted to use one of these but never got a chance. I turn it sideways, and the screen rotates. "Now when I test-drive, I won't have to worry about whether I'm on Eighth or Ninth Street. Can I borrow it?"

Technology that cool has to have some use, right? I just need to find it.

Max snatches it back. "How about you borrow a wrench and get to work?"

So much for a toy to take my mind off things. Instead a numbing progression of fixes occupies me until eleven-thirty (2003 Pontiac Grand Prix, stalls at highway speed) when Max bellows my name with enough force that I nearly fall in the engine.

Tim and Ari look up from their respective vehicles, and they trail me to the front desk.

I stop at the door, and Tim bumps into my back. Max has Carlos at his flank, looking murderous. On the other side of the counter is cold-eyed Mr. Chauvinist, accompanied by a tight-lipped woman. He's a lot shorter than I remember, but still built like a brick.

I didn't touch the man's car. I didn't even touch the keys. Why are they here?

Max turns to them. "That's her."

I'm so dead, it's a wonder I'm standing.

Ari has his hand on my elbow, a wordless offer of backup.

The woman turns to the man. "Well?"

The man mutters, "My wife tells me I was rude yesterday."

I don't relax. The conclusion he reached might be, *It would have been politer to shoot you.*

The woman says, "We ordered you pizzas. They'll be here in ten minutes."

My eyes widen. "Uh— Thank you. That wasn't necessary."

Max exclaims, "What are you talking about? Of course it's necessary!" He turns to the couple. "Thank you for your sincere apology. Take a business card and tell all your friends about our excellent service—"

Ten minutes later, Pino's too-familiar driver brings a six-pack of Coke and three pizzas he assures us are not spiked with anything more deadly than the usual. Crammed in Max's office while our walk-ins wonder what the hell just happened, we feast like starving wolves, pizza boxes balanced on junk mail and atop the monitor.

"A toast to the lady of the house," Max says. "Long may she reign."

The guys cheer.

Ari turns to me. "You still don't look happy."

Carlos gives a mock gasp. "How can anyone be unhappy about free food?"

The pizza is tasteless. I had no idea you could do that to a pizza, and it's not what I'd expect of Pino's.

My next thought is worse: everyone else likes it. So it's not the pizza.

Allison swallows a bite of pepperoni. "I imagine he ranted at home until his wife said, *Husband, meet couch. Couch, meet husband.* So we got pizza. But you notice he didn't leave us his car."

"A toast to the mighty check engine light," says Max, raising his Coke, "without which many drivers would walk around with a wad of bills in their back pockets."

I smile despite myself.

Ari raises his can. "A toast to the genius who thought of the every-three-thousand-mile oil change, without whom we wouldn't see our best friends every two months."

"Here here!" cries Carlos. "A toast to the under-inflated tire, whose inefficiency brings us more tune-ups than any other easily-corrected problem!"

Tim grunts.

They turn to me. I raise my can. "A toast to *Won't Go, Won't Start,* and their good buddy *Runs Rough,* without whom life would be boring."

"And unprofitable," adds Max.

"Here here!" cheers Ari, and we drink to all our friends here at the shop.

"I don't get it." Avery dabs two pieces of ship railing with glue, then fits them together. "Are you living with us?"

"Just a couple of nights."

Randy insisted I stay overnight again, so I packed a bag and left Beth a note. I didn't bother checking voicemail or email because the only one I want to speak to isn't going to leave a message.

It's nine o'clock, long after Avery's game. The volleyball team did great, and I told her so, but even I could sense the chill. The volleyball coach is shuttling Avery to the side in that "Don't be oversensitive" fashion calculated to leave the victim knowing she's been slighted but unable to prove it. It's the social isolation flavor of bullying, old as Sarah and Hagar.

Avery and I are equally subdued as we piece together the Titanic from the parts dominating the table. We've worked since dinner ended, when Corinne forced me away from the sink and urged me to Avery's side. Brennan helped for five minutes before declaring it boring. Maybe Avery is bored too, but she hasn't complained.

We've got the outline of the ship already. There are approximately 50,000 steps, and we're on number fourteen. At this rate, we'll finish in September.

Avery says, "What happened?"

"Falling-out with my best friend."

"Oh, God!" Avery sounds horrified. "I thought that ended when you left school!"

We install more deck railing.

Avery says, "What are you going to do?"

I'm not sure Bucky wants me to do anything. If he's decided I'm hopeless, then me trying to win him back is going to be futile, maybe anger him, and maybe make him sad if he didn't want to go through with it. On the other hand, maybe he wants me to do something to convince him to come home. And maybe my inaction makes him angry or sad too.

Never contact your ex.

That's Bucky's rule, and presumably he knew what he would have wanted. I have to honor it.

We install one of the lifeboats.

Avery still wants an answer, and for reasons I no longer remember, I'm supposed to be her role model. "You can't force someone to accept you."

"You can." She blows at her bangs. "You can do whatever they want."

"And then they despise you for having no backbone."

She snorts. "Do they think about it that much? Or do they just feel glad they got their way?"

I'm on solid ground here. "Then they don't like *you*, do they? They just like having control, and it doesn't matter who gives it to them."

Avery bites her lip. We install more of the deck.

Corinne appears in the doorway. "Avery, honey, it's time for bed."

Avery rolls her eyes.

"Don't give me that." Corinne lays a hand on Avery's shoulder. "You have school tomorrow."

"We're not at a good stopping point."

I say, "I'll work a bit more."

Avery leaves. I register when she comes back after brushing her teeth, hugs me and says goodnight. A while after that, I realize Randy is seated beside me at the table, and when I look up, he chuckles. "Ah, you're alive after all."

I frown. "There was any doubt?"

"Kind of. It's ten." Randy sighs. "I'm going to bed, and I think you should too."

"I can't just yet. There are too many pieces." I look over the skeleton of a ship that hasn't sailed for nearly a century. "I'll just keep going, and then I'll have more of it put back together. At least I can put something back together."

I stop short. My heart races.

"Ah, you're smarter than you let on." Randy rises from the table. "Turn off the lights when you're done."

I return to work, but my heart hammers. *At least I can put something back together.* I can't put things together with Hal, and I can't put things together again with Bucky. But the model of a ship—

Fifteen hundred people died aboard the Titanic. Thousands more lives must have been changed. One fated hour, a chain of thoughtless mistakes insignificant in themselves that added up to permanent estrangement for fifteen hundred people dead beneath miles of water.

Smoke stacks go up. Rigging gets strung. Life boats appear on the decks, but not enough, not enough, not enough. My hands tremble. It's midnight. Half a ship. I've got half a ship.

I'm too tired. I can't finish tonight, alone.

Sitting at the table, I put my face in my hands. I can't finish.

I wish I could talk to him again and explain. I wish he wouldn't have believed the worst of me. I wish I weren't a liar and he didn't think he couldn't trust me ever again.

Bucky, I think. *Bucky, you're such a jerk.*

I return to work, return home, return to my regular life.

The minute I clock out on Thursday, I'm at the drug store buying a fist-sized container of dental floss. I will floss every tooth as if I were in dentistry school.

Next I hit Park Slope Optic for prescription-free colored contact lenses and ask for lessons in turning my eyes green. I have to practice to make it work. I practice every day.

I spend a week dazed, encased in myself like a ring behind a jeweler's glass.

Life isn't fun any longer. I move between work and home. For dinner I scrounge something of the just-add-water variety from the cabinets. I purchase odds and ends for Mrs. Goretti. I scarf down hundreds of Cheetos and play lots of angry music.

I watch TV until I'm bored. I don't play my PlayStation. I skim my email without answering any. When none comes, I immediately click "get mail" again, as if that will summon a message. I surf the web long after I should go to sleep, reading websites I don't care about. Waiting until I'm too tired to think means I crash with less time to miss having someone tell me good night.

I flinch when I delete Bucky's playlist from my iPod.

I play lots of ABBA instead.

I shut the Bucky statue in a drawer, wrapped in newspaper.

So many changes, things I didn't expect. It was automatic to reach for Bucky when I started the engine, to ask which roads are clear, or to ask him for help finding a space—and then I remember—and then I don't say anything.

I can't tell him when I want to strangle a customer, or Max, or the woman arguing over three cents with the Key Food cashier (although I did hand her a nickel). There's no one to make fun of the shop displays. It's just me, and I must not like me very much, because it's not worth making jokes just for me.

I can't ask God to make this right. I want to, but the thought of Bucky in on the conversation and me not feeling it is worse than wondering if an angel is around and not knowing where or whom. Maybe God is as sad as I am that Bucky left me, but I don't think God could be sad, so I really am alone in this.

My body aches. Just sitting, there's a physical ache in my arms and over my eyes.

Bucky's print has arrived. I shoved it in the back of my closet, unopened. The concert ticket arrived as well. I put it in the china cabinet. I'll decide what to do with it later. Probably sell it on Craigslist.

I've been to the gym. When I saw Bill, he immediately asked whether things weren't working out with Hal (transparent me). We went to a movie, and afterward we played the lobby arcade games until security gave us the evil eye. But it wasn't a date. Since then, Bill has left two messages and two emails, and I haven't responded. I'm avoiding the gym, too. It's taking everything to hold myself together. It takes too much effort to talk. I just can't, not without falling apart. And I don't want to fall apart.

Chapter Twenty-Five:

"Fire me, Max."

After I finish changing the brake pads on a 2005 Chevy Caprice, I find Mrs. Zhou and her five-year-old at the front desk.

"Oh, for crying out loud!" I head to the computer. "The trunk?"

"A tire."

"Are you kidding?"

No, she is not. Lying in state in her now-safe trunk is a tire, as empty of air as I am of reasons why this keeps happening. Every breath jets from me like a dragon's smoke as I examine the tire in full sunlight, and sure enough, I find a cracked sidewall.

It's not one we've already replaced, so it's out of warrantee. She's fine with this. "We just have bad luck with tires."

"You're way beyond bad luck." My mouth twitches. "I can't believe tire fairies siphon your air through the sidewall while the city sleeps." I hop on the stool and lean my elbows on the counter. "Does anyone hate you? Anyone with a rap sheet for vandalism?"

She insists on bad luck. The tires have died in other locations, so it's not just their neighbors practicing with ninja stars. And no, they don't joyride through razor wire. They barely drive at all.

I love a challenge, but this one has me baffled. "I'll talk to Max."

But first I replace her tire. This time the trunk doesn't try to gobble me. It's a shame: right now, I'd let it.

I go to Max's office to get his opinion, but he's not there, so I swipe a leftover Coke. Before I finish, Ari sticks in his head and holds up two keys. "We just got two walk-ins. Take your pick: an oil change or the Henpecked Pizza Man."

A sudden desire for an oil change overwhelms my mechanical heart. Ari underhands a key across the room, and I snatch it from the air. 2006 Camry, and lo—it's the valet key. Someone actually uses his valet key!

Inside the car, I jot down the mileage to replace our competition's oil change sticker. "Next oil change: 54,700," and here it is 54,745. Prompt driver.

In the next moment, I catch a whiff of Old Spice.

Heart pounding, I scour the interior for any mark, even a wisp of the owner's identity. No junk mail, nothing whatsoever. No sandwich wrappers. No tissue discarded on the floor. That in and of itself means trouble.

I eject the CD and find Manhattan Transfer. Oh criminy.

Hating myself, I grope beneath the maps in the glove box for the insurance cards. Bingo: I'm in Hal's car.

I've never been a vindictive ex-girlfriend, assuming I was his girlfriend in the first place. Hal could trust me to change all four tires, not fretting for a second that I might accidentally-on-purpose forget to tighten the lug nuts or slip my screw driver beneath the brake pads.

Since odds are he's *not* giving me the chance to prove my virtue, why is Hal even here? This was not only a walk-in, but also I got the choice of which walk-in I took. Beth couldn't have set this up: this reeks of coincidence.

In the grand scheme of things, therefore, I must have Hal's car for a reason. I can't just give it back to him.

I spend extra time under the hood testing fluid levels. I check the timing belt too, just because no one ever thinks to do that. I eyeball the tire treads and the other wear-and-tear suspects, but nothing else needs doing.

The shop-vac is a puppy following me across the garage: the thing lingers far behind, then the hose recoils like a spring and the shop-vac scoots to my ankles, where it lingers until the tension increases on the hose once more. I vacuum the inside of the car, put a nickel and a dime into the ash tray after I find them in the back seat, then Windex the windows and mirrors.

I think I'm done. I must be done: I'm shaking.

Afraid I'm going to wing the garage door, I back Hal's car outside and park nose-out so he can make a quick getaway.

I return to the garage, Hal's key in my pocket, and meticulously wash my hands. Then, out of ways to delay the inevitable, I face myself in the mirror.

Max would check him out. Ari would do it if I explained. But instead I take my place behind the counter and without raising my eyes, wake the computer. With my peripheral vision, I see Hal look up. And freeze.

I enter the uneventful oil change into Hal's account, and the mileage. It's his first visit.

I slide my own credit card through the reader, wait for the machine to spit out the slip, then sign.

His laptop shuts with a click.

I staple the report to the work order, then lay the key on the papers and slide it across the counter to where he can reach. Looking across the room, I force myself to meet Hal's wide eyes. He's pale.

"You're all set," I manage.

He won't come to the counter. "I need to pay."

"It's taken care of."

"Oh." A long moment. "Thanks."

He takes the key and the receipt. "Can I talk to you outside?"

I shiver at his voice. Hal can't drop the temperature ten degrees like a snow god, so that's got to be my imagination. "Sure."

I grab my jacket. From behind I hear, "Where do you think you're going?"

"Fire me, Max."

I step outside before he replies.

On the concrete, Hal turns to me. "This is the job so shameful you couldn't tell anyone?"

I shove my hands deep in my pockets, cramming my unused gloves to the bottom. "There's a coffee shop a block away if—"

"I'm not sure I care to spend that kind of time on you." When he huffs, Hal's breath vaporizes like a cloud. "The free oil change is a nice gesture, but it doesn't erase the way you played games with my head."

"I'm sorry." The tremble begins again inside. "That wasn't what I wanted."

"I'm having a hard time deciphering what else you intended."

"I didn't want you to know."

"Isn't that special?" Hal's eyes narrow even as he stares across Fifth Avenue. "You also didn't want Bill to know, I note, or Stuart, so it's not just my exalted opinion that had you trembling in your sneakers."

My shoulders drop. My chest aches.

"I conjured up a dozen noble reasons for hiding your job." His voice is sharper than any one of his chef's knives. "The witness protection program. Or if you worked for the NSA. Maybe you'd been fired and were ashamed to admit it. But now I discover it's *this?*"

I wrap my arms around myself. "It's better than being a drug dealer. Or a hooker."

"I shouldn't have said that." He sighs. "But damn it, Lee, I *wanted* you to explain" He kicks a pebble across the concrete. "I can't figure you out."

Beth's words are too little, too late. "I was afraid what you'd think of me."

"Well, now I think you're a liar," Hal snaps. "Who on earth would hate you because you fix cars?"

"My mother."

It slipped out, but I gasp.

He stares out into the street. "She didn't look like she hated you."

But I'm right, aren't I? It's built up to this for years. Over time I've grown apart from her and formed my own tastes and my own opinions. Every time I stepped out on my own, she reined me back with the message that if I wanted her to love me, I had to be like her.

I never pushed back. I always sidestepped.

Hal says, "I'm not a psychologist and I won't go wandering through the maze that's your head. The way you mined me for anecdotes, I've wondered how many people you told my accounting stories to as if they're yours. It's my life, not yours. That was Bill's life, not yours."

I swallow. "You're right."

"I know I'm right." He glares at his car. "Is it safe to drive, or have you wired a bomb?"

"Your car is perfect. You can trust me that much. I might screw up a relationship, but I'd never hurt someone's car." I look at my feet. "How did you find me?"

"Someone thumb-tacked business cards for this place on the church bulletin board. Was it you?" His eyes narrow. "Maybe you wanted to be found out."

"I'm sorry," I say again.

"I'm tired of hearing how sorry you are!" Hal turns to leave, then strides back to me. "For pity's sake, the time to be sorry was before you lied, or when I asked you what was going on. Not right now when I found out by chance you're an auto mechanic and you're standing in front of me looking like five miles of rough road and you can't even look me in the eyes!"

I swallow. "That's not your fault. I've had some other things blow up in my face too."

"Is Avery okay?" he blurts out.

"She's fine." I shake my head. "I'm not trying to make you pity me. And I wasn't luring you here. Max had me put those business cards on the board months ago."

Hal nailed it—I can't look him in the eyes.

"Please—" I stare at the pavement. "Please forgive me. I'm not asking you to trust me or to speak to me again. I knew what I was doing was wrong, but I wasn't doing it to hurt you. I just didn't want you to find out about me."

"So it was—"

"—entirely selfish. But I'm asking you to forgive me anyhow."

Hal mutters, "Why do you care?"

"Because I was falling in love with you." My eyes are screwed shut. "I don't want you to hate me. I just want you to be able to forget me and move on."

When I finally look up, strain of sadness crosses Hal's face. "Yeah, well," and then he trails off.

I put my hand on his arm.

Hal jerks away. "Please don't. You and I wanted different things from the start. You'll never marry and you'll never have kids. Whoever I end up with, it'll be for the long haul. Not a game of leap-frog."

"Yeah. You're probably right." I stare hard at the ground. It's hard to breathe. "I need to return your whisk."

"Keep it. Some things are easy to replace."

I can't bear to watch him get into his car, so I just go back into the shop.

Max says he likes a woman with spunk, and that's why he took the liberty of clocking me out for those five minutes.

I don't know why he bothered because no one's in the waiting room, and the one remaining repair I can't begin until the part arrives. I could spend my lunchtime surfing the web because I'm not hungry.

But I should eat. Bucky would tell me to eat if Bucky cared any longer. Hal would tell me to eat if he didn't hate me. Beth would tell me to eat because she does care and doesn't hate me. And my mother would tell me to eat because as my mother she spent the first year of my life feeding me and why should anything change?

Shortly I'm on the street. I have spread before me the international a la carte buffet that is Brooklyn, but I can't think of a thing that appeals.

The guys at the bagel store know me by name. They slop extra tuna salad onto a salted bagel, with tomato and lettuce but no pickles because although I love pickles and I like tuna, the ingredients don't match. Strange ingredients. Ouch.

I buy a Coke and carry the sandwich outside. With the can stuffed in my jacket pocket, I walk uphill eating the sandwich while mentally chewing over what I said about my mother.

Was it fair? I'm not sure it is. But far scarier, I can't discount it.

By the time I reach Seventh Avenue, I've eaten half the sandwich and mulled through half my life with my mother, how I've kicked at everything she's insisted on even as I've let her steer me. She pushed me into college when I wanted a job, so I didn't study. She steered me into nursing, which I left. She kicked me out of her apartment when I started working for the lawyers, and then I revolted even harder and ended up a mechanic, something I knew from the start would horrify her.

I can't imagine a job more interesting. If I could, wouldn't I already be doing it? Bucky might even have called it a vocation: I'm comfortable with the idea of doing it twenty years from now, when you turn wrenches via electrodes wired into your eyeballs. I could be telling Avery's grandkids how my restored Mustang and I terrorized the highways.

But the rest of a future—there's nothing, no husband or children. Just a handful of apartments, dates and hobbies, with me leapfrogging from one to the next to the next.

A kid on a really big playground.

Bucky told me to diagnose my own problems the same way I diagnose a car. If a problem only happens when you're in reverse, it's got to be the transmission. If the problem doesn't repeat when the car's on the lift, inspect the tires. And if the problem only happens in a relationship, then take a hard look at intimacy: if you don't know yourself, how can you be comfortable letting someone else know you?

Despite the intense cold, I keep walking. Past Hal's subway stop; past the collectible crap store. Plastic curtains surround the Korean grocery, insulating the fruit bins from the frost.

If years of my mother's criticism have made me uncomfortable with myself, is that her fault, or is it mine for listening? Or am I'm uncomfortable with myself because the rebel isn't the real me either? Maybe all I know is what I'm not, but not what I am.

Realizing my sandwich wrapper is empty, I chuck the wadded paper into a corner trash can. Buses pass. Cars roll by on their way to wherever.

I am not pink and frills. I am not a reader of Bride magazine. I am not my mother's idea of a respectable woman. What am I instead?

Would any definition fit after so long? Who would even be able to find it under all the layers of flannel and failed careers and ruined relationships? The only one who hasn't despaired of me is Randy.

So who am I? I start to think outward into the universe, but then I stop. Never contact your ex.

I turn a corner only to change direction. With no destination, it's good merely to be moving. I can't run away from myself, but I can force myself to work hard catching up with me.

Eventually, though, I need to return to work, and that's less meandering. I descend to Seventh Avenue—only to I stop in front of the boutique where Bucky told me the display dress would look good on me.

It's still yellow, still too summery for the next four months. I could never deal with the lace or the print or the color, but something about it snagged his attention.

The shop's name is *Luxuriant*. That alone makes me flinch. I don't have time for this. I don't have the money. I sure as heck don't have the class. I need to be back at Mack's, only instead I open the door.

My heart pounds as if I'm about to bungee jump. (Actually, bungee jumping is fun. I'd much rather hurtle off a platform than shop for clothes. What am I doing here?) The chime of the door is the claxon of a prison alarm. Muzak. Eucalyptus scent. Price tags. Forget this.

"May I help you?"

I turn as if captured behind enemy lines. "I—" What's my rank and serial number? "I need some clothes."

The sales gal is younger than I am and has a pierced helix. "You're in luck." Her smile makes her round face even rounder. "We sell some."

She gestures that I should step away from the door. "What kind of clothes?"

I back into the door. "I shouldn't waste your time. I'm sorry."

"I'll take the next person on line then." She shields her eyes as if scanning Shea Stadium for anyone she knew in high school. "You appear to be the only one. Please, relax. There's only so many times I can re-fold the sweater table."

My voice breaks. "I need you to turn me into a woman."

She laughs. "You already have the equipment, I presume?"

When I nod, she adds, "These are clothes. You put them on and take them off again. If you try on something you hate, you take it off and forget about it."

I pull my jacket closer. "I have no fashion sense. But I need to get some."

Cha-ching! That's the sound of a commission in the sales gal's head.

"Do you see anything you like? We'll go from there."

"You have a dress in the window." This hurts. "A...friend of mine...said it would look good. But I don't know."

"The yellow dress? She's right. The cut would flatter you, but it's too flowery. I may have something similar in a darker shade." She sizes me up. "Hunt around and see if you find something else you like, and that'll give me a starting point." She takes a step, then returns. "Don't tell my manager, but if you want to build up a wardrobe, you mustn't do it all at once. That's the surest way to end up with a closet full of clothes you hate. In the long run, I make more money if you're happy."

I force a smile. "Kind of how an honest mechanic gains a lifelong client."

While she's rummaging through the racks, I browse too. Despite it being February, spaghetti straps and cap sleeves abound. I've never understood the sales calendar. I've gotten stuck more than once with a wedding the next weekend and nothing in an entire mall to wear to it.

Why am I here? It's not as if there's a reason to buy a dress, nor will it lure back either Bucky or Hal. It won't change my mother's opinion. I'll look like a kid playing dress-up in her mother's closet, and isn't that what I just finished telling myself I didn't need to be doing?

The sales gal returns with a burgundy dress. "This was the closest I could find." She holds it at length. "Although on second thought, you don't have enough hips to make the best use of the skirt." She frowns. "Have you found anything?"

Feeling like an idiot, I lift an ankle-boot from the display of shoes. "I like this."

Rather than laughing in my face, the sales clerk lights up. "Perfect! Find your size in the boxes, and I'll be right back."

By the time I've fished out the right box and steeled myself against the price tag, she's back, arms laden with clothing. "Time to play!"

I follow to a changing room. "Clothes are a game?"

"The best kind. It's easy when someone points to a blouse and says, *That in size ten.* But you slunk in with a look of terror, and if you walk out with an outfit you adore, I count it a victory."

Thinking of an EGR valve, I smile.

"By the way," she says, "my name's Shari."

Shari and I experiment with clothes like girls raiding their sister's closet. She's got skill. Like Hal's surprising ingredients, a skirt and blouse that don't match on their own suddenly meld into one another with the addition of the right camisole or a scarf worn with a clip (which, bless her, she shows me how to clasp.)

In the end, I'm dressed. And even weirder, it looks like me. We've found a denim blouse with satin ribbon on the seams, mother-of-pearl buttons, and a geometric pattern gracing the collar's edges. Bohemian, but feminine. I'm wearing an ankle-length crinkle-cotton prairie-style skirt (four tiers) in black, a fabric sheer enough to see through but decent due thanks to double-layers. The ankle boots blend into the outfit perfectly, and somehow Shari found a belt that enhances both the triangles on the blouse and the pattern on the boots.

Even with practice, the scarf feels awkward, so we lose that in favor of a chunky necklace with several strands of tiny beads.

It's wild, but I look terrific. I look like me.

My cell phone peals the opening notes of "Carry On Wayward Son," and it's Mack's number on the ID. Cringing, I flip open the phone.

"Lee," Max barks, "do you really think I fired you?"

"Do I still have a job?"

A banner day! I had fun buying clothes, and I got out of his question without lying!

"Not if you don't get yourself back here to do it! Where the hell are you?"

"About a mile away."

"Well get a move on already. You've got to replace a serpentine belt, and I'm sick of Allison griping that I ran you out of here."

I snicker. "I'll be right there."

As I snap the phone shut, Shari says, "I'll ring you out. Throw the clothes over the top of the door as you get changed."

Two minutes later I'm back in jeans and a flannel shirt, and inexplicably, I feel more like me than I did before. Maybe Hal was right that I looked like five miles of rough road (or any two-hundred foot segment of the Van Wyck.) My eyes are still the wrong color, but for the first time in days, I'm smiling.

As she rings me up, she says, "You work nearby?"

I nod.

She says, "Doing what?"

I start to speak, but my throat closes. When she looks up, I force out, "I answer phones."

She chuckles. "Yeah, you don't need a wardrobe for that."

I hurry back to my job swinging a shopping bag. This was fun. This was good.

And ouch, this was expensive. Thank heaven Uncle Mickey usually sends a check for my birthday, because I'm going to need it. Although, come to think about it, if I tell my mother what happened today, she may be in Park Slope before the evening is out, begging Shari to finish turning her daughter into a female.

Chapter Twenty-Six:

I really did do everything wrong

With joy my mother agrees to move my birthday dinner to the Sunday before. She intimates that I have romantic plans for Valentine's Day, and I tell her they are romantic—for Randy and Corinne. Then she's not so pleased.

On the other hand, she stares for the duration of dinner at Shari's outfit (which Beth already laid dibs on for Valentine's Day.) When Mom asks the name of the shop, I foresee a gift certificate in my future.

The extended family invades an Italian restaurant for my birthday dinner: Randy and Corinne and the kids, plus my brothers Morgan and Kerry and their families. The waitstaff brings dessert while singing Happy Birthday To Me, and I sing along with them.

Avery treats me to a ten-minute monologue during a trip to the restroom. She can't wait for the school year to end and is applying to the city's magnet high schools in an effort to get out of Dodge. I don't blame her. She has a litany about which girls did what to her and when, and who said what behind whose back. It's a big bowl of spaghetti. Even Avery can't keep it straight.

On the way back to the table, I try distracting her. "Have you ever heard of geocaching?"

When she shrugs, I say, "If you have a handheld GPS unit, you can go to coordinates people list online to find boxes they've hidden. They call it a 'geocache.' Like a high-tech treasure hunt. I'm dying to try it."

She looks uncertain. "Have you got a GPS thing?"

"Um...not yet?" I chuckle. "But if I can, do you want to try?"

She reaches her seat. "No offense but it sounds as fun as dumpster diving."

As I sit back down, I mutter, "That can be fun."

At the end, there's loot. My brothers Kerry and Morgan gave me gift cards to Toys R Us ("Because you're really a big kid") and Randy gave me a model of a 1965 Mustang the same color as my own. That's awesome.

Out in the parking lot, my mother has me walk her to her car, where she pops the trunk. "This is for you." She hands over a gift bag. "I included the receipt so you could return it."

"You didn't have to."

"It's the actual receipt because sometimes they don't refund the whole thing with gift receipts." She shuts the trunk. "You really do look nice in those clothes, but I prefer your eyes brown."

I'm colder than the weather. I wish I could ask my mother outright if she would love me even if I never married, never wore nylons again, never wore pink or grew my hair past my ears. Instead I start to thank her for coming out tonight.

She interrupts me. "Have you spoken again to Hal?"

I nod. "I have. It's over."

She looks as if she's offering condolences. "I know it's your birthday coming up, but many women find true love after thirty."

I'm sure she'll think my chuckle sounds natural. "I'll just stay immature forever. Don't worry."

While I'm walking to my car, Randy's kids wave as they pull out. "See you Thursday!"

My engine starts, and "Go Your Own Way" comes from the radio. I kill the music. For the first time that night, I miss Bucky. I miss him terribly.

My birthday dawns the same as any other day. I struggle to brew drinkable coffee, shower without having to force out a voyeur, and bike to work hoping it won't snow.

My customers don't care that it's my birthday. They argue about the diagnostics and claim I quoted lower than I did even though they "lost" the written estimate. Max doesn't care that it's my birthday. He keeps me thirty minutes late replacing an axle. Tim, Carlos and Ari don't care because they don't even know. Carlos and Ari spend lunch comparing their Valentine's Day plans while Tim glowers like a gargoyle. And Bucky doesn't care that it's my birthday because he doesn't show up.

I spend an illuminating half-hour on the phone with our tire distributor, discussing Drakkens and sidewalls. I've hunted for a recall or a technical service bulletin but found nothing. On the other hand, from Drakken headquarters we have the intriguing combination of silence and the unavailability of this particular tire. "Even I can't get any more of them," says our distributor.

I think we have our answer, Watson. I leave a message with Mrs. Zhou asking her to phone at her convenience.

I'm home long enough to say hi to Beth as my outfit passes me in the hallway. In the mail I find a gift certificate from Luxuriant with enough for another outfit or a couple of pieces that will coordinate with what I've already found. Thanks, Mom!

An hour later, Corinne's navy dress swirls around her ankles as she rushes through her apartment with last minute preparations. The instant I walk in the door, Avery phones for pizza while Brennan stacks board games on the table.

Susanne jumps in front of me with excitement, grabbing both my hands. "Aunt Lee! Guess what I learned today? A flame-broiled beef patty is actually a *hamburger*!"

While I laugh, Randy comes out of his bedroom saying, "Hey, Grease-Monkey, get over here."

Before he can show me the list he's holding, I put out my hand, looking him right in the eye. Steady. "Don't call me that."

He double-takes. "What?"

"Grease-Monkey, or Wrench-head, or anything else you've been calling me." My hands tremble, but what's the worst that can happen? He'll tell me I can't babysit his kids? You might say I have the power here.

But there's no need for power right now. Randy says, "I'm sorry. I thought you thought it was funny."

I say, "It stopped being funny. What were you going to show me?"

Subdued, he hands me a list of phone numbers: his cell, Corinne's cell, the pediatrician's office, the neighbor, the building's superintendent, the police, God, their congressional representatives, and the attorney who has their wills. He's paper-clipped the kids' insurance cards to the page.

"You don't do this often, do you?" I wink at Corinne, who's emerged from the hallway holding her coat. "Or don't you trust me?"

Corinne gives me a hug. "Get them in bed by nine, and don't do anything life-threatening. Beyond that, there are no house rules. There's dessert in the freezer."

The kids cheer.

Avery hangs up the phone. "Pizza in half an hour!"

Randy hands me cash for the pizza. "Thanks for doing this. We both appreciate it. And I'm sorry about the grease-monkey thing."

"Just get out of here." I beam. "Have a good time."

Then they're out the door. Behind them, I lock the chain and the deadbolt almost at the ceiling. (Sneakitude. I'm such an idiot.)

"Games first," Brennan calls.

The first game involves sliding tiles to manipulate a maze, enabling your wooden pawn to make his way to assorted targets. I choose red and tell the kids "red always wins." The game is angelable—Bucky would have loved it. Well, tough on Bucky. The kids play cooperatively: if they can get to their target without needing to slide a tile, they'll use their move to help each other reach their next goal.

After that, Brennan chooses a glorified game of Memory (just don't uncover all twelve clocks, or time runs out.) Every time we uncover a clock, the kids intone, "Dong!"

Pizza arrives midway through the second game (and bad Avery ordered cinnamon sticks to go with it, meaning I need to shell out extra) so we eat while playing.

Hands-down, this beats munching Cheetos and toasting eternal singlehood at home.

We open the freezer, and I laugh when I find an ice cream cake proclaiming "Happy Birthday Lee!" in blue icing. The kids protest that my slices are far, far smaller than what their father hacks off for them. I tell them to shut up and eat.

Avery excuses herself to the bathroom while I set them up with a video I saw last year (twice) even though it involves singing animals and a G rating. *You're a big kid in a playground.*

After about five minutes, I head to the bathroom to ask if she's going to watch. She might be having cramps or lots of bleeding—which would be my luck, that Avery would hemorrhage while I was in charge.

I rap a couple of times on the bathroom door. "Avery, you okay?"

She cracks the door. "I'm fine. Really."

"You wouldn't be the first to double over with cramps." As I start to turn away, I catch something out of the corner of my eye.

It's an Advil bottle, and beside it the child-safe cap. My mind prickles. "You took some?"

Avery looks around. "Oh, uh—yeah, I'm a bit crampy."

As I return to the living room, she clicks the door again.

By the time I've got the movie set up, Avery reappears in the living room. Her voice sounds strained. "I'm going to bed."

"You pigged out on the cake?" Brennan says, but instead of whapping him with a throw pillow (what other use do throw pillows even have?) Avery walks away.

Within five minutes Susanne croons along with the singing ducks while Brennan and I recite an embarrassing percentage of the lines. I need to get a copy.

During a fade between scenes, I hear Avery's voice but not her words, so I pause the DVD. I find her in the hallway.

Avery's clutching her throat, and my heart pounds—she's ash white. No, she's grey. Blue. Oh my God.

"Brennan!"

Avery stumbles toward me, and as she pitches into my arms, I shout again, "Brennan! Get over here!"

He skids up to me. I fix him with my eyes even as Avery goes limp against me. "Call 9-1-1!"

I lower Avery to the floor, and in her fist I find a brown prescription container. Before I can react, she stiffens and jerks, her eyes roll, and she's still blue.

Seizure.

The stupid kid took a bottle of Advil and some other crap, and she's seizing.

"Brennan!" But he's already talking to 9-1-1, stammering that he doesn't know what's going on but he needs an ambulance. "Tell them she's having a seizure!"

Avery vomits all over herself, the carpet, my jeans. She's still blue. God—oh, God—

Brennan's back.

"Put on your coat. Get Susanne's. Now!"

He runs.

That's when I hear, "Roll her onto her side."

Bucky.

I start up.

His voice raises. "Roll her onto her side!"

My own voice is shrill. "They'll be here in three minutes!"

"She doesn't have three minutes!" His eyes are fire. "Onto her side!"

I fight Avery's stiff limbs until she's side-lying. "Hit her back." He points to a spot between her shoulder blades. I hit her. "Harder! Hard enough to hurt her!"

I hit her three times, and abruptly she coughs with a throaty hoarseness that's half liquid, then spews out more garbage. She gasps like a diver, so hard the skin goes concave between her collar-bones, then coughs again and again.

"Grab a cloth." Bucky crouches beside me. "Put it over her mouth and force in air."

I yank a napkin from the table, and steeling myself against the acid smell of vomit on her lips, I breathe into her. This I remember from nursing, but Bucky talks me through anyhow. "Pinch her nose." I need more hands or more space, but it works. Blowing out, I feel her lungs expand, like inflating a balloon. It wasn't this panicked in training. I inch back so she exhales. Again. Breathe for her. Stupid kid. Stupid lying kid. Don't you dare die on me. You have to breathe. God, let her breathe.

She coughs again, and her limbs relax, but she still won't breathe on her own. I keep breathing for her.

Pounding at the door. They're here.

I can't leave Avery's side. The door is locked.

"Brennan!" I shout again, but the deadbolt is too high. I turn to Bucky. "Bucky, please—"

The apartment door opens, and then EMTs in uniform push me aside to strap an oxygen mask on her. I register orders shouted, and Susanne in my arms sobbing, and Brennan holding his coat. My jeans are cold and sticking to my thighs, and everything smells bad, but I look at Bucky who's still there, who came back to save Avery.

He only regards me. No expression.

Thank you. I close my eyes as the tension overwhelms me. *Thank you.*

I have to dial Randy's number three times before getting all ten digits in the right order. No way should I have driven to the hospital, but somehow I followed with the kids, and now I need their parents. I remembered their insurance information. I have their doctor's name. But I need Randy to take over for me. I need to sit before I collapse.

Randy answers. "Hey, Lee. Are they giving you a hard time?"

"You've got to come now," I choke. "We're at Kings Highway Hospital. It's Avery."

Afterward, I know I talked to him. I think I asked if he was okay to drive. I overheard him telling a waiter he needed a check *now*. But here I am, holding a dead phone, and I don't know for how long.

Susanne clutches my leg. Brennan sits across the waiting room on a metal and vinyl chair, hands clasped between his knees. They're blank. I'm blank.

Stupid kid. Stupid lying kid.

The doctor talks to me. Not good. ICU. Heart problems. Kidneys. Toxicity. Overdose.

Before he leaves, the doctor puts a hand on my shoulder. "You'll probably never want to babysit again. What a nightmare."

We return to the room where they're working on Avery, but we don't enter. Through the glass I count two doctors and three nurses. A ventilator breathes for her, and she's got two IV bags. I could translate the monitor if I plugged back into my nursing skills: 97.5, 107, 55, 63%.

Susanne's slips her hand into mine. She wants to know what's going to happen. I don't know.

They transfer her to the ICU, and I don't know if we should wait in the ER for Randy to show up, but we go to the upstairs waiting area. I use my cell to call Randy, and Corinne answers with "What now?" They're ten minutes away. I ask her to make sure Randy doesn't drive like a maniac. "Too late," she says.

About to ask Bucky to make sure Randy doesn't get his butt pulled over, I stop myself. I lost track of Bucky between leaving the apartment and getting the kids in the car. I haven't sensed him since.

Eventually I register two other families waiting. One a woman with her elderly father, the other a couple with a woman who could be the other woman's sister, but the conversation eventually reveals she's the man's sister. They're worried about their mother.

I huddle on the plastic chair and cover my face with my hands. I listen to myself breathing hard, and the next instant I'm sobbing. Avery, you idiot, after all we did for you, this wasn't worth it—who cares what your friends think?

"Don't cry." Susanne climbs up my filthy lap. "It's okay, Aunt Lee."

I wrap my arms around her, head to head so I inhale her strawberry shampoo and kid-sweat. I was supposed to be in charge of her. Her father gave her to me to look after, and I couldn't do it, didn't do it because she stymied me by lying about the danger that she'd made for herself.

Just like me—Avery and me, liars.

Bucky and I stood in the same place: not a parent, not a friend, no way to force compliance, dealing with someone whose own lies might endanger her body, endanger her soul.

I clutch Susanne all the harder and cry until my ribs sting when I breathe. I feel hands on my shoulder. Bucky? No, just the hospital volunteer, pattering nonsense while handing me a box of Kleenex. "It will be all right."

"It can't," I choke. "I've messed everything up. I did everything wrong."

"You haven't done everything wrong," babbles the volunteer. "You have two beautiful children."

I can't help but laugh, only at a hysterical pitch. "I really did do everything wrong." I take a tissue and crumple it in my hands. "These guys aren't mine."

When Randy marches into the ICU and demands they page a doctor, he brings the oxygen back into the room. He consults several nurses while Corinne hovers beside an unconscious Avery, stroking her hair and murmuring encouragement.

Half an hour and two doctors later, Randy returns to the waiting room. He rattles off an update on her condition, which I translate as "no good" and says, "Can you bring the kids home? I don't think we're getting out of here tonight."

I hope not. I can't imagine Corinne would leave Avery while she's still alive.

I locked the spare keys in the apartment, so Randy hands me his and tells me not to bother sending the kids to school. "Are you okay to drive?"

"No," I say, "but what choice is there?"

I drive home in my own "blizzard conditions," keeping forty car lengths between me and everyone else, always five miles per hour under the limit. Brennan has to open the apartment door because I can't fit the key in the lock. Once inside, I tell them to get into pajamas while I set up the pull-out couch, then loot Randy's drawer for a t-shirt and sweat pants. I take Avery's pillow because, well, she's not using it.

Stupid kid. I'm such an idiot.

That done, I find Susanne lying in my bed already and Brennan setting up shop on the floor. It would take strength I don't have to argue. I lie awake while Susanne form-fits to me, checking the clock every time I doze off and then awaken with a dull grief. At five-thirty, I'm awake for good.

Coffee bootstrapping is especially tough in an unfamiliar kitchen with a strange coffee maker, but the pot has filled by six o'clock when I leave a message on Max's voicemail. Knowing Beth will be awake by now, I phone her as well. She cries when I tell her what happened.

I'm debating calling Mom when Corinne shambles in the door.

She looks like death, but the first words out of her mouth are, "She's stable, still on a ventilator. Randy sent me home."

Thank God. "How's he holding up?"

"Other than threatening a few doctors with dismemberment, he's all right." Corinne sits at the table, then raises her head. "How are the other two?"

"Asleep in the living room. No one wanted to be alone."

After managing to pour hot liquid in or around the cup, I set a mug of coffee in front of Corinne, then hesitate. "Maybe you need the sleep more."

"Trust me, this won't make a dent." She drinks it black, unsweetened. "I'm going to get a shower, then try to get a nap, and we'll figure out the rest as we go along." She rests her head in her hands to massage her temples. "You know what's the dumbest thing? I can't even take my antidepressant because Avery took them all."

I shiver. "Corinne, I'm so sorry. I had no idea she was doing it."

She raises one hand. "Please don't apologize. I know how sneaky she is."

"It happened on my watch."

"*She did it* on your watch. Unless you staked the kids down and gave them supervised restroom trips as a group, she would have done it." Corinne looks right at me. "Randy told me to say it's not your fault the instant I walked in the door, but I thought that would sound too much like 'The lady doth protest too much.'"

I frown. "Could you put that in English? I'm a Philistine."

"You'd think I was blaming you by absolving you straight off." She dances a fingertip around the lip of the mug. "Should I send the kids to school today? They won't learn anything, but at least they can lean on their friends." She shivers. "Someone needs to phone Avery's school, and if you don't mind, I'd rather it be you. I'm too apt to give them an earful."

Brennan and Susanne have allowed their cereal to turn boggy before Corinne returns from her shower, hair damp and eyes sunken. While she hugs them, she explains that Avery is still very sick and needs lots of prayers. The kids opt to go to school. While Corinne lies down, I get them dressed, make sure they have lunches and gloves and hats.

After dropping off the kids, I sit in my car, watching students trudging or sprinting into the school, and every gait in between.

I've resisted a disturbing thought all night, but now that I'm alone, I can't resist thinking it: Bucky appeared. He appeared to save Avery, fine. But the fact that he appeared at all means he could have shown himself at any time. He'd just chosen not to.

Bucky looks at his assignment from the perspective of eternity. I understand he's got different priorities, but at the same time it stings because what that means is Avery's life was important to him, but our friendship was not. He gave up on me, but not on her.

I hold it together for the drive back, and while Corinne naps, I resort to the oldest trick in the book: in the shower, I sob where the water will swallow the sound and wash away the tears.

Chapter Twenty-Seven:

I'm going to learn to play electric guitar

Avery spends the 15th in and out of consciousness, seizes a few times, spends time with a psychiatrist, has scans of her kidneys. And more. I lose track.

Thank God for my mother, who plants herself alongside Avery's bed and doesn't budge. She talks the talk far better than ever I did, and afterward, she translates Doctorspeak into Human.

It's a four-day nightmare. Hospital-smell permeates my nose again, and I don't think it'll ever be purged. I can't keep losing people: losing Hal, losing Bucky, losing Avery.

There's one bright spot, I guess, other than Avery's incremental progress: a classmate visited, one never named in the tales of woe. During one of Avery's awake times, she sat alongside the bed with a ponytail of black ringlets, lost inside a sweater so big she might as well have crawled into a cave and worn it to the hospital. She belonged to the drama club and the yearbook, and underlying her chatter was an invitation to join a different clique.

Sunday morning, I crawl out of bed at ten to bootstrap some coffee, shower, and floss until I bleed. Beth and Stuart have donuts, and not caring so much about being a third wheel, I park myself and my coffee at the table. I hear Stuart speaking, but only dimly. His inflection tells me the right places to nod. Beyond that, I'm checked out.

Beth says, "That's sweet," and I rewind the conversation until I realize Stuart said Hal asked about Avery.

My eyes widen. "You told him? Why?"

"I figured after all that." Stuart seems uneasy. "That whole thing—I don't get what happened between you, but he's not heartless. He was pretty upset."

"About Avery," I fill in, and before Stuart can speak, I say, "Yeah, he did ask about her when I saw him last time."

Beth says, "You saw him?"

"He showed up at work last week." Was it last week? Or longer? Then I remember. "Oh, can you do me a favor?" I go into the kitchen and hand him Hal's little whisk. "That's Hal's, but it's better if I don't bother him again. Can you return it for me?"

"Sure—the book group meets next Saturday, so I'll give it to him then." He plays with the wire loops so it makes a chimey tone. "Why'd he go to a preschool?"

Looking at Stuart, I suddenly think: I don't care anymore. What is he going to do? Laugh? And then what? Kick me in the shins?

"He brought his car for an oil change." I look Stuart dead in the eye. "I'm an auto mechanic."

My lips tingle and my vision goes spotty.

Stuart says, "What?"

Beth rolls her eyes. "She told you once. You acted like a jackass about it."

Stuart says, "You change oil? And tires?"

"And rebuild transmissions, yeah."

He says, "Wow. I had no clue."

But he doesn't laugh again. He doesn't leave. My shins go unkicked. He chats with Beth while I finish my coffee and my blood pressure returns to normal.

That afternoon, the doctors discharge Avery, and once the nurses have bundled her into Randy's car, my mother and I head for the parking lot together. As we walk, she says, "You were a rock of strength."

I give a sarcastic huff.

"Randy's not sure how they would have gotten through this without you."

We've reached her car. "He'd have figured it out."

"You could be here all the time because you didn't have kids to shuttle around." She brightens. "Maybe that's why you haven't gotten married yet, so you could be here for Randy."

I roll my eyes. "God's that short-staffed?"

"You know what I mean." Before I can insist I don't, she hands me a heart-shaped box from her front seat, emblazoned with *50% OFF!* "Here, since you didn't get any Valentine's Day gifts, I thought you might like it."

Fifty percent off my heart. That about cuts it right now.

Then I drive off with my gut like a brick because I'm about to go home and make it 100%.

I've planned for a couple of days now, planned while waiting in the hallway for a doctor, planned while standing on line at the hospital cafeteria with a bag of Cheetos and three quarts of coffee. Planned all the itty-bitty details. I just need to do it.

On the way home, I acquire a spider plant.

Alone in the apartment and fighting a feeling of frenzy, I write a letter. Ignoring the urgency, I carry it to the dining room.

I set Bucky's print on the table, still in its shipping carton, and then the plant and the concert ticket. Once I finish, I'm going to list the ticket on Craigslist so it's out of my house by tomorrow.

I light a candle and then play "Songbird" at a low volume.

Taking a deep breath, I center myself.

God, please give Bucky this message. My heart thrums. *I need this settled.*

I lay the letter on the table. "Dear Bucky." My voice comes barely louder than the music. "I'm sorry I was nothing but a disappointment to you, and I'm sorry I lied. I tried to do something nice and ended up destroying our friendship. I know that's my fault. You can't guard me if you can't trust me, and I finally understand why what I did was so awful."

My eyes sting, and my pulse races. I don't want to do this. My heart screams not to go through with it.

"You deserved better than me, and I can't stand to keep you chained when all you ever wanted was a person you could get into Heaven. As long as you're bound to me, you won't have what you want. That's why I'm asking God to release—"

Stop!

My head snaps up. I can't see Bucky. But I sensed him.

I rub the back of my hand across my eyes. "It's for the best."

Another protest—Bucky's feathers would be fluffed. First off, I can't fire him. Secondly—

"I can't fire you, but I can release you from my end and ask God to release you at yours. Then you can have a new person. Someone you won't give up on." Tears on the tabletop. "You can have the person you wanted for four thousand years, someone who would be with you in Heaven too."

He never gave up on me. Bucky's sensation is very close: he loves me more than anyone but God, and he will never give up on me.

I fold my arms and lay down my head.

My shoulders and throat tingle. A hug. I don't respond.

You left me. The thought churns in my head. *You left me. You left me. You left me.*

A blossom in my head: he didn't leave. Except for a few hours initially when he asked a friend to stand in, he stayed, doing all the normal guardian things.

You don't want me anymore.

A protest: Of course he wants me. How can I doubt he does?

You wanted me to be someone else. Again it repeats five or six times before I go still inside.

Bucky's not active in my mind, but I'm still tingling.

Never wanted me.

Inside me, his voice is stunned. He would promise this before the throne of God Himself: he loves me and always will.

I reach for him with my mind, and he engulfs me. I send him the kaleidoscope whirling through my head: that he left me, that he's done exactly what my mother's done, but I can't continue the relationship that way. I need to be sure of him, not fearing one wrong word will cause him to exit stage left. I'm not going through this again. If he stays, he has to stay. Otherwise, I want him to go.

On his side, assent. But tentative.

Then immediately, the angelic equivalent of a gasp: I'm right. Knowing me as thoroughly as he does, he intuited which techniques would get me on the right path and keep me there. The most effective was leaving me off-balance. I assumed instability in relationships; when no other tactic evoked honesty, he threatened his loss to ensure compliance.

Well fine, I understand he has an important job and not many weapons in his arsenal. But I can't live under that threat any longer.

From him: hesitation.

I wait. I'm not doing this halfway. Either it's a forever-promise or it's not going to be anything at all.

I feel prompted to look up.

When I raise my eyes, I can see him. His feathers are drab and his gaze downcast, but I can see him.

"Are you going to stay?" I swallow. "Or should I finish the letter?"

"I have to stay." Bucky forces up his gaze. "You'll kill my plant if I don't."

"You know I'll kill your plant anyhow." I bite my lip. "Well? Forever?"

"Forever." He reaches across the table, and I extend my hand to his so we can almost touch. "For keeps."

I don't know how many angels can dance on the head of a pin, but I do know one angel can dance on the back of a seat in Madison Square Garden.

Bucky enjoys the concert even more than I predicted, and he glows all the way home. In time with the subway noises, I hum "As Long As You Follow."

"Isn't Lindsey Buckingham something?" The lights flicker as we enter the tunnel beneath the East River, but Bucky shines enough that I see just fine. "I'm going to learn to play electric guitar."

I frown. *Can you do that?*

"Why not?" The lights flicker again, and when they come up, Bucky holds a black hardbody electric guitar, an amplifier at his side and a Mel Bay book open on his lap. "How hard can this be?"

I get to hear the riff of "Don't Stop" until the Union Street Station, with experimental chords following me from Fourth Avenue all the way to Sixth.

Bucky and I have cleared the air for hours since Sunday night. At the beginning he left me with a friend because he didn't want to cave when I reacted. He returned by the time Randy phoned (I get the impression he pushed Randy to call) and while it relieved him to learn I hadn't ventured into felony theft, he had to follow through.

He reacted with horror when I said he loved Avery more than me. "I couldn't let her die!" Then he avoided my eyes and shoved his hands in his pockets. "Her guardian wasn't going to let me let her die, either."

At lunch we brought my gift certificate to Luxuriant, and he talked to Shari's guardian about clothing combinations while Shari squealed about her upcoming commission. We've made plans to go to Toys R Us to pick up a copy of Brennan's maze game.

Breathing is easier now: things are the way they should be.

Bucky asked me to quit it with the contact lenses, but I don't know. They're cool. I did throw away the dental floss.

Back home, I do little more than put on pajamas and flop into bed. *Would you mind checking on Avery for me?*

Don't buy anything while I'm gone. And a moment later, *She's fine. Sleeping.*

Good night, Bucky. I tighten the blanket around my shoulders. *I'll see you in the morning.*

I'll be here. He sets aside the electric guitar to rest his hand on my forehead. *Honest and for true.*

After two days home with her daughter, Corinne wants to get out of the house, get groceries, get her sanity, and when Randy's home she wants (strangely enough) to spend time with Randy. So as on previous weeks, I bug out of work early Wednesday to visit Avery.

After mutual reassurances, Corinne leaves, but I'm still jittery because the last time didn't work so well. I set up Susanne and Brennan with their homework ("But Aunt Lee, we don't *get* homework!") then brave the living room where Avery has bundled herself in a quilt on the threadbare couch.

As I enter, she shrinks. Avery hasn't looked me in the eye since Thursday. We haven't even been alone together.

We've always had doctors and her parents and uncles and my mother between us.

"You doing okay?"

She nods.

With that, I run out of things to say.

Brennan calls from the kitchen, "Aunt Lee, do you know how to find the square root of a fraction?"

Bucky isn't visible when he says, *Tell him you'll help later.*

Like I remember how to do anything with fractions.

"I do." Bucky appears atop the television, a remarkable event because it's the first time in ten years there's been something worthwhile on the TV.

"Later," I tell Brennan. "Do your other homework first."

After another silent minute, Avery says, "I'm sorry, Aunt Lee."

My blood pressure rises. "It's not me you should be sorry to."

"Yeah, but..." She swallows. "I wasted your time."

"My time?" I stare. "You nearly wasted your *life*. You nearly died, and you're worried that I missed a few days of work and ate a ton of fast food—" I pause. "Well, that probably did shave a few weeks off my life, but not the rest of it."

She sighs. "Mom said you should be pissed because you'd done so much for me, and that you'd have blamed yourself forever if I'd died, but I only figured if Mom and Dad didn't see it happen then they wouldn't be as upset."

"Are you out of your mind? Like there's any way that could hurt them any less?"

"Mom said that too." Her mouth twitches as she fights tears. "I didn't mean to make you feel bad."

"Doing it on my watch was a big *fuck you*." She cringes. "Yeah, so I should be angry. But what you did was stupid. I'm not mad."

She wraps her arms around herself. "You're not?"

I glare at the floor. "Maybe a little."

Jane Lebak

"Mom yelled at me." She tucks up her knees tight. "She was most mad about the stupidest things, too. Like I told my friends she took antidepressants."

My head jerks up. "That was you?"

Avery nods. "She thought it was the pastor's wife. I found out when the pastor's wife came in the hospital, and she was totally cold to her. Then she dragged her into the hallway, and when she came back, they both were crying." She bites a fingernail. "I thought it would get them off my back, and it just made it worse for everyone."

"It's always that way." I run a hand through my hair. "It's part of being human."

Angels too, Bucky puts in my head, and I glance at him on the TV. *We have a clearer perception, but only God sees all the way down all the roads.*

The doorbell rings. "It's Jenny from school," says a voice through the intercom.

I don't push the reply button. "Avery, should I buzz her in?"

She nods with enthusiasm.

While Jenny and Avery talk up a storm in the living room, Bucky talks me through the fractions and I repeat after him to Brennan, kind of like those movies where someone tells a phone operator to tell the hero how to defuse a bomb. Susanne copies her spelling words while humming under her breath *The More We Get Together.*

It's cool being someone's crazy aunt. It's cool that they know it.

Chapter Twenty-Eight:

Honest And For True?

The *Rumours* Album blares "The Chain" while I straighten the shop after closing at noon on Saturday. Mrs. Zhou, she of the tires, waits in the front. I've placed my tenth phone call, this time laced with enough threats that our supplier took us seriously. I sent Bucky to go lean on them. We're getting a call from corporate this afternoon.

Bucky sits on the hood of a green 2007 Saturn playing his guitar, his face a rigid concentration as he slides his hand along the neck doing bar chords. All is right with the world.

Well, I still miss Hal. I guess all isn't right.

Bucky stops playing to look at me. I thrust the broom into the closet and slam the door.

I don't turn down the music, but I no longer dance as I clean up. Bucky plays without the same enthusiasm. He can't read my thoughts, but sometimes you don't need to read them.

The phone rings. In a flash, I'm at the front desk, in the spotlight of the stage that is Mrs. Zhou's world. "Mack's Auto. Lee speaking."

"This is Frank Aston from Drakken Tire."

"Let's talk turkey." I gather myself. "The customer standing in front of me has needed to replace four of your Ultimate Series D all-seasons before any of them had more than twenty-five thousand miles, all due to cracks in the sidewall."

Aston says, "If her driving patterns—"

"No possible driving pattern would result in this. I understand that Drakken stopped making these tires about six months ago and is only using up surplus." I pause. "It's not highly publicized for some reason. But you'd be stunned to learn that many of our customers have had to replace their tires far too soon for the same reason."

I pause. See if Aston hangs himself.

"You're jumping to unwarranted conclusions."

"Looking at our shop database," I say, "all the conclusions are jumping to me."

Mrs. Zhou contains a giggle.

When Aston doesn't reply, I push. "I've informed our distributor we're not taking any Drakken deliveries unless you make things right for our customer. We're the ones on the line when tires fail and you don't have the decency to recall them. Who do the customers blame? The customers blame us, not you. We can't have that."

This time, no matter how long, I'm going to wait him out.

Finally he says, "What do you want?'

"I want my customer reimbursed for the tires, plus labor."

Mrs. Zhou beams.

Aston says, "We'll replace the four tires."

"Unacceptable." I lower my voice. "She's already replaced four of your tires. The are four more on her vehicle. You'll cut her a check for all eight."

"Absolutely not."

"Put it in writing." He's on the ropes. "Say that you want your customer driving her children over New York City highways on tires which are prone to blowouts. Say you don't think that constitutes depraved indifference for human life."

I love that phrase. I've wanted to use it for the last ten years.

Mrs. Zhou waits. I wait. I feel Bucky waiting, and I think he's praying, too.

Finally, Aston humphs. "Agreed. Fax the receipts for the work done. We'll reimburse that, and we'll replace the four tires on her vehicle with Drakken High Performance XM-3s."

I give Mrs. Zhou a thumbs-up. "Done!"

Five minutes later, the fax machine sends four pages to Drakken corporate, and Mrs. Zhou has an appointment for after (we hope) the check will clear the bank. "You should have a check in hand by the end of the week, too." At least six hundred bucks.

Our supplier will take the remainder of our bad stock on Monday. Mrs. Zhou exits with a smile. I head into the garage to clock out.

"Well," Bucky intones, "our work here is finished."

I grab a wrench and sing into it. "We are the champions! We are the champions!"

Bucky laughs out loud.

Max storms into the garage. "Good grief! I thought a stray cat got locked in here."

I pound my fist on the air. "We did it! All eight tires reimbursed, plus labor costs! You're not out a dime. You have a customer for life in anyone she tells this story!"

Max folds his arms. "Good girl."

I hold out my hand. "And—?"

With a frown, he withdraws his GPS unit from his back pocket. "A deal's a deal. Keep it safe or it's coming out of your paycheck. And trust me—you're a better mechanic than a singer."

After that ego-boosting encounter with my warm-and-fuzzy employer, I bike home, brilliant inside: I've solved a mystery, protected a customer, and forced the corporate evil to kneel at the feet of Lee Singer.

Yeah. That rocks.

I chain my bike out front and run upstairs to get the backpack I loaded last night. A sweet little tool like this deserves to guide its owner up a cliff face to find the golden fleece, but it's kind of cold to climb a mountain, so instead Bucky and I are going geocaching. I hunted online for a cache in Prospect Park, so we're going to bike up the hill to play with our global coordinates.

But first, a hit of sugary caffeine. I pull Mom's box from the freezer, rip the plastic proclaiming *50% off*, and discover a chocolate heart as thick as two fingers and wide as a lunch plate. Frozen, it's hard as concrete. I pull the hammer from the kitchen drawer, smash it into the chocolate brick, and then harvest enough shards of frozen heart to give me a buzz. The rest returns to the freezer.

While I'm packing lunch, I get a call from Beth. "What's up?"

"Stuart needs to move the book group to our apartment."

"What?" Reflexively I glance at the dining room table, elbow-deep in origami and other detritus. "He can't do that!"

"He's having a plumbing disaster, and they're coming in half an hour."

"Screw that. Let me grab my tools." I open the pantry and dig through plastic bags to find the black box. "What's going on?"

"Water's flowing over the top of the toilet tank."

I laugh. "Shut off the water supply."

"Where's that?"

"Find the supply pipe leading from the wall to the toilet tank. On that there's a shutoff valve, near the floor. Turn it until the water stops."

I lock the door on the giant mess that is our dining room. May no one open it.

Beth says, "I can't find it."

"It's the handle on the six-inch silver pipe. Turn it." I start down the stairs. "I'll be there in a minute, but have Stuart turn the shutoff valve if you can't find it."

This is why every woman should learn to fix a toilet: because she shouldn't have to ask her boyfriend what a shutoff valve looks like.

I sprint down Sixth Avenue to Stuart's building. I'm sure it was stately before a landlord hacked it into six apartments. Stuart lives on the second floor. I don't know where the landlord lives. I assume on Long Island.

Beth meets me at the front. "Stuart can't find it either."

Good grief. Shouldn't it be obvious? This is why every man should learn to fix a toilet: so he doesn't look like an idiot in front of his girlfriend's roommate.

She leads me to the studio apartment where I head into the bathroom and find—

"Where's the shutoff valve?" I drop the toolbox on the floor with a clank. "There's supposed to be a shutoff valve!"

A pipe, its silver lines undisturbed by a tiny knob that could have saved the day, goes from the floor straight into the toilet tank, which ripples like a waterfall in steady—and apparently unstoppable—beauty.

"What did they do? Save a dollar on plumbing parts?" I set the tank lid to the side, then pull up the float arm. The water should stop when the arm fully raises, but it doesn't.

"Have you called the landlord?"

"He hasn't answered."

"Can you can turn off the water to your apartment? Or the whole building?"

No, Stuart has no idea where or how to do that. It's probably in the basement, which is always locked.

Well, we'll do this the hard way. "Get some towels. Old awful ones are best."

Beth says, "That's the only kind he has," and Stuart snaps, "Hey!"

"A bucket too if you have one."

I love a challenge. Really, I do, but this is ridiculous. I tug the chain to flush the water from the tank, then grab my ratchet screw driver from the box. Straddling the toilet backward, I remove screws from the flush lever while the tank refills.

Behind me, I hear a voice that makes me drop a screw in the tank. "Whoa. What's going on?"

I turn to see Hal, a foil pan in one hand and a book in the other. "Put that down and get over here."

I look into the bottom of the tank to make sure the screw isn't going to flush out. It's safe. I ought to have rolled up my sleeves, but at this point it hardly matters: my jeans are soaked.

Hal approaches.

"You're going to do the most important job in the world." I raise the chain that attaches to the flush valve. "I need you to hold this so the water from the tank keeps going into the toilet."

Hal leans over me to get to it, and when the water drains, this time it stays out.

I turn to Beth. "That's not enough towels. Go to the neighbors downstairs—anyone else you can think of, but the downstairs neighbors have a vested interest in helping. Get at least one more bucket, too."

Stuart says, "You try upstairs. I'll go downstairs." And they take off.

I remove the float arm. The valve plunger is going to be the tougher problem because in order to do that, I need to remove the riser tube from the bottom of the tank while the water is running.

"Damn it," I whisper. "Damn it. Damn it. I can't do this."

"You're doing fine." Hal grips my shoulder. "This is going to be a mess no matter what, but you'll get it under control."

Well, that's one of us with confidence. I extract myself from between Hal and the tank to grab my tool box. Beth reappears with a second bucket. "They're coming up with another towel when they can find one."

What I really want right now is a truckload of sandbags. "Hal, grab a rag. You can let go of the chain now." I oil the area around the inlet tube and get my wrench. "I'm sorry, but you're about to get soaked."

Above me, he sounds rueful. "Go for it."

I clamp the wrench around the water supply pipe and unscrew it. I flush the tank manually, then pop it off. As soon as it's free, water blasts from the open pipe. I smother the front end with Hal's rag and plug it with my thumb, spraying water out the sides but stemming the flow. I bend the tube end into the bucket, which starts filling with a roar as the spray hits the plastic.

"When this tops off, swap in the second bucket and dump it in the tub."

I climb back onto the toilet. With the nut off the bottom, I can slide the refill tube out of the tank. Using my pliers, I extract the rubber washer on the end of the flush valve. Yes, it's worn enough that it's not stopping the water. I root through my tool box, but I have nothing that will work the same way.

Beth and Hal do a bucket-swap.

"Good grief," I whisper. Then, "Stuart! I need you to run to the hardware store!"

I show him the washer and start explaining what I need, but then I stop. No—it can't be that easy, could it?

I turn the washer over and replace it upside-down.

"Please work." I kneel on the toilet lid as I reinsert the valve plunger. Once that's in, I straighten the riser tube (getting sprayed in the face) and screw it back to the tank, with water jetting out the sides until it seals tight. While the tank fills, I fish in the tank to retrieve the screw I dropped and reattach the float arm. "Please work," I whisper. "Please."

For sixty seconds there's silence while four ostensibly normal adults watch a toilet tank fill.

And then, as the float arm hits the top, just when I think it won't, the water stops.

Stuart whoops. Beth cheers. I slump against the ceramic, laughing helplessly, while Hal claps me on the shoulder. A moment later, I realize how Hal's got his arm around my waist and his breath is ghosting over my neck.

I skitter away from him. "Thanks." My cheeks are hot—hah, we fixed a toilet, but it's me who's flushed.

Hal looks similarly flustered. "That was incredible."

Stuart laughs. "Who said having a book group was boring?"

Hal smirks. "I'm just glad I showed up early, or I'd have missed the excitement." He turns to Stuart. "Could you put that in the oven, by the way? 350 for twenty minutes."

Beth calls after him, "And you know, since we're all soaking, maybe some extra clothes would be in order."

"Look in the drawers. Hal can wear my jeans, but Lee's going to be lost in anything I have."

Beth vanishes as well.

Avoiding Hal's gaze, I clank the top onto the tank, then begin mopping water with the towels. I'm already soaked, so it's not a big deal. Hal joins me.

My heart pounds harder than when I got sprayed by the inlet tube. I glance up to find him looking at me.

"Ah—" He averts his eyes. "How is your niece?"

"Home now. Doing better. In therapy." I fidget. "I'm sorry."

"Don't." He reaches for another towel. "You already apologized, and I think I understand. It's done."

As I lean toward the tub to wring out the towel, he intercepts me. Wrapped in his arms, I'm find I'm hugging him too, my eyes scrinched tight, my left cheek to his right shoulder. He's all here, his arms, his chest strong against me, my head nestled against him.

I wonder, if he squeezes me, will a gush of water stream onto the tiles? I raise my head to ask, but before I speak, he's kissing me.

I should untangle myself and run. I'll only hurt him again if I stay. But I stay, and he holds me so tightly it aches.

He releases me. I slump to my knees.

"Oh." I stare through his shoulder, breathing hard. "I'm sorry."

Hal pulls me close. "Quit apologizing." He kisses me: urgent, remorseless.

A minute later, I'm out of breath, I've got my hands in his hair, and Hal doesn't seem to have a problem with getting caught. There are more kisses, followed by us flying apart when Stuart shows back up with jeans for Hal and sweats for me. We're fighting giggles and shooting looks at each other.

"Thanks. Here, take this." Hal thrusts Stuart the bucket. "Go downstairs and tell them the day's been saved."

Stuart looks confused. Beth drags him by the elbow, and Hal pulls me onto his lap to kiss me while they're out of the apartment.

I whisper, "We're supposed to be cleaning up the mess I made," and Hal whispers back, "I think we are."

Oh, wow—I was right! I knew the best thing a woman could do was learn to repair a toilet!

We separate before Stuart gets back, and we clean up the worst of the water. The apartment is beginning to smell of apple crisp.

"I'll just get changed, then." Hal grabs the jeans and steps out of the bathroom, leaving the sweats for me and pointedly shutting the door behind him.

My saturated jeans splat to the floor. My shirt is a loss, but I'll zip my jacket and hope not to freeze. My tools go back into the tool box. My socks are drenched, but again, my boots should do okay for the walk home.

I emerge from the bathroom to hear Stuart relating the story to a couple of guys I assume are from the book club. Wearing clothes that don't fit, Hal has his eyes all over me.

Worse, I see what he's got in his hand: that tiny whisk. And he's grinning.

Stuart says, "Tell these guys what you did."

With Hal watching my solo version of a wet-flannel-shirt contest? Sorry, no. I zip my jacket to the neck. "No thanks. I'll send your stuff back with Beth."

I shove my jeans and socks into a plastic bag and grab my tool box.

I'm in the hall when Hal grabs his jacket to follow. "I'll walk you home."

"No, don't." As he shuts the apartment door, I descend a step. Now he's about two heads taller than me. "It's your body talking." I back down another step. "Think about it when I'm not near enough to distract you."

He grins. "I really like being distracted."

"That makes it worse." I run down the steps. ""Goodbye!"

He laughs. "You're insane."

"I'm protecting you from yourself, you goober." And I shut myself on the other side of the door.

Hal's not following me, but I run. I run thinking, *What am I going to do— What am I going to do—* because that shouldn't have happened. What was that? What was he thinking? He gave up on me. I lied to him. He wants a big white wedding with a thousand guests and fifty bridesmaids. He wants to marry someone forever. Why would he spend time splashing around on a bathroom floor with me?

Home again, I pull off Stuart's pants and my shirt. I get dressed again in warm clothes.

Bucky appears on the back of my couch with his elbows on his knees and his wings flared. "Are you going to turn on the computer and wait for Hal's email?"

I pivot, but he's not making fun of me. He looks pleased. "But—"

Bucky raises his hands. "Just a suggestion."

"No. No, no, no." I pull Max's GPS unit out of my jacket pocket. "I already have a commitment, remember? We've got geos to cache."

Aloft, he follows my bike with me the only one to appreciate that yellow and brown wingspan, the way he covers my world. Pumping hard to get uphill, I work up heat despite the late afternoon chill. My breath is visible.

Once in the park, sides heaving, I ask the GPS device to tell me where in the world is Lee Singer. Bucky reads over my shoulder, teasing me with, "Colder... warmer... warmer... lots warmer—" until I shoot him a filthy look.

Our coordinates match the target numbers at a specific grove of trees. From that point, it takes half an hour to pinpoint the correct tree to climb in order to locate a Rubbermaid bin the size of a breadbox, propped between two limbs.

Sitting on the branch, I open the box to sign and date the log book. I look at the two dozen tokens left by previous geocachers, then leave a token of my own: an origami pair of wings.

Bucky peers down the trunk. "You're going to take the slow way down, right?"

My cell phone sings. After a glance at the screen, my stomach goes hard as a rock. "It's Hal."

Bucky leans over my shoulder to read the text Hal sent: "I want to see you again."

Bucky brightens. "Well? Write him back."

I lower the phone. "But—I don't need him. We have everything right here."

Bucky says, "Honest and for true?"

"Honest and for true."

I expect Bucky to make a smart remark about a box of junk jammed into a tree limb being everything. Instead he says, "Maybe once you realize you don't need anything else—maybe that's the time to reach for one thing more."

The phone sounds again. Hal has sent, "I have a whisk for you."

You couldn't loosen the smile from my face with a tire iron.

I text back, "I'll call you tonight," and then turn off my phone to keep watching the clouds. Nothing unusual here: just a mechanic and an angel sitting in a tree in New York.

Acknowledgments

I've had the pleasure of so many amazing beta-readers and critique partners. I need to thank those who read the initial chapters as I turned them out: Ivy Reisner, Wendy Dinsmore, Maria Franzetti and Kenneth Elwood. Wendy gave me a lot of help with car parts, too, and the description of the spoiler is hers nearly verbatim. I'd also like to thank those who offered comments on early drafts: Amy Deardon, Normandie Fischer, Kimberly Horsburgh, Kathleen Bailey and Peggy Rychwa. Thank-yous go also to Evan and Madeline for advice and experience.

Many thanks to agent Janet Reid who gave some amazing editorial advice and to agent Roseanne Wells, who guided me through crafting a finished piece.

A final thank-you goes to all the clunker cars in my past, from the 1972 Dodge Dart to the Studentmobile. You've enriched my world as well as my mechanic's pockets.

Find out what happens with Lee and Hall

Forever And For Keeps

Once you have the right tools, anything's easy. I talk Avery through her first tire change, beginning by showing her how I positioned the jack so it supports the car without raising it. Next we remove the lug nuts, plinking them into the hubcap. We jack the car higher to slide the wheel off, then lay that beneath the car so if the jack gives out, the car will fall onto that rather than someone's hand. She slides on the donut, then replaces the nuts on the axle. I tighten those myself, then finally heave the flat tire into Great Aunt Alice's trunk.

Avery high-fives me. My mother tsks at her. "Go wash your hands. You're full of grease."

Have I introduced my mother? I could single-handedly tune up every car in the Presidential Motorcade while it rolled down Fifth Avenue, and she'd wonder aloud why I did it wearing jeans.

It's while I'm jacking down the car that Morgan says to Hal, "So when are you two getting hitched?"

Even as I glare at my brother, Hal replies, "Isn't five months a little soon to be talking marriage?"

"You know how one year is seven dog years?" Morgan glances at Randy with a grin. "Well, five months dating Lee is the equivalent of three years dating a normal woman."

I get to my feet. And you thought the tire blew up. "You mean a normal woman who can't change a tire?"

Morgan grins. "I mean a normal woman who hasn't dated three hundred guys."

Uncle Mickey breaks it up before I can find out whether Great Aunt Alice's cross-wrench would be able to remove the lugnuts bolting Morgan's under-used brain into his skull.

Thank you so much for reading Honest And For True! If you enjoyed the book, I would love to hear from you. Please consider joining my mailing list at http://eepurl.com/bcnCNX. I don't send out much on the list, but I'll use it to notify readers of any new books, potential discounts, and ask for people who want free books in exchange for honest reviews.

Speaking of honest reviews, good books can always use them. Forget what Mrs. Miller told you in third grade: a book review can be a couple of lines and doesn't have to be anything more than "I loved this story! I laughed so hard I fell off the subway bench" or "Boring. Don't bother." You can post a review on the book's page at Amazon.com or Goodreads, and I hope you will.

Thank you for the gift of your time and the privilege of allowing my angels into your home.

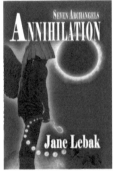

Made in United States
Troutdale, OR
10/24/2023

13969191R00192